My Angel
The True One

Samanthya Wyatt

Love Endures

My Angel The True One

Also by

THE BROTHERS GREYSTOKE
The Daunting Greystoke (Book 1)
Greystoke Heir Apparent (Book 2)
Greystoke's Confliction (Book 3)

ONE AND ONLY COLLECTION
The Right One For Me (Book 1)
My Angel The True One (Book 2)
The Only One My Love (Book 3)

I will never forget the editor who gave me my first break. To
Stella, who gave me the chance for the first book in this series.
And most important of all, to the readers—my fans.
I sincerely hope you enjoy my books.
Keep the Spirit!
Samanthya

Contents

Prologue

Cape Verde Islands, 1824

The noise from the taproom flowed through the open door. Jedediah stood to the side while one man staggered out. When the way was clear, he slid through the door into the dimly lit room. His eyes searched through the smoke and barrier of bodies until he found a large man with a red beard. His informant had not exaggerated when he said the man had arms the size of tree limbs, and a chest as wide as the trunks in England's glens.

Finally, his search was at an end. In the ten months it took to find the captain, Jedediah had apparently been one port behind him at every stop. Now, his quarry was in sight. Soon he could return to London.

The bearded man threw back his head and roared with laughter. His arm snaked out and grabbed a barmaid, landing her firmly in his lap. Mayhap this man was not as fierce as Jedediah had been led to believe. But then, appearances could be deceiving. After all, his employer certainly kept his clandestine dealings separate from his noble status. Especially when he ventured to the London docks.

Disreputable men lurked everywhere.

Jedediah stared at the captain of *Serpent's Ghost*. If tales were to be believed, this particular ship sailed in and out of ports as slick as a mate's whistle. Disappearing into thin air. Named appropriately, he supposed. And its commander was a man to be feared—yet awed.

Some said he was ruthless.

Dangerous.

Deadly.

Diverse few said his haughtiness was more confidence than conceit. His temper flared as fierce as his red hair suggested—seemingly rooted from passion. Everything Jedediah had learned painted the man ruthless, devoid of mercy. Yet from more than one man's lips, the words trust and loyalty were added to the intense captain's qualities.

Those redeeming traits had convinced Jedediah's employer that Captain Stephen Radbourn was the right man for this task. Being a staffer, Jedediah had been sent to find the notorious captain.

Without drawing attention to himself, he stayed in the shadows of the island's tavern. He had come here for a reason. He could not back out now. Slowly, he stepped forward, making his way around the raucous room to the table of the man with hair so thick, green eyes blazed in the middle of a red cloud.

"Go on with ya," the barmaid cooed.

"Give me a taste, wench." The captain pulled at the scanty top barely covering the girl's bosom, and lowered his head. She giggled and pretended to push away while giving him a generous view of her globes. The captain playfully drove a hand down the front of her blouse. The claim of his fondness for women was unquestionably true.

Clearly enjoying his advances, the girl wiggled closer. Her slender fingers grasped a lock of red hair and she whispered in his ear. The captain growled, removed his hand and squeezed her hip. He tilted his head and laughed again. The girl jumped from his lap with a siren's grin and a promise in her eyes.

The captain lifted his mug, giving a salute. Another sailor, obviously in his cups, bumped into the raised arm, spilling the ale. The red-haired giant growled and lunged out of his chair, swinging his arms like a ship's sails dithering in the raging sea wind. After a good blasting, the poor sod trembled in fright and scurried away.

Indeed. Jedediah had found the right man.

Inching closer, he stood beside the colossal man's table. "Excuse me. Would you be the captain of *Serpent's Ghost*?"

The huge man spun around, amazingly swift for a man his size. He lifted his brows in a gesture that very effectively managed to convey his displeasure. Jedediah swallowed. Maybe this was not the best way to approach the man, especially in a place like this.

With eyes as green as the palms on the island, the giant's gaze held a calculating chill, dissecting every pore of Jedediah's skin. The bushy beard covered a good bit of the captain's face, but not enough to hide his scowl, which made his scrunched brows look about as malleable as granite.

"And who are you?" Captain Radbourn said with such a booming voice, surely the rafters shook.

Jedediah ignored his quaking knees and put on his best business face. "My name is Jedediah, but I am not important. If you are the captain of *Serpent's Ghost*, I have a proposition for you."

The hulking captain crossed his massive arms over his chest. "Go on."

"You will be rewarded handsomely." Jedediah gestured toward the table where the man had been sitting. "If you will allow me to buy you a drink, I will explain everything."

The captain's eyes narrowed with skepticism while he contemplated his decision. With a jerk of his head, he pulled back his chair and lowered his bulk. Thank goodness. Jedediah had a stiff neck from looking up. The man stood over six feet and a half foot more. The muscles on his frame looked like he'd pilfered the butcher's shop and tied hams around his arms and thighs.

Trying to maintain his composure, Jedidiah pulled out a chair and motioned a barmaid to their table. Knowing this large man could break his thin frame like a twig did not embolden him. Nevertheless, he had a job to do. "My employer is a very wealthy man." He wished his voice sounded stronger.

The captain propped his forearm on the wooden table, and leaned in close. "And just who is your *employer*?"

"A gentleman in England who prefers his name be kept private. However, he has instructed me to make you an offer."

"Me," the captain repeated.

"The captain of the *Serpent's Ghost*," Jedediah said and then held his breath.

The big man leaned back in his chair, making the wooden legs creak under his weight. "Why would *your employer* be wanting the *Serpent's Ghost*?"

"Your reputation, of course. It is told that your ship can go places none other can. There are stories about its captain. I have heard he is ruthless and fears no one. It is said that his men—*your men*—are steadfast and loyal. Your ship has been known to slip in and out of ports of interest without notice."

"And you would want my ship not to be noticed?" Lines creased the captain's forehead.

"Undetected, yes." Jedediah gave a sharp nod.

"The destination?"

Jedediah's mouth was suddenly dry. He swallowed, then answered, "India."

No movement. The captain, still as stone, gave no clue to his thoughts. Then his jaw tightened, and his eyes narrowed. Jedediah's stomach coiled from the heated glare.

A mug of ale landed on the table, right in front of him. He nearly jumped out of his chair. Deeply involved in his purpose, he had not noticed the girl's arrival. But the interruption gave him a moment of reprieve. With a saucy smile, the bar maid placed another mug in front of the captain. His eyes remained on Jedediah. Unable to coax a response from her previous admirer, she swung around to the next table.

"Why?"

Only one word. But the abrasive tone insisted Jedediah answer. "My employer has an interest in the Indian states."

Captain Radbourn braced one arm on the table, leaning forward in the same position as before. "If you have learned anything about me, you should know I am a man who is informed about things happening on the other side of the world. I am familiar with the skirmishes among the Indian princes with the British military taking away the rulers' independence. I assume your employer is aware there are warlike Rajputs who fight against being ruled by the British."

"There are those who fight for good, and there are those who fight purely because they are evil. Should you run into such a group, they would be relentless."

The captain's eyes bore into him. "I have no intention of running into, as you say, such a group."

As the captain—thankfully—relaxed back on his chair, Jedidiah sighed in relief. The captain lifted his mug, and Jedidiah took the moment to do the same. He took a quick sip, the cool, wet ale assuaging his thirst.

"I suppose you did your research before you singled me out for this undertaking."

"Yes," he replied, sitting his mug down. "We delved into your background."

A devious smile lifted one corner of the giant's mouth. "So, what were my credentials for this particular job?"

"Your brash manner captured my employer's attention. You strike fear in the hearts of men. A more ruthless character would not be found."

"Ruthless?"

"And fair," he added quickly, not wanting to offend the captain. "Those two . . . qualities do not usually go hand in hand. Your men are loyal, to the point they would lay down their lives for you."

"And you learned all this? You have been asking around more than a few places. And how do you know the loyalty of my men?"

"Such allegiance speaks exceedingly well for a man. Word gets around." Every port Jedidiah had visited knew the red-bearded captain.

When the captain's eyes blazed, Jedediah hoped he had complimented the man and not mistakenly insulted him in some way. He took another approach. "This undertaking would make you a fortune."

Captain Radbourn leaned back once again, crossing his arms over his massive chest. "I will not trade in opium."

"No . . . no one expects you to." Jedediah hated the catch in his voice. He shifted his weight, suddenly aware of the wood beneath his seat. Hard, unyielding. Like the man in front of him.

Jedediah took a steadying breath. "There are Indian spinners and weavers who do not want to fight. These men believe in fair trade but are being forced by some armies to follow certain rulers, to give up their independence. Those are the ones my employer wants to help." He waited a moment for his words to sink in. "I must have your answer before I give you more information."

The giant seemed to be considering. Then he asked, "Would I be carrying guns?"

Jedidiah hoped his answer was the right one. His employer wanted this captain, but he would not lie to get him. "Yes. You would travel as a merchant transporting goods manufactured in Britain." He reached to his inside pocket and carefully removed a dark cloth. He watched the captain as the man realized an object hid inside the folds. Making sure no one could see, Jedidiah pulled back one corner exposing a ruby the size of an egg.

The captain's eyes darkened, but no other expression appeared on his face.

Jedediah waited breathlessly for a response. The man was maddeningly composed. He stared at the ruby, not with greed, but as if he were trying to discover the reason behind this meeting. Lives depended on their secrecy. Jedidiah would not let his master down.

"As I said, my employer would pay you well."

He grew uncomfortable under the captain's stare. Sweat broke out on the back of his neck. He willed his hands to remain still. Even though he desperately wanted to loosen his neck cloth, he dare not move a muscle. Trying not to blink, he prayed the giant would not plant a fist in his face. Or worse, choke the life out of him.

The master had assured Jedidiah that this was the one. The captain they could trust. He had based his decision on Jedidiah's findings, of course, and he had been thorough. He needed to trust his employer's instincts.

And pray.

"The money does not play a part in my decision," the captain finally replied. "I own three other ships. And make a tidy profit. However, I feel a bit restless and suddenly find myself in need of a distraction." The captain slammed both hands on the table with a bang. "I accept."

After Jedediah nearly jumped out of his skin, relief unlike anything he'd ever known poured through his limbs. He had taken a risk, not knowing if he would be permitted to walk away. He quickly covered the gem, and put it out of sight. Men had killed for less than the priceless stone he housed in his pocket. "Are you certain? Once I disclose the details of this voyage, you must follow through. I need your word."

Anger flared in large green eyes, and Jedediah feared his life had come to its end.

"Let me assure you of something, *little man*. Once I give my word, it will suffice."

The captain's harsh tone unsettled Jedediah to his bones. "Our matter is of a timely nature. It has taken me months to find you. My employer hopes you will set sail right away."

"Is that so? Your employer must be an impatient man."

"Quite the contrary. As I said, it has taken me months to find you. I will meet you tomorrow morning, at your ship, with more instructions." Jedidiah collected himself and waited, hoping the captain would accept.

"I will speak to my men."

"I bid you, do not say anything of our plans to your crew. At least until after you sail. I trust no one." If anyone got wind of the reason behind this voyage, it would spell disaster—for everyone involved.

Stephen watched the squirrelly man slip away, wondering what he had just agreed to? He lifted his mug and doused his apprehension as quickly as he slaked his thirst. He'd been in sticky situations before.

"What was that all about?" Stephen's first mate, Abe, plopped his ale on the table and lowered his frame into the chair the wiry man had just vacated.

"Our next voyage." Stephen's gaze remained on the little man until the crowd swallowed his form. "I just received an intriguing proposal."

"Who was that?" Abe gave a jerk of his head.

"A man of a man." Stephen shifted in his chair. "Who just offered me a fortune."

"Another boasting of treasure?"

"Something a mite different."

"You have the look of mystery. If there is secrecy, there must be a threat."

"There is always an element of danger." Stephen regarded his first mate. "What would you do if you had a fortune, Abe?"

"Same as you. Get my own ship and sail for the rest of me life." He lifted his mug and took a hefty swallow.

Stephen absentmindedly rubbed the handle on his mug of ale. "With one large score, I could go home for Katherine."

"And be right back on a ship in a matter of months. Your sister is fine with relatives in London. You love the sea."

Stephen gave a knowing smile. "That's why I still captain *Serpent's Ghost*." His eyes darted to the tavern door. Who was the little man? More important, who was his employer?

It mattered not at the moment. He had made a bargain. He would follow through.

"So, what's it to be?" Abe asked after some moments.

Stephen looked to his mate. "The men have tonight. I'll not disappoint them." He lifted his mug and drained it. "Tomorrow, round up the crew."

"Rounding them up will be a chore. May require a day or two. Most of them scattered the instant we docked."

Stephen swiped the foam from his beard. "We leave as soon as the ship is stocked with supplies."

"The little man in a hurry? Where are we headed?"

Stephen elevated one brow. "India."

"India?" Abe stared, hesitating. Finally, he said what they both already knew. "We have not sailed in those waters before."

"Aye." Stephen frowned.

Again silence. Abe was trustworthy, and close as a brother could be. But he would not ask his captain to explain his decision. When Abe did speak, his voice was raspy. "Are you expecting trouble?"

"Hopefully, we will avoid it. We will not discuss it here. And not now." He would learn the details in the morning. Tonight was for ale and women. He called out, with a wink. "I'm off to find me a willing woman."

Abe laughed and turned to the barmaid heading in their direction. "I have a hunch you won't need to go far."

Chapter 1

India, 1824

Cannons exploded, sending balls through the deck of *Serpent's Ghost*. Wood splintered propelling wreckage, making those fragments as deadly as a bullet. Smoke and shouts rent the air. Stephen bellowed orders to the crew, demanding to be heard over the chaos swarming on deck. Men drew their swords, but the magnitude of the opposite force climbing on board far outweighed the number fighting for their lives.

The ship was badly damaged and already taking on water. He would send *Serpent's Ghost* to her grave before he let these assailants take his ship.

"There's too many of 'em, Captain. Even for us." His second in command told him what he already knew.

"Damn it to hell," Stephen barked.

"I'm with you. The men will fight to the death."

"I know that, Abe. I did not plan on surrendering, but I will not serve these men up like lambs to a slaughter. *Serpent's Ghost* is going down. Our only choice is to jump ship." His gut twisted with his decision. Out manned, out gunned, he had no choice. As Abe said, the men would be fighting to their death. Any hope of winning was gone.

Now they fought to survive.

"Aye, Captain." While Abe swung his sword, he made his way to the center of the action.

"Abandon ship," Stephen shouted. The order tasted like bile as the words rolled off his tongue. At all times the crew followed his orders without question, but their hesitation portrayed their reluctance to obey—never before having to forsake their ship.

Three of the enemy devils confronted him at once. With a cutlass in one hand and his sword in the other, Stephen braced his feet and took a stand for their onslaught.

"Come on, you slimy bastards. The man hasna been born who can take me down." The devils charged. He swung with all his might. The first man dropped. Stephen thrust his sword into the second while slashing the third. The cutthroat screamed as blood poured from his face. Another swipe and down he went to the fate of his mates.

Pain seared Stephen's side. With a ferocious growl, he spun to face another attacker. More thrusts, and more. They kept coming. Abe signaled, letting Stephen know those left of his crew were now treading water. He leaped forward, slashing his way across the deck littered with lifeless bodies. During the skirmish, his crew had slain their share. He hoped most, if not all of them, escaped over the side. He fought like a madman, desperate to reach the stern. The last thing he saw, just before he jumped, was a flash of steel too damn close to his neck.

The cold sea sucked him down into her powerful depth. Rays of light pricked overhead, showing him the way to the surface. His lungs near to bursting, he broke through and gulped his first breath of air. He looked furiously about, searching for his men, praying they would make it to safety.

With determined strength, he wrestled away from the swirling current and headed for the beach, staying below the surface. Only when his lungs demanded air, he made his way topside. He maneuvered around a large rock, came up for another grasp of air, and found his men crawling onto shore.

Thank the merciful heavens.

He clawed his way to the water's edge only to find more heathens waiting for them. His gut curled as he watched his men being bashed and slammed to the ground. Fury clawed his belly, driving him. He bounded from the surf, the breakers tugging him back. The enemy was waiting. Men grabbed his arms, jerking him from the water and then restraining him. Already winded, he had little fight left. But it took six to knock him to his knees and hold him.

One man stood out, obviously the leader of this blood-thirsty bunch. Dressed in an array of colorful robes. Clumps of black hair sprung down from a winding turban. Eyes just as black, glowed from a sense of triumph the cur must surely feel.

Stephen lunged, taking his holders off guard. Someone struck him with the butt of a gun before he'd gone two feet. Hands gripped his shoulders, slamming him to his knees.

The leader looked down the line of kowtowing males.

Serpent's Ghost's crew may have looked defeated, but Stephen knew hatred filled their eyes as well as their hearts. His men would not surrender. Would never give up. They waited for a sign from him. Loyal to the death.

He had not intended for his crew to be thus, but each man held his regard, and somehow the bond had formed. Every man would lay down his life for him, and he would do the same.

Evil filled the air. These devils attacked *Serpent's Ghost* without warning, no hail, nor signal of any kind. The bastard showed no mercy as the crew crawled onto the beach. For their sake, Stephen must handle the situation carefully.

"Which one of you is the cap-i-tan?"

"I am," he replied, his voice strong and sturdy.

"Well, well." The leader's eyes took on a gleam as if he'd just found a tasty meal. "So, you are the commander."

The devil sauntered closer, but kept a good measure of distance between them. *Smart.* He probably sensed Stephen would attack the bastard if he came too close.

He met Stephen's gaze without tipping his chin above his nose. No easy feat since the man barely stood to Stephen mid-chest, if he were standing.

"What are you doing here?" The nasal tone set Stephen's teeth on edge. The man knew he had the upper hand. He displayed his self-assurance in his slow, drawn out words.

"We've come to trade." Stephen answered with as much calm as he could muster, when what he really wanted was to strangle the man till his eyes popped out of his damned head.

"Trade? What cargo do you have on your ship?"

"Sugar." Even if the man found out he lied, Stephen would not disclose the guns hidden in the hold.

"You have entered into territory you should not have discovered."

The story came easily to his lips. "A storm blew us off course. We were headed for the East India Port."

The man studied Stephen as though he knew the captain lied. "But, Cap-i-tan, you sailed into my cove." His grin twisted with malice.

His cove? Stephen glared, but held his tongue. This must be one of the Rajput princes who defied the emperor. One still clinging to his religious identity and resenting the English.

Chills shivered down his spine, and it did not have a bloody thing to do with his sea wet clothes. He feared this leader housed an evil soul. Malice filled his dark eyes. Black as night, and deadly.

"We were on a course for the Bay of Bengal," Stephen said. "We anticipated making our way to the Port of Tuticorin by following the coast line."

"Ahh, you expect me to believe this tale?"

"I speak the truth." Lie or truth, Stephen did not like being called on his honor. His anger reflected in his voice.

"We will see how much of what you speak is the truth." The prince twisted to the right, and raised his hand.

A shot rang out. One shipmate toppled to the ground with a gaping hole in his chest.

Stephen sucked air in between his teeth. Rage seeped through his bones.

The bloody whoreson.

He lunged in a roaring frenzy, every cell in his body wanting to kill. The pounding he received rivaled a bunch of bees pricking his hide, until their sting finally plummeted him onto the wet sand.

"Now." The bastard showed no remorse. No feeling at all. "Has your answer changed?"

Stephen spit blood from his mouth. "I will kill you with my bare hands."

The only reaction the leader gave was the narrowing of his eyes. "I will never understand you Englishmen. Foolish words. As you can see, you are at my mercy."

No matter how much he hated the idea, the bloody bastard was right.

The man raised his arm in the air and with a flick of his fingers, several of his men came forward.

To Stephen's horror, he saw chains. The bastard was going to put them in chains.

"What do you want?" he growled.

"I want to know how you found my secluded cove."

"I told you . . ."

Another shot rang out.

Judas Priest!

Before the smoking gun cooled, his band of men placed shackles on the remaining crew. Stephen's gut coiled. If they thought they could chain him . . .

Agony speared his temple and he thought his head would explode.

Darkness descended.

❧

Pain rolled over him in crashing waves. He prayed devoutly for the return of sweet, blissful unconsciousness—but it was not to be. There was that moaning again. How very strange. It seemed to be coming from him.

His arms were stretched over his head, his wrists bound by chains. Muscles strained where he hung, nearly pulling his arms from their sockets. At some point, the ache in his shoulders had dulled to a smarting throb. He thought he was still in one piece, although his legs hung loose. He could feel shackles, his ankles were tethered. Once again, rage jammed his skull. The pounding in his brain caused nausea to fill his throat.

Mindful his ribs were more than likely broken, he slowly gasped for breath.

His men.

Slaughtered before him. Their suffering increased his guilt. *He had* brought them here. To a land of chaos and bloodthirsty bastards who surely were spawned from the devil himself.

He wondered how long he'd hung here this time. Every few days the bleedin' dogs would suspend him in these manacles like a prize trophy, take him down, throw him in a filthy corner of a cell, only to take him out and start the process all over again.

When would he wake from this horrendous nightmare? It seemed he'd been in this hell-pit forever. Between the beatings and other indescribable torture, he had lost count after the first few months. His body a shadow of what it used to be.

His size had always intimidated men. There was nothing intimidating about him now.

He enjoyed pounding his fist in a man's face now and again. But, when a man was chained to a wall, the only blows he got were the ones he received. Time—and the Rajput prince—had taken their toll. For his legs were unable to carry him out of this bloody asylum.

Men's voices drew his attention. They were back.

Their native tongue was unknown to his ears. He did not need to speak their language to know their intent. His worn muscles—what was left of them—continued to flex even though his limbs were limp from hunger. How much longer could his body hold out?

Flickering light bounced off the dungeon walls creating shadows. The shuffle of footsteps and then, the man he had come to hate, appeared from the dimness. He stopped, just out of reach. Then, he motioned to a sentry. The man dipped a ladle into a jug and poured water into a cup.

So, they were to play that game, again.

From swollen lids, he kept his stare straight forward. His empty belly ached. The *prince* thought starving him would . . . what? Make him crack? The bloody vultures sunk his ship. They'd murdered his men. There was nothing left.

The bastard simply tortured him for his own senseless pleasure.

The man stood with his arms crossed over his big belly concealed by layers of silk. With eyes as dark as his black hair, his sinister gaze glowed with a sense of triumph the deuced man must surely feel. A sickening smile, more like a sneer brandished the harsh angles of his face. Stephen hoped the man choked on his own spittle.

"Now, Cap-i-tan. Are you ready to talk?"

"Go to hell." Although Stephen growled through gritted teeth, his voice emerged barely more than a croak.

The Rajput prince raised his arms. "What else can I do? You allowed your men to die when all I seek are answers."

"Devil curse you for your vile acts."

"Vile? You, Cap-i-tan, are responsible. You sentenced your men to death rather than tell me what I want to know. Tell me how you found my secluded cove."

Stephen held his tongue. The bastard would never believe that by a stroke of fate they had stumbled into that particular cove. Stephen had considered it a stroke of luck, until cannons fired on his ship. The worthless monster raised one arm and gave a slight flick of his hand. Fire lanced Stephen's back. Too weak to remain quiet, he cried out. Damn his fragile state.

"I would think, Cap-i-tan, you would do anything to end this."

"And then you will spare my life?" Stephen rasped from his dry throat. "Like you did my crew?" Nothing could erase the images in his mind. The screams of his crew—tortured and slaughtered like animals—their bodies drug across the stone floor. His shame in knowing he could not save them. He had begged for their lives, and eventually ... their welcoming deaths.

The whoreson smiled in triumph as his eyes narrowed. "You choose a slow miserable death?"

Stephen tried to spring forward with what energy he had left. His shackles jangled, making a mockery of his failed strength. He wished he could rip the chains from the damp rock, wrap them around the bloody man's neck, and send his soul to hell.

Laughter echoed off the walls. "Your actions are foolish. Tell me what I want to know."

For a harrowing moment, the man's eyes held a crazed madness. Stephen knew it did not alter the words he uttered, the Rajput Prince derived too much pleasure in torture to allow his captive to go free. His chin lifted, and he gave another flick of his wrist.

Pain exploded. His damn lapdog packed a hell of a punch. By the force of the blow, the devil incarnate must have fractured Stephen's jaw. The only bone in his body the bastard probably had not broken, up to now. Agony seared his face and sparks flashed before his eyes.

"You are a stubborn one." The Rajput prince nodded again to his companion, turned in a flurry of colors, and strode back into the darkened tunnel.

Stephen braced himself for what came next.

A mallet pounded in his brain. Stephen lay on his side, his face upon cold stone, his hip against bars set in walls of rock. Eyelids swollen from the most recent beating, he could not get them to open enough to see even a glimmer of light. Not that there would be more than a flickering flame from the wall outside his cell. Still he struggled to raise his lids in hope the dizzy spinning would slow somewhat before he retched again.

The stench alone was enough to make an ordinary man hurl. He'd been given very little to eat. He tried to swallow, but his enlarged tongue assured him that his throat was bone dry. Something trickled down his cheek. He knew it wasn't sweat. He tried to raise his arm to wipe the blood—instant agony let him know it was broken. He did a mental check of other body parts. With this much pain, they all had to be present and accounted for. Although, it just might be worth getting rid of a few if he could shed the pain right along with a few limbs.

Sorrow clogged his lungs.

His shipmates. Men he had been responsible for. He should be with them. Lying in the ground beside them. But he would not give up. He lived for the day when he could rip the guts out of the evil monster, make him suffer as he had made Stephen's crew suffer. He would afflict such pain and torment, the bastard would prefer hell instead of being at Stephen's mercy.

He could not move an inch, a limb, a muscle. A limp mass on top of filth. Weak as a new born kitten. Every curse word imaginable crossed his lips. The bastard gave no chance for escape. His damn dogs kept a close watch. Even when they took him down from his restraints and threw him in his prison, they never left him alone. These cutthroats were worse than rabid animals.

Now his chances were even dimmer. With two broken ankles, there was no chance he'd be running away. Hell, he couldn't even stand. And thanks to the latest beating, he had no idea how long it would be before he could eat again—when they allowed it. Not that you could call the swill they served as food. When was the last time he'd eaten?

Stephen urged his mind to other things. Pleasant things. Anything to provide the distraction he needed to survive the anguish that consumed him.

Home—Aunt Elizabeth—Uncle Albert—Katherine.

Sometimes, Kat was too much for his weary mind to handle. Ever since their parents' deaths, he'd tried to give her what she wanted. Hell. Every time he looked at her, he saw the pain of loss in her young, sad eyes. They pulled at his heart strings. He had made his sister his priority, her needs his own.

True he'd spoiled her since she was a baby. He had let her have her way many times. With a temper to match that fiery red hair— like him— she would not stop until she got exactly what she wanted. And Stephen had never been able to deny her.

She looked so much like their mother.

While he sailed the seas, his little sister had grown. A beautiful young woman dancing at parties and balls. He imagined her in a whirl of lace and petticoats. No more freckles, or running around in pigtails. If for no other reason, he needed to get out of this hell for her. Get back to England, and keep her safe from rogues. And men like him.

Home.

Voices again. Oh God. Terror held him in its grip even though he tried to shove it away. Footsteps. A guard bent to retrieve something from the floor. What could it be? They had already exhausted everything imaginable. Death didn't scare him, but he'd thought his end would come while on his ship. Maybe sink to a watery grave. Not die like a mutilated rat in a hellish dungeon. He would rather go down fighting—even if they had already bled his strength.

A heavy thud echoed. A body landed on the filthy floor.

What the devil?

Unable to see clearly, his other senses sharpened. He listened intently. Someone moved outside his cell, and not the usual trio who guarded him. Enthusiastic whispers rendered him to consciousness. The concerned voices were not the ones of his enemies. To his disgust, he would have to be carried if someone were to free him from this hellhole. It would be a miracle, if after all this, he would escape still a man.

Keys clanked against the metal lock. They were coming to him. What more could they do to him? Yet the frightening unknown set off his survival instincts. His head screamed at his body, *move*! Too bad he did not have the energy. He was going to die soon. At least he would be with his comrades.

Someone entered his cell, stepped close. He heard a voice, deep and raspy. It might be the man in the next cell. Another voice. Then, there were two men standing over him.

Facing what he knew would come next, and the stench of his own blood, caused his stomach to roll. Unable to fight the dizziness any longer, he thankfully sank to a world of darkness.

"It's about time you got here. Hurry up." Clothed in black, the rebel leader's men were hard to see. But Tarak's eyes had grown accustomed to the darkness. A clinking sound and the cell bars opened. He stepped through.

"Took us a while to find you, Tarak," his second in command said.

"Did you silence the guards?"

"They're all dead. We did not leave anyone to sound an alarm."

"Give me those keys." He jerked the metal ring from Dinar's hand and hurried to the captain's cell.

"Tarak, what are you doing?"

"He's going with us." Keys clanked against callous steel. Tarak hurried, his shaky fingers made opening the lock more difficult.

"Have you lost your mind?"

Maybe he had. Who wouldn't after the torture he had witnessed. If not for the captain, he would have been the recipient of the Rajput's ruthlessness. "I said he's coming with us."

"You're the chief," Dinar conceded.

Once the lock clicked, Tarak jerked the cell door open and rushed inside.

"Not much left of 'em." Dinar spoke over Tarak's shoulder. "He looks like he's dead."

"Any other man would be." Tarak knelt on one knee and put a hand to the captain's throat. Silent in his own cell, Tarak had watched in revulsion as the evil prince ordered cruel acts upon the captain—and wondered if *he* would suffer the same fate, knowing most likely he would not survive. Yet, the captain lived, after all the man had endured. And he deserved to die somewhere other than this rotting hole.

"He's still alive. Help me get him up."

"He's a tall 'un. Limp like he is, how we going to do this and not make him worse?"

Tarak turned and gave a harsh whisper. "Gafur!"

A large man filling the doorway, ducked his head and squeezed inside.

"Gafur. Take him. If you have to carry him on your horse, do it. I'll not leave him behind."

Silent as a crypt, and with the ease of picking up a boot, the large man hefted the captain in his arms and carried him like a babe. Shifting his weight from side to side, he made his way through the cell doorway.

"There are other prisoners." Tarak said.

"Apu is releasing every last one. The prince will have a fine time trying to round them up again. Course the only one he may come after is you."

"Then we shall put distance between us." Tarak rushed down the dark corridor with his men. He had known they would come. All he'd had to do was wait. He had been spared at the sacrifice of the British captain. He cringed. This Rajput was not a man. He was Satan.

They rushed to the opening. Once outside, Tarak found more of his men waiting with horses. He jumped onto a saddle and grabbed the reins. Kicking the animal's sides, he fled into the night.

Darkness aided in their escape. But the presence of the captain cost them precious seconds. After they had ridden a good distance, Tarak nudged his horse beside Gafur. "How is he?"

"He's barely breathing. I do not know what is keeping him alive."

"Sheer will. There is a village ahead. I'll send a man to scout for someone to take him off our hands."

Tarak gave orders to dismount. No fires were lit, the men kept watch. His men never questioned, simply followed the orders he gave. The group of rebels may have wondered why he brought along a man who was sure to die, but none asked. Even Dinar withheld his opinion. They waited in silence.

When Tarak checked on the captain, Gafur shook his head. If the captain died, he would be free of the pain, as well as the horrible prison. Tarak would bury the captain with honor.

"Someone comes." His second spoke.

A wagon rolled into camp, with two of his men following.

"Thanks to Buddha. We're too exposed in the open," Apu added.

Tarak hurried to the wagon. A little man climbed down. A long plait of hair, bound by a strip of leather, hung down his back. He stood with his arms folded and his hands inside the sleeves of his too-big shirt. Another person climbed from the wagon, same size, same dark clothing. The little man gave a nod and let out a string of gibberish. About to hurl an oath, Tarak stopped at the soft voice of a young girl.

"My father has agreed to help. Where is the hurt man?"

Tilting her head, she avoided direct eye contact, but her voice crooned like a singing bird. Tarak realized his mistake. This was a young woman. The little man bobbed his head up and down. Tarak wondered if the small man understood the words the girl spoke.

"Hand him over and let's get out of here." Dinar spoke from behind.

Tarek's men had succeeded in their well-organized escape, but they were not yet in the clear. The quicker they got rid of the captain, the quicker they could cover their tracks, and lead the prince in the opposite direction. For there was no doubt the Rajput Prince would follow once he found them gone—if for no other reason than his pride would demand satisfaction.

"This way." Tarak led the little man and girl over to the spot where the captain was hidden. They could not take the risk of him being discovered.

The little man slumped to his knees, then ran his hands over the captain's body. He spoke to the young woman in their tongue.

Hurry it along, would ya?

The prince had been after his rebel army for a long time. When Tarak had been captured, he knew he would be tortured, and was willing to die. But he had been astounded at the lengths the prince had gone to torture the British captain. As though the cruel Rajput had a personal vengeance against the man.

The little man stood and spoke, again a slew of rapid words. This time, the girl did look at Tarak. "My father asks for you to place him in our cart."

Mei Li dipped the cloth in the bowl and dabbed at the corner of the man's mouth. For three days, he lay still as death, yet he breathed. She mixed her father's curing sage with some water and finally got a few drops inside the injured man's mouth—and hopefully into his stomach. Her father had wrapped a cloth around the man's head to hold his jaw in place, which made it difficult to give him any nourishment.

She had never seen so much hair on a man's face, or his body. The color of fire, as the sun sets in the evening sky. As she wet the cloth, she smoothed thick curls back from his bruised face. Yellow and purple tinted his left cheek. She smoothed the cloth over his face, applied ointment on the open wound, and then retied the cloth tightly under his chin.

His hands and feet were sizeable. The torn clothing that hung on his body implied he'd been a large man at one time. Skin hung on his bones. Deep cuts oozed with poison. Every inch of his body had been wrapped with healing herbs. Her father had arranged the man's limbs and bound them tightly for his broken bones to mend properly. As she rewrapped his ankles, she wondered what cruel person had done this to him.

"Mei Li."

She stepped to the back of the wagon and raised the flap. "Yes, Father."

He stood with his hands folded inside the sleeves of his long robe. "Come. Let us eat."

Mei Li climbed to the ground. "Father, the movement of the wagon hurts him. His body rolls with each hole the wheel falls into."

Her father gave a sharp nod, then turned to the fire. Mei Li lifted the kettle and poured a portion of tea into two cups. She handed one to her father.

"I am afraid, my daughter, the bounce of the wagon over rough ground will not allow his bones to mend."

She kept her silence, as she had been taught, not wanting to intrude on her father's thoughts. She sipped her tea. After a long moment, he spoke.

"The one who did this will search for him. We cannot hide him, daughter. The journey is rough. If we stop, we give aide to those who seek him. We put him and ourselves in danger. We must find other shelter."

Chapter 2

The hateful man left.

Reluctantly, Jennifer held her tongue and turned to go back inside the small house. Her haven, barely more than a mere shack in need of repair. It was not much, but it was all she had.

She closed the door, lowered the bolt firmly into place, and then pressed her back to the wood. Making a face, she contemplated her chances of getting away with shooting the loathsome man. Could she hide the body? Would she be able to drag him away, or bury him without being discovered? She shook her head. What a flight of fancy.

Only a few hours remained until darkness, then she would go to her lonely bed. But no matter how desolate she got, she would never welcome Barincott to her bed.

Jennifer carried a well-worn pot over to the stone-laid fire pit. The first year in this isolated land, she had been miserable. Blinded by love, she had eagerly left her home in England two years ago.

Born and raised in a comfortable London house, her father was a member of parliament, and her mother a favored member of the Ladies Social Club. Like any other young maiden, Jennifer had dressed in the latest fashion. She had been ecstatic when the time came for her coming out. She attended parties and balls, and danced with the most handsome of men. It was at one particular ball she met and had fallen madly in love with a second son. Only the first son could inherit land and a title. So, with stars in her eyes, Jennifer had gone with her sweetheart to a new land full of promise and adventure. She had left the security of her home and the warmth of her family to follow a man full of dreams, ready to make his fortune.

If only he had.

She'd gone from blind love to keen-sighted misery. Foolishly, she had believed his promises to love her forever—assuming he ever had. She could barely recall the happy times she'd shared with her newly married husband. A young girl with her delusions of fairytales, her head in the clouds, she thought she loved him.

Johnny lost his boyish, good looks too soon. Failure after failure crushed all hope of finding his pot of gold at the next rainbow. Broken dreams turned him into a stern, obsessed, and finally, a dejected man. He took to the bottle. His drinking made him careless, and by accident, he'd ended his young life.

What would her existence be like if he had found his golden goose? What would her life be like if she had remained safely ensconced in the bosom of her family?

Jennifer closed her eyes and willed the tears not to fall. She had cried enough when she came to this desolate country. She could never go back. Not after the way she'd left. Disobeying her father, she had sneaked away like a thief in the dark of night. He would never forgive her.

Kneeling before her grate of stones, her hands worked quickly to start a fire. In short time, flames licked the logs and warmth penetrated the small space. She stood and wiped her palms across her skirt.

At least the dwelling was hers. She looked around the room. An uneven table, on which she had put the wooden legs herself.

If she had waited for Johnny, it would never have gotten done, for he was always chasing his next aspiration.

Her husband's death had left her at the mercy of the fates. But, Jennifer was made of strong stock. There was no one to take care of her, she had to rely on herself.

Chopping wood gave her blisters, but she swiftly learned to tie cloth around her palms before tackling the chore. How proud she'd been, building a bench for the table. Her back straightened and she stood a bit taller.

It was not easy. But she was a survivor. And she would waste no more tears over a man who had the insolence to die and leave her alone in this brutal country.

Placing a precious potato on the table, Jennifer picked up a knife. The thought of carving an ear off her disreputable neighbor popped into her head. After their harrowing confrontation, she deserved a boon. So, she picked up a second potato. As the dull blade scraped the brown skin, she made a note to add sharpening to her lists of tasks tomorrow. She cut the potatoes into pieces and dropped the bits into the pot above the fire. Adding a leftover portion of squirrel from yesterday, she left the stew to cook.

She made her way to the connecting room. The only private room in her modest house—after she pleaded with her husband to put up a partial wall, which she had to finish. She stepped to the small trunk, where she stored all her worldly possessions when she had fled, and married Johnny in Gretna Green.

Lifting the lid, memories crowded her mind. Her family gathering for the evening meal. Her mother and sister dressed in silk gowns and her father with his sharply tied cravat. Balls and parties, a different social every night.

And then she met Johnny.

How divine he had looked in his dandy finery.

Shaking away the cobwebs in her mind, a trace of blue caught her eye. She lifted the first of the only two gowns she had brought with her. Holding the smooth material against her cheek, moisture filled her eyes. Her vision blurred. She had no reason to dress for dinner now, other than the simple pleasure it gave her. Stroking the fabric with shaky fingers, she stared at the cobalt satin. After a few more moments, she refolded the elegant gown and carefully placed it back inside the chest.

Not tonight. She would wear it another evening when she felt a bit stronger.

Jennifer picked up her brush and returned to the outer room. She sat in the rocker in front of the glowing fire. Lifting a long lock of dark hair, she stroked from the crown of her head down her shoulder and on to her waist. One. The first of one hundred strokes that had become her nightly ritual. As she stared into the dancing flames, she lifted the brush for another stroke.

To look at her now, no one would know she had been born a lady.

If she allowed it, melancholy would settle over her.

If she allowed it, she would wish she were home.

A long time passed before she realized dusk had settled and shadows from the fire pranced on one wall. A noise resounded from outside. Her head tilted as she listened. Then she recognized the sure sound of a creaking wagon. It stopped right outside her door. Who would be calling so late? For a moment she thought it might be her disagreeable neighbor, but even he would not come back again tonight. Arriving after dark, he would be taking the chance she might shoot him.

Turning up the wick, she used the flame to light another lantern, and then she carefully replaced the globe over the flame. She lifted the lamp, and made her way to the one window in her small house. She pulled the curtain back just enough for her to peek outside. Foolish girl. Whoever was out there would see her before she saw them.

With the moon's glow, she made out the shape of a small lone figure, climbing down from a squared, canopied wagon. She jerked back from the window before he could see her watching. Her heart pounded. The man was small enough she should be able to fight him off if necessary. Perhaps he meant her no harm.

A moment later there was a rap on her door. He had seen her light. In all the months she had been here, only two callers had stopped at her house. One was the man who wanted to replace her husband.

Revolting idea.

The other was a native of the land. He had looked her up and down, then turned his head and continued on his way. Johnny was still alive then. She supposed the native had reckoned she already had a man and left her alone. She wished her distant neighbor would leave her alone, as well.

Another rap. Reluctantly, she crept to the wooden door.

"Who is it?" She called through the barrier.

The stranger let fly a rapid string of words in a language she did not understand. In a weak voice, she called, "What do you want?"

She heard a shuffling sound, and then a soft voice. "My father and I beg your forgiveness. We care for an injured man. We need help. Will you open the door?"

A female.

A girl by the sound of her young voice. A woman living alone could not be too careful. Jennifer opened the door a crack and held the lantern high. A girl stood there, about half Jennifer's size, and with long black hair. Bright pleading eyes stared out of a serene face, and immediately Jennifer trusted the girl. Her head dipped, tilting downward, as if she was trying to show that she was no threat.

Jennifer opened the door wider.

"I am Mei Li. This is my father. The hurt man is in our cart." She moved her hand slightly toward the covered wagon. "Please. Will you help him?"

The little man hurried to the back. He moved something, stepped back and gestured inside with a sense of urgency.

"He is hurt badly," the young girl said.

Jennifer looked at Mei Li and then to her father. Mother always said things happened for a reason. Of course, that was before her daughter ran off with a husband-to-be.

Thinking this girl and her father presented no danger, Jennifer took a deep breath for courage. Dear God, don't let this be anything more than exactly what it appeared to be.

She trusted too easily.

Jennifer carefully stepped through the door keeping her eyes alert for any sudden movement. Reaching the back of the wagon without mishap, she peered inside. What she saw horrified her. A skeleton of a man in filthy rags lay on a makeshift bed, wrapped in bandages from his head to his feet. At a glance, it was alarmingly obvious the man had been beaten within an inch of his life. Who could be so cruel? And how had this couple come by him?

She did not need an extra burden. But she could not turn her back on the helpless man. He would probably die. Unless . . . Jennifer turned to the petite girl with sad eyes. "Is he alive?"

"For now. It is up to Buddha how long."

The little restless man spoke again.

Mei Li looked at her father and pointed to the wagon. "My father fears he will die if he does not remain immobile. We tried to heal his wounds, but he was very near his last breath when he came to us. Travel is not good for him. The cart rocks, and the road is full of harsh bumps. My father asks if we can leave him here."

A thousand questions flooded Jennifer's mind at once. But one thing the girl said surpassed the lot.

Leave him here?

Chapter 3

J ennifer looked down at the man in her bed.

Her bed.

Compassion overrode good sense. She had allowed empathy to triumph, overpowering any sensible protest she might have made. Her stomach was tied up in knots. Had been ever since the injured man turned up at her doorstep. Who was he? Where had he been? Who did this to him? She figured it was perhaps best not to dwell on the who. She prayed *the who* would not come to her door looking for him.

She had never seen anyone in such bad shape.

Mei Li said his jaw was broken. Jennifer studied the battered face of her patient—the part not wrapped in bandages. She wondered what he looked like under the bruises and swelling. Unconscious and limp as a wet cloth, he'd not made one sound when they carried him inside, which was no easy deed. He must have been a large man at one time, for his frame and loose clothing portrayed a man of massive build. Clearly, he had been starved as well as beaten.

Shreds of cloth wilted from his shoulders down his sides. The marks on his wrists indicated he had been chained or somehow restrained. Lifting the bandage from across his ribs, she gasped. Burned flesh. Her stomach rolled. She recognized the serious-ness of the wound from a time when her husband, in one of his drunken stupors, had stumbled into a campfire and burned his arm. The scorched flesh took weeks of careful nursing before his skin regrew.

Fortifying her courage, she took a deep breath and immediately realized her mistake. A mixture of decay and dried blood assaulted her nostrils, along with the herbs and ointment coating his wounds. The back of her arm flew to her mouth in reflex. Inhaling the clean linen helped to settle her stomach. She was not queasy by nature, she harbored a strong stomach. But the shock of the evening and the sudden realization of the brutality done to a human being, shattered her already tired bravado.

Leaning over, she peeled bandages, one by one. Several cuts and burns covered his torso. How could anyone endure such agony? Although some festered, the wounds seemed to be clean. Undoubtedly thanks to Mei Li and her father's healing herbs. Jennifer wondered again how the pair had come by this man. Thank the good Lord they had. She applied fresh ointment on his charred skin, and replaced the bandages with clean strips of cloth. He moaned.

Automatically her fingers went to his brow feeling for fever. With his body fighting so hard, it was a miracle he still lived. She planned to do her best to keep him that way. He moaned again.

She took a damp cloth and brushed his brow. "You are safe. Please remain still. I will take care of you. You are safe."

He did not wake. Hopefully her voice and gentle touch would calm him. With any luck, somewhere in his pain-hazed mind, the poor man would comprehend.

Her gaze traveled down his body to rest on the bandages covering his swollen ankles. Her heart screamed at the viciousness of his wounds. His tattered trousers would have to be cut off. She stepped out of the room. Wrapping a cloth around her hand, she reached into the stove for one of the stones she kept inside. She dropped it into a bowl which she pumped full of water. She opened the cupboard and procured a knife. Then scooped up a tin of lye soap and carried everything back into the small makeshift room.

As gently as she could, she grasped his trousers, which was not much more than rags, and slid the knife beneath. The sound of the tearing fabric sent chills up her spine. She refused to admit the chills had anything to do with seeing a man's exposed flesh.

How long it had been?

Any stimulating or amorous thoughts died a sudden death.

Her gaze followed the seeping wound from his knee several inches on his bare thigh. Raw and jagged. Someone had taken a dagger to this man, and enjoyed doing it. Anger coiled in her chest. She rolled him, just a bit, and carefully pulled the blood-soaked pad away. More torn and marred flesh on his backside. She stared, disbelieving. Her stomach churned. Amazing he had any blood left. She wished the brutalizing monsters who had done this to hell.

She bit her bottom lip as she probed. Once the wound was clean, she stitched the gaping hole closed. Adding the herbal medicine from Mei Li to a folded square of linen, she covered his leg.

Removing the remainder of his shabby covering, Jen quickly cleaned and dressed the rest of his wounds, losing count of the stitches it took to close the many gashes. This man was her patient. No time for timid modesty. After all, she had been a married woman. She had seen a man's body.

Although, certainly not like this. The task demanding, determination drove her movements.

By the time she finished, she was completely exhausted. She wiped her face with her arm, and pushed several hanging strands of hair out of her way. She stretched her neck from side to side and rolled her shoulders, relieving the tension. With steady fingers, she reached out to stroke his russet brow. His skin was flushed, it burned her palm. Danger lay in the degree of infection. She desperately hoped he would not develop a fever. She did have a bottle of laudanum, but with his injuries, she suspected he would not wake up at all. Possibly he would not live out the night.

The young girl's words had been fitting. This stranger was in God's hands now.

Should she pray? Pray for his soul? She had given up prayer long ago. It had not worked for her.

But then, *she* had chosen to run away. *She* had left her home, fleeing with a boy who thought he was a man. Believing love was all she needed. Believing love would last forever. Not only had she been reckless, she'd been stupid as well. If her situation was not so serious, her actions would be laughable.

Knowing there was nothing more she could do, she tidied the room. The fire had died down, so she threw on another log. Pulling her rocking chair close to the flames, she grabbed her quilt and prepared for a long night.

It was not the first time she'd slept in this chair. Sadly, she spent more time in her rocker than in her solitary bed. Sometimes due to hardship, sometimes due to cold, and sometimes her loneliness was too much for her to gather the fortitude to get up.

What did she have to complain about? Just look at the man in the next room. At least she had her health. With determination and fortitude, she had managed these last several months on her own. And if the stranger died during the night, she would be alone again.

She'd done all she could. She repeatedly told herself the litany, until she drifted off to sleep.

She dreamed of home.

Jennifer climbed the steps in anxious anticipation. The Derbyshire ballroom dazzled with bright chandeliers while strains of music floated among the whirling couples. Excitement pumped in her veins. She had plagued Aunt Sara with her nervous fidgeting over her hair and beleaguering decision of which dress to wear. All in an effort to please Johnny. He promised he would be here.

Impatiently, she searched until she found him. With his dapper evening attire of black silk, and his crisply folded collar, he looked absolutely debonair. Everyone else in the room faded. His blue eyes flashed his admiration, making her pleased she had taken such care with her appearance.

Her heart fluttered as she accepted his invitation to dance. He swept her a bow and took her hand, raising it to his lips while his gaze generated alluring warmth throughout her body. She was ever so glad her parents had not attended that evening, for her father's brow would have surely jutted upward in disapproval. Johnny's gaze remained on her as if she were the most beautiful woman in the world. Shivers ran along her spine. Then he slipped her hand within the bend of his arm, and escorted her to the edge of the dance floor.

He was every bit as smooth on his feet as the dance instructor her parents had hired. Johnny swept her around the ballroom, turning and swirling until her mind became a blur of utter delight.

Although she had pleaded with Aunt Sara, she was denied a second dance with her handsome beau.

Immensely charming, he had swept her off her feet, and carried her heart clean away.

Suddenly her father's angry face appeared. He shouted. "No, you cannot marry a nobody."

Tears streamed down her face. How could her father call Johnny a nobody?

"You should set your eyes on his brother."

She did not want his brother. She wanted Johnny. "Please, Papa."

Jennifer jerked awake.

Her hands were fisted in the blanket. She swiped at the tears on her cheeks. It was only a dream. The same dream.

How many times had she cried herself to sleep over her foolishness? How many times had she cried because there was no one to soften the pain? Her loss of innocence, her husband's death—but the greatest awareness of emptiness was the loss of her family. Which she had thoughtlessly thrown away.

As much as they tried to raise her a lady, she had been a trial to her family. Her education stood beyond reproach. Her tutors had diligently sought to instruct her in proper English diction and etiquette. She could out read, and on occasion, out think her tutor. She frowned, remembering how naïve she had been when she thought her parents overprotective.

But she'd been too smart for her own good. At the age of seventeen, she'd developed into a woman with a determination to show them her responsible nature. She had matured, and she detested being thought of as a child. She had attended many parties and balls, and then she met the man of her dreams. Since she was old enough to marry, she'd asserted her independence. Her father's stern voice still haunted her. He had denied her request to marry a second son, and threatened to lock her up at the idea of her leave-taking to another country.

Now she wished she were ensconced safely back in her family's loving arms. Regret was a harsh lesson. Wishes, she had learned, were a waste of time. Time was the one thing she had in abundance.

Time alone.

She shrugged away the melancholy, remembering she had a house guest. Tonight she was not alone. The house had grown chilly. Lifting the cover from her lap, she slowly rose, and carried another log to the dying fire.

Sunlight streamed in between the crack of her one boxboard window. Jennifer sighed and opened her eyes wider. The stiffness in her neck reminded her she had spent another night curled up in her rocker. She uncoiled the blanket wrapped around her legs and jolted. Events of the previous night prompted her to awareness.

She cocked her head sideways. No sound came from the adjoining room. Her uninvited guest still slept. *Maybe.* A shiver ran down her spine at the alternative. She stood, ignoring the pain in her back, and padded to the doorway. Again, she hesitated, listening for any sound from within.

Nothing.

She gently shoved the rough door open. The man appeared to be sleeping.

She hoped.

Making her way to the bed, she held her breath in anxious expectation. With every step, dread clogged her throat. His chest unmoving, she searched for any sign of breathing. As she leaned closer, she heard a raspy sound. He was sucking air into his mouth. Weak with relief, her shoulders fell and she closed her eyes in a silent thank you.

Why did she worry? Maybe death would be welcome to the man. His suffering, more than likely, agonizing. There was no way of knowing the extent of damage done on the inside. With him being unconscious, she had no idea of his pain.

She looked for signs of fresh bleeding. From what she could tell, he had not moved. If he were to recover, he would need nourishment. She tucked the coverlet around him and returned to the main room.

She had stew from the night before. He would not be able to chew, but if she could get some broth past his lips, the liquid would trickle down his throat and he would at least have a chance of survival. The poor man had been starved, his stomach could not handle much, even if he were able to eat. Again, her gut revolted at the cruelty done to him.

After her morning grooming, she glimpsed the sky through her window. Heavy clouds loomed close overhead. Most likely there would be a storm today, which should keep her pestering neighbor away. Her crude larder held very little food. She attained a biscuit for herself. Preferring tea—her one weakness from England—she thought perhaps the brew would serve a stimulating tonic for her patient. She noted her quickly diminishing supply, so she tucked the idea to the back of her mind for later. Taking a bowl from the cupboard, she added some broth. She had accepted the task of nursing him back to health. Since he had managed to live through the night, she decided the fellow was destined to be here.

She pulled a chair close to the bed. Being careful not to move him more than necessary, she tucked pillows about his head. She gathered the bowl and spoon, and settled herself to her task. Scooping some broth, she touched the spoon to his bottom lip, permitting a few drops of liquid to trickle inside. She dipped a second time and held the broth under his nose, willing him to smell the aroma and hopefully stir a response. Maybe he would lick his lips. Maybe he would recognize the scent as food, and by self-preservation, his instincts would kick in and he would want more.

She scooped more liquid. This time when she touched his mouth, he rolled his lip. The bob in his throat moved. He swallowed. She smiled, thinking her patient was stronger than he looked. A few more sips, and then she placed the bowl to the side. Too much too soon would have his stomach revolting. The idea was to keep food in him.

Several times throughout the day she repeated the process. Sometimes his tongue laved greedily at the moisture. Other times she encouraged him to swallow pitiful amounts of water. Anything to get something in his stomach.

⸻ ele ⸻

It was a good day for sailing. However, the matter of getting Katherine on board his ship proved more difficult than maneuvering the roughest waters. Not even his towering height, nor his best brooding look, intimidated the young girl by his side. Despite her desperate pleading to go with him, he refused to weaken. He would not let his love for his sister sway him from doing what, he believed, was best for her.

He looked down at the girl who looked so much like their mother. Her beautiful auburn locks hung below her waist. Her face was shadowed in the evening twilight. It had been difficult enough to accept his parents' deaths, but her pleading eyes were nearly his undoing. He knew nothing of raising a girl of fourteen. He could not take her to sea, no matter how much she wanted to go.

"Please, Stephen." she begged. "Keep me with you. I won't get in your way. I promise."

"It has already been arranged. Aunt Marguerite and Uncle Albert are eagerly waiting for you." He lifted her pelisse and strode up the boarded plank. She had no choice but to follow.

Cannon fire exploded from hell. A ship brimming with guns emerged from the windward side.

Bloody hell!

She'd been lying in wait for them. Smoke rolled up in billowing clouds, the sails encumbered in flames. His ears rang from the fire of cannons, splintering wood, his men's shouts. His crew fighting to their last breath.

Serpent's Ghost is going down.

"Abandon ship!"

Wide God-fearing eyes fixed on him as if in silent communication, loyal to the bitter end. Unbelieving their captain had given the order. Unbelieving their fate had come to this.

Men dived over the sides. He swung his sword, lashing everything in his path. Hell fire on these vile devils that dared to attack his ship and sink her to a watery grave.

Water surrounded him. His lungs craved air. He surged to the surface, clawed his way to shore.

His men in chains.

Roaring gunshots.

His crew dropping wordlessly to the ground.

Limp, lifeless, slaughtered.

Chapter 4

Moaning sounds roused Jen from her uneasy nap. She swept a glance to the man lying in her husband's bed. He twitched and jerked. His head thrashed from side to side as though he were caught in the midst of a bad dream.

She laid a hand across his brow. Leaning back, she sighed in relief, *no fever*. But, he dwelled in a world of demented delirium. Struggling with an enemy known only to him. He battled his nightmare and she wished she could save him. Let him know he had escaped his tormentor.

Being alone, often times the only voice she heard was her own. The sound of her expression in song had been her companion many solitary evenings. She loved music. Unfortunately, the only harpsichord within fifty miles belonged to her neighbor, Barincott. She shuddered wondering how much longer she could thwart him. Since her husband's death, the man made regular visits, constantly assuring her she could not subsist on her own. The one thing she would not do was sell her soul for comfort. She had already given herself to one man, and once was most assuredly enough.

Another moan drew her attention back to the pitiful figure upon the bed. She pressed a damp cloth to his forehead and hummed. Almost immediately he calmed. Encouraged, she sang a lullaby she remembered from her childhood. Thinking of her mother caused a pang to her already desolate heart. She would like to think her family had forgiven her.

When she finished her song, she dipped the cloth and rung out the excess water. He mumbled. She took a glass of water and spooned a few drops into his mouth. He rolled his lips greedily.

"More." The words were faint. Relief engulfed her, unlike anything she had felt in a long time. After several more attempts at swallowing, he quieted, and slipped into an easy slumber.

He spoke. He actually roused enough to speak. And he asked for more. He had been coherent, if not fully awake.

Now that she knew her patient would live, she decided to give him a bath. His matted, smelly hair entwined with his scraggly beard. It was hard to tell where one ended and the other began. She studied the man in her bed. Strong cheekbones, a crooked nose, she wondered at the color of his eyes. Profuse russet brows, she would guess they were green or blue.

She wondered if the color of his hair had anything to do with his temperament. Would he be a man of honor, or a blackheart? A soft-spoken man, or a man with a loud booming voice? Would he be gentle, or would he be a hard taskmaster? Something told her he measured significantly different from her young husband.

What had he done to land himself in trouble? This country was harsh, and the people lived very differently. She rose to get a basin with water. A beautiful landscape painted on the base with gold trim along the rim. She had spied the colorful treasure upon entering this land, and Johnny had bought it for her.

Gathering soap and rags, she prepared what she thought she might need. Although her supply limited, she carried her bundle to the next room. She pulled back the blanket, lifted the bandages and checked his wounds. Thank goodness none of the gashes had opened during his delirium. She dipped the cloth in the basin of water, frothed it up with soap, and gently scrubbed his face. She ran the cloth down his neck and across his shoulder, mindful of the scorched flesh. The burns were healing.

Tugging the blanket lower, her eyes flew wide. *Goodness*, she gasped under her breath. *Soft and big*. She quickly covered him with the linen, trying not to think of that part of him while she soaped his thigh. Red curls spiraled greedily, as they engaged the dampness. She rinsed and soaped the cloth again. The water was murky, so she threw it out and poured fresh, then applied the same ministration to the opposite leg. For a moment, she stared. Hesitantly, she trailed one finger along the jagged puckered flesh. Her fingers tingled. A man's skin.

Her eyes darted to his face. His lids were closed, she hoped the man slept. She lightly touched her fingers to his bruised jaw. He possessed a ridged chin. Even in his sorry state, his lush mouth made her think of kissing. She should not stare at his body, but her curiosity took over her good sense. Neither the gashes, nor abrasions, repelled her. She had never looked upon a man's nude body before. Even Johnny had undressed in the dark, and on those few occasions where she could have spied on him, her own timid nature made her look away. Opportunity presented her this moment. How wicked she was to take advantage.

Her eyes soaked up every inch of him. From the cords in his neck, across his wide shoulders, down his torso to the indented button just above the part of him hidden under the blanket. She stared. Temptation nagged her to lift the covering. Did not that section of him need to be washed as well?

Her mind railed. Her role as a healer declared she treat his private part the same as any other limb on his body. But her woman's curiosity desperately wanted to look her fill. And if she touched him—there—permitting her fingers to linger . . . Oh how she craved the courage to . . .

Good Lord. Get hold of yourself. The man is helpless and you are having improper thoughts.

She shook her head and resumed his bath. She removed the wrapping around his ankles and applied more of Mei Li's special herbs. One last place to finish. Clearing her mind of impure thoughts, she raised the linen around his privates, stuck the wet cloth underneath, and hastily washed. The thing moved. She jerked her hand away and swallowed. That would have to do. She covered him up again.

Washing his hair presented more of a challenge than she expected, but she managed. Satisfied with her work, she wiped the back of her arm across her forehead and stood. She placed both hands on her aching back above her waist and stretched.

With a heavy sigh, she grabbed the bowl and padded into the front room. She tossed some logs onto the welcoming fire. Her stomach growled in hunger. How long had it been since she'd eaten? She retrieved a bowl and dished up some of the stew she had made the day before. Sitting at her table, she stared into the broth. At least she was not alone.

Which made her wonder what would happen when the man woke. For he had a better chance of waking now that he'd made it through another day. Who was he? What happened to him? Would the people who did this find their way to her home? Then what?

She had enough trouble with her neighbor. She did not need more men knocking at her door. The type of evildoers who tortured a man this way would show not a care for anyone who gave him shelter.

❧

Sunlight streamed in through the window casting streaks across the figure sleeping more peacefully. Jennifer blinked. Too peacefully. With dread in her heart, she rose. Placing one finger under his nose and the other on the side of his neck, she checked her patient to see if he still breathed. She gave a sigh of relief.

Her morning ritual consisted of washing, and running a brush through her hair. She drew on a pair of her husband's breeches and tied his long shirt at her waist. A gown restricted her movements when chopping wood and other chores. Who was here to see her anyway? Except for her distant neighbor—who did not keep his distance.

She caught the long tresses of her hair and wove them into a knot at the nape of her neck. Then filled the kettle with water and went to her cupboard for tea. She tidied up her scant belongings, wiped her table, and then set about her chores.

Opening her door, she drew in a breath of crisp morning air. A new day. Only today would not be like every other. Today she was not alone. The air seemed fresher. The sun seemed brighter. Due to her houseguest? Why should she feel any different just because she had a man staying at her home? In her bed?

Memories threatened of her familiarity with Johnny. Some days their life wasn't so bad. Sometimes she had enjoyed their intimacy. Especially when he held her until she fell asleep in his arms.

Those days were gone. Now her days were filled with solitude. Best not to dwell on something which would only intensify her lonesomeness.

She picked up the axe she kept inside. One never knew when a being might come to her door. Best not to leave it outside, giving them a weapon to use against her.

Slipping to the corner of her dwelling, she scanned the trees, searching for any sign of movement. Satisfied no creature stirred, she made her way to the chopping block. The small pile of brush and tree limbs she'd gathered last week had dwindled. She would need to gather more, soon. The sun heated the ground during the daylight, but at night the air grew chilly. Only a meager amount of wood was used for cooking, for quite often she had nothing to put in her pot.

Dragging a limb, she hoisted a branch upon the block. She lifted the axe and brought the blade down with a thud, splintering wood. Again and again she wielded the blade. After some time, she brushed a stray curl behind her ear, and gave a satisfied smile. The pile of timber should last her a few days.

She carried her axe back inside and checked on her patient. Asleep. The rise and fall of his chest indicated he still breathed. She padded to her wash bowl and splashed in cold water. Another item she needed to replenish. Now was as good a time as any.

Sweat ran in rivulets down her back. Her mother's words rang in her ear. *A lady does not sweat.*

Well, this one did. A trek to the lake carrying a heavy bucket would no doubt produce more.

She plucked her husband's knife from the wood box and stuck it in the band of her breeches. Grasping a pail, she headed out the door.

Mindful of her surroundings, she noted the distance with every step. Even though she'd grown accustomed to the country, lack of awareness risked mistakes. Miscalculations presumed doom. Being alone, she could not afford to be careless. Most of the animals kept to themselves, but she steered clear—ever watchful—just in case.

When she reached the water's edge, she lowered her bucket. How nice it would be to take a dip and refresh her sweltering body. How unfair the cool water beckoned, and she stood here roasting. The more she thought about it, the more oppressive the scorching heat grew. Reckless yearning battled within her. She searched every direction. Throwing caution to the wind, she quickly shed her wilting clothes, and jumped in.

Cold shock impaled her. She kicked her feet hoping to generate some warmth. Closer to the surface, the stream held less of a chill. Her body temperature adjusted quickly. Soon she reclined on her back and enjoyed the soothing swirling motion, saturating her limbs. The sun warmed her face. Water kneaded her aching muscles, making her body weightless. Caught up in the moment, she allowed precious minutes to slip by unheeded.

She stepped onto the grass, a movement caught her eye. She froze. A snake suddenly appeared next to her clothing. Her knife lay in the pile. No matter how many times she'd been careful, she had let down her guard today. Fear kept her immobile, she dare not move. No matter how badly she wanted to run, logic told her there was no benefit in retracing her steps back to the stream. A snake could swim far faster than she. The creature would swiftly overtake her. She would drown, or her body would be found naked in the grass. What was she to do?

Blood drained from her face. She hoped she would not retch. She closed her eyes and prepared to meet her maker. Now would be a perfect time to renew her faith.

Arrow prayers.

When she needed something fast, she would send a short prayer to heaven in a spearing fashion. Growing up, she had launched a number of those.

Dear Lord. Blessed be thy name. I beg your forgiveness in forsaking your name. It was not you who brought me here. My own foolish choices landed me in this country. But it was you who gave me the strength to go on after my husband's death.

If it be thy will, restore me in your grace. When I feel the snake's bite, help me to be strong once again. When the poison takes the breath from my lungs, I ask that you will allow me peace. Peace and joy of knowing you will accept me into your loving arms. Comfort in knowing you will grant me a place in your kingdom.

A single tear coursed down her cheek. Who knew it would come to this? When she fashioned the end in her mind, she never envisioned the embarrassment of someone finding her body bereft of clothing. She choked on a sob, desperately swallowing. Not allowing a sound to escape from her lips. Any sudden movement, or gasp, would make the creature strike sooner.

Her mother. Her father. They would never know what happened to their daughter. At least they would be saved the disgrace of how she died. Or how she would be found.

The shiver that struck her body derived from a mixture of shame, cold and dread. Her thin shoulders drooped in misery.

Seconds ticked by. The longest seconds of her life.

Reluctantly, she opened her eyes to slits. Seemingly uninterested, the slimy form slithered away. She watched the slithering creature until he was gone completely from her sight.

She dropped to the ground. Tears spilled from her eyes while gulping sobs tore from her chest.

Chapter 5

He was dead.

He had to be. For serenity enclosed him. Fresh air cloaked him. A cloud of softness wrapped him. Comfort would mean he'd gone to heaven, when he had been destined for hell .Slowly, Stephen became aware of soreness, then stinging, then blinding pain. Sure signs of hell.

The lilting voice of an angel drew him to an unbelievable place of calm. The honeyed sound soothed his mind to a state of ease. Alleviating his anxiety. Diminishing his pain. The most enchanting dream he'd ever held.

He opened his eyes with excruciating sluggishness. The first glimpse of light splintered his skull with a sharp stabbing. He slammed his eyes closed, and groaned in agony. He had been denied sunlight for so long, he thought never to see the light of day again.

His insides still stuck to his backbone. He breathed as deeply as his broken ribs allowed, then grinded his teeth over the agonizing ache. Slashing pain shot through his jaw stirring more memories. Oh yes. That had been broken, too.

Flashes of torture penetrated his skull—men with curved knives and jeweled handles, shackles, a pit for a prison cell. He was struggling with the bonds squeezing him when the sweetest sound pulled him from the dark fog. He seemed to recall a woman's hands. Impossible, but he fell into the dream. Reassuring hands swabbing a wet cloth over his feverish skin. Liquid. She coaxed him to swallow. Blessed relief to his parched lips.

A bed? He took a moment to grasp his surroundings. Unfamiliar hands. Gentle hands. He thought he'd felt movement at one time, dreamed he was in a wagon.

Was this real? How had he come to loll in a bed?

With a sense of unease, he pondered his situation, wondering what state of play brought him to this consequence. He inhaled, taking in pleasant air. No stench. No slimy creatures. Where was he? At this point he did not care. As long as he no longer suffered the Raj's torture.

Slowly, and more cautious this time, he lifted one lid to a narrow slit. The swelling around his eye had gone down considerably.

Definitely a bed.

He glanced down to find a hand-sewn quilt, like the ones his mother had made. Which also resembled his English heritage. Had he somehow been transported back to England?

He rolled his head against the pillow's softness, his mind wandering restlessly through a mirage of shadows. His ribs were on fire. He searched the room, finding an open window, and the thin covering wavered as if the wind blew gently to make it dance. He saw a crude piece of furniture beyond the bed with items scattered about the top. Perhaps a hair brush, ladies things. Then, to the right was a door. He wondered who was on the other side. Friend or adversary? Seeking relief, he closed his eyes for a moment.

He heard a sigh. Ignoring the pain in his skull, he turned his head to the right, and saw the delicate creature from his dream. An angel of mercy, with dark hair falling about her shoulders. Long sweeping lashes brushing velvety cheeks. Her chest rose and fell with her breathing, drawing attention to her generous bosom. Instant awareness surged through his body. At least the devils had not killed that part of him.

On the heels of that thought, he wondered if she were a maid or the wife of some possessive husband. If she were his wife—perish the thought—he would never leave her alone in any room with a strange man, incapacitated or no. Especially not in close proximity of a bed.

And he was naked. Bare as a new baby's bottom.

He studied the sleeping woman. How long had she slept in that chair? Watching him? Caring for him? Was this the only bed? How long had he been here? Where the deuced hell was he? When he drew an agitated breath, his ribs reminded him they had not yet healed. He glanced down at the bindings covering his chest. Running his hand down his torso and onto his thigh he found more compresses. His left thigh burned like the very devil. At least he still had his legs. He wiggled his toes and saw his ankles twice their normal size. More bandages. Time would tell, but he would walk again. If he had to rebreak, reset, crawl on his belly to a post, he would climb to his feet and walk like a bloody man.

He hated weakness. He hated his loss of time. While he'd been unconscious, any number of things could have happened, and he'd had no control of the events. Huh. Face it. He'd had no control of anything for a long time.

The bed's softness drew him like a flower drew a bee to its pollen. Releasing the tension in his muscles, he relaxed in comfort and clean linen. He turned his head to the side and sniffed. Hmm. *He* smelled better too. Relying on his intuition—which at the moment was telling him he was free—he calmed. Things had taken a definite turn for the better. He needed rest for now.

Take this time to regain his strength. When he was better, he would figure out his location and circumstance.

Couldn't be too bad. Not if he'd traded the Rajput prince for a guardian angel.

⁓ ele ⁓

Jennifer jolted awake. She jerked up straight in the chair, and glanced at the man's still form. Something woke her. She thought she had heard a noise. Her ears strained, listening for any sound. Nothing. Maybe it had just been her imagination.

While one hand rubbed the bones in her neck, she placed the other at her waist and arched her spine. Good Lord, sleeping on the floor would hold more comfort. The kinks in her back were many. She dragged herself up and padded to the main room. The fire had died, so she added more wood, stoked the fire, and set the kettle for heating water. She performed her morning duties, then gathered some broth which had become her routine. She took a hunk of bread, also. Since her patient was unable to chew, she would sop small bits in the broth for him to swallow.

Entering the smaller room, she placed the bowl on the stand, then stood beside the bed looking down at him. He had flung one arm over his forehead. The cover had slipped to his waist. She could not help but stare. Russet curls covered his chest and arms. So far, the special herbs had purged the infection. She may as well check the rest of him. She moved the blanket to the side, keeping his lower middle hidden. Purple, green and blue splotches covered his torso. Bruises often looked worse when they were healing. She wondered if his ribs still pained him in his sleep.

She ran her hand down his thigh, tracing the jagged line generating new red skin. The blanket slightly moved. The area around his lower middle formed a lump. Quite a large lump. She knew what a man wanted when *that part* of him grew big like that. Her eyes darted to his face. Thank goodness, his lids were still closed. Her shoulders sagged in relief. She should not be thinking about his manhood. But she had been married. She knew what went on in the bedchamber. Thinking about this man in that way sharpened her unsettling awareness.

Her hand hovered over him. This was absurd. She was just about to bring the blanket back over his leg when a rough, callused hand grabbed hers.

Her gaze flew to his in shock. Green sparkling eyes pierced hers. Well, that settled the color of his eyes. A wicked smile slowly curved his lips.

Her stomach lurched.

"I do not mind so much the direction of your hand, my lovely angel, but am I to be at the mercy of a fallen angel?"

His raspy voice knocked the breath right out of her lungs. His words, though hoarsely croaked, took her a full minute to grasp what he had said.

"Might I know your name," he swallowed and took another breath, "while you have your way with me?"

"I intended no such thing," she gasped.

His eyes creased at the corners and he gave a slight chuckle, sounding much like he had swallowed a mouth full of dry desert.

"I do not find the situation as amusing as you. I do not know how you can joke after what you have been through."

"Ah, and you know what I've been through?" His words muffled from the bandage tied firmly under his jaw.

"Well no, not exactly." She bit her lip. "You really should not speak. Your jaw needs more time to mend. I do know someone horrible has done this to you."

The humor left his face abruptly.

"You must have a strong will to live, for your injuries were severe. We thought you would die."

"We?"

"The people who brought you here."

He frowned, and seemed to be deep in thought. Jennifer had said too much. "Where exactly is here?"

Her eyes darted to where his fingers held her arm.

"I'm sorry." He let go. "I am not used to kind words, nor caring hands."

She tried to keep her mind from forming an image as she thought of who he meant.

"What is your name?"

"Jennifer."

"A beautiful name for a beautiful woman." The cocky grin was back. "Might I trouble you for a drink of water?"

Good Lord. Her surprise, and his husky voice, not to mention his tropical sea green eyes, had addled her wits. She twisted to get the bowl of soup.

"Is that a cup of coffee I spy?"

Hesitating, she grasped the cup instead. "It is tea."

"Tea?" His bushy brows rose to a slant.

"Yes. I keep a supply on hand." She held the cup forward, with a spoon to his lips.

"I can sit up."

"No!" She did not normally shout, well never. She lowered her voice and started to explain. "I spent a lot of sleepless hours sewing you back together. I do not want you to reopen your wounds."

The corner of his mouth lifted in a masculine grin, sending heat clear down to her toes. His eyes held the look of a lion that had just cornered a deer.

"So, you sewed me back together, did ya? I'm mighty grateful."

She blinked,

He was grateful.

"Then lie still. She perched on the end of her chair. "Take some of this." She spoon-fed him the warm tea.

"Mmm. Good ole English tea. You have yet to tell me where I am."

"I gave you my name, would you care to tell me yours?"

"That's easy enough. Stephen. Stephen Radbourn."

Stephen studied her as he said his name. With her gaze on the cup, she gave no reaction. Not a bold woman, a mite timid he would guess, since she would not meet his eyes. Slim delicate fingers, strong in their ministrations. He had dreamed of soft hands. Her hands. On his skin.

She brought the spoon to his lips again, and when he did not immediately open, her gaze locked with his. The most beautiful lavender eyes stared back at him, their color reminding him of the morning hours just before sunrise. When the sun's rays streaked above the ocean's horizon announcing the coming of a new day. Trepidation filled their impeccable depth.

Fear? Worry?

No.

Uncertainty.

"You have me at a disadvantage." He lifted his good arm drawing attention to his person. "At my present state, I can do you no harm. Even if I were completely whole, I would not harm a hair on your lovely head." He gave her a smile that had won many a fair maiden in many ports. And his chest lifted when she smiled back.

"Drink."

The clear liquid tasted better than any ale in any pub. Although the cloth tied around his head impaired the opening of his mouth.

"How long will I have to wear this blasted thing?" His voice unrecognizable to his own ears, he managed to coax words between his teeth.

"Your jaw was broken. It will be weeks before it is entirely healed."

"I have to sit here and let you spoon-feed me?" he asked, his voice curt with anger.

"Unless you would rather go hungry."

The imp. Days of her attendance sounded divine to him. It just might be worth the confinement to see her rousing smile. She switched the cup for a bowl. He watched as she added a few bits of bread, and then she offered him a bite.

The bread dissolved in his mouth. "This is good."

"I am sorry that I have to give you such small amounts."

"Lately, I've received much smaller portions."

"I would say hardly no portions. The way your clothes hung on you . . ." Her face flushed and she quickly dropped her head.

He knew what she was thinking. He wondered if she blushed so prettily when she removed the strips of cloth from his body. He swallowed the chuckle in his throat.

"We'll see what you have to say once I regain my appetite. I am a big man with a big stomach. I'll eat you out of house and home."

"We will see. You have a long way to go." She brought the spoon to his lips.

As she leaned nearer, he inhaled. Other than the stew, he whiffed no trace of perfume. No scent of woman, other than clean and fresh. Which he liked.

"Where are the others?"

"Others?"

"Earlier you said *we*."

"Oh. A man and young woman brought you to my door, and then left. There is no one else here but you and me."

He gave a soft whistle through his teeth. It took a lot of guts for a woman to admit to a man she didn't know that she lived alone. "This is your house?"

She nodded.

"Where is here?"

She held the spoon in midair. He crooked his head to the side. "I think my eyes are bigger than my stomach these days."

She set the bowl on the table beside her and stood. He watched as she rubbed her upper arms and paced to the doorway. He thought she would leave without answering. She turned.

"Who are you?"

"I told you my name. I captain a ship. Mostly, I live on the sea."

"You are English."

"So are you." Her eyes flashed with surprise. "Your voice. I recognize my homeland."

She gave a slight nod. "You are on the Malay Peninsula."

"Then I am still in India." *Damn.* So much for wishing he had somehow managed to get home.

"Y . . . yes. Did you sail your ship here? To India, I mean?"

The memory of his ship, and his men, scraped his soul. "Yes, bloody . . . Uh, sorry. Forgive my . . ."

She held up a hand stopping him. "That's quite alright."

He began again, this time being conscious of his language. "My ship sailed into a storm that blew us off course. We sailed the coastline hoping for a sign to get back on direction when we were blasted out of the water."

"You were attacked?"

"Yes. By blood-thirsty cutthroats. My crew was taken in chains." His anger boiled anew. Pain shot up the side of his face as he clenched his jaw. Guilt stabbed his conscious over the senseless slaughter. His hands fisted. He wanted to kill the bastard prince. "I will not tell you more."

"There is no need." Her soft voice echoed the sound of his own desolation. With quiet steps, she padded to his side. "How are your ribs?"

"I've still got 'em."

She sat down and gently poked his chest. Nimble fingers stroked his ribs, as if she was trying to see how many were broken. When she hit a tender area, he gave a sharp hiss through his teeth. She stilled.

"Is this hurting you?"

"No," he replied hoarsely.

"No?" Her raised brow, knowing he lied.

Damned if he would admit it.

"No," he said again.

"There is no shame in . . ."

He gave a bark of laughter, then immediately regretted his outburst as pain stabbed his chest.

"Are you going to tell me that did not hurt? Your expression says otherwise." She pulled the blanket to his chin. "From your reaction and the bruising, I'll warrant all your ribs are cracked."

"I could have told you that."

Her eyes softened to pity. The one thing he could not stomach.

"I am still a man," he said in a harsh voice. "My bones will heal. In no time at all, I'll be able to hold my own and no longer a burden to you."

"You are not . . ."

"I am not a burden?" He gestured toward his feet. "Even in my most stubborn state, I'm smart enough to know I cannot walk on these. So, I will be indebted to you a while longer. Have no doubt, I will compensate you well for your trouble. If that does not suit you, I will leave now."

Her sappy expression turned to confusion, then suddenly changed to anger. She braced her fisted hands on her hips. "All right, Captain Radbourn. Get up. Walk right out of here. Or would you rather I drag you out. I can do it you know, you stubborn jackass. Is it too much for you to just say thank you?"

With a huff, she whirled around and stormed out of sight.

He adjusted his earlier calculation.

Timid, hell.

What a spitfire.

She just might have a temper to match his. He snuggled his head into the pillow and stared at the ceiling. The corner of his mouth lifted in a smile.

He just might enjoy being in bed for a spell.

Chapter 6

What did the blasted man think he was going to do with this anyway? Stuck in bed, yet he demanded she bring him wood. Did he plan to whittle shavings onto her floor? If that was his intention, he had another think coming. Jennifer dug in her heels and heaved the limb, a trickle of crackling leaves evidence of her labor.

He did not handle confinement well. She supposed he had been the same way with his captor, which more than likely had resulted in his punishment being more severe. His body grew stronger each day. So did his voice—loud and insistent. He had an opinion for everything, and pouted when he did not get his way.

With too much time on his hands, he had come up with his latest idea. If it kept him from complaining, she would do anything. It was obvious he was used to commanding men, but she was not one of his crew. They butted heads, but here she was, in the middle of a maze of trees, following his instructions.

She walked for what seemed like hours before she found some limbs lying on the ground. One branch seemed large enough to provide several of the sizes he listed. Chewing on the end of her fingernail, she wondered if she could drag the whole thing back. After a few minutes deliberation, she decided to do just that.

She pulled and tugged, and hoped she would not meet anyone, especially her neighbor, Barincott. So far she had kept her house guest hidden, but it was just a matter of time before Barincott found out. If he saw her dragging this tree limb, he would not let her go without finding out every detail of what she did, and why. For now, she wanted to keep her houseguest her secret. For her own protection, it would be better he not find out. Barincott knew a great number of people. Those who imprisoned the captain could still be out there.

Several steps later, she dropped the base of her burden. Raising the canteen, she sipped fresh water. Cool liquid soothed her throat. She replaced the cap, and dropped the canister back on her hip. She raised a hand, shielding the sunlight from her eyes. A cloudless sky assured another hot day. She rolled her shoulders, lifted the tree limb, and continued on her way.

When her little shack came in sight, the band, the one she hadn't realized she had around her chest, eased.

I am not alone.

Knowing someone waited for her encouraged her steps. It did not matter the man was a stranger. He breathed air, and blood flowed through his veins. A real person. The past few weeks may have been a trial, but she had felt more alive than anytime this past year.

Stepping in from the afternoon sun, she hurried to the side room, unwilling to admit her eagerness to see him. Propped up on the bed, arms crossed, a sour expression covered his too-fetching face. She hid the smile that teased her lips.

His head jerked up when he sensed her presence. "Are you alright? You've been gone a long time."

His concern sent a tingling thrill of warmth through her. "I'm fine. You did send me after wood."

"Figured you'd get that right outside your door."

"I was not gone long."

"Long enough." He mumbled, and it sounded like he was cursing under his breath. "I will feel much better when I can get out of this da . . . er . . . bed."

"Not for a few more weeks," she said, ignoring his slip.

"Weeks. Bah. I'm getting sores on my backside."

"Then roll over," she said, more exasperated than any thought of wickedness.

"Why, Miss Jennifer." A wolf could not have looked more menacing. His wicked expression sent a tingle down her spine. "Are you wanting to have your way with me, again?"

Heat rushed to her cheeks, along with the memory of his bath, when she had thought he was unconscious. From complaining to seduction in one breath. The man was exasperating. "You can rest on your side and give your . . . *backside* a break."

He winced. "Please do not mention the word *break*. I have gotten accustomed to the idea of my bones mending."

He was adorably handsome when he scowled like a little boy. But he was a man. A robust man. When he completely recovered, he would be a mountain. Thinking about him in a personal way opened up other thoughts—like how suitable he looked in her bed. The blanket rode low at his waist. Enticing. Her fingers begged to dance among the spiraling curls, to learn if they were as silky as those fine hairs looked—without soap.

In her imagination, she saw him on a ship. The wind in his titian hair. Corded ropes for muscles. Feet braced apart while tight breeches caressed his thighs. Master of his ship, he would be the master of any woman.

The breath caught in her throat.

Good Lord, get hold of yourself.

"Uh . . . Captain . . ."

"Now might be a good time for you to call me by my given name," he said. "Seeing as how we are getting pretty familiar here."

The two of them, being in close proximity, she supposed they were bound to get … close. She had certainly become comfortable having him around. Had she given herself away? Had he read her mind? She flushed at the possibility. Desire must have been written on her face. And him, being a scoundrel—he must be since he sailed the seas, probably a pirate—could read her all too well.

She flounced away from him before he could do any more damage.

If she thought to cool off out of doors, she thought wrong. Since it happened to be mid-day, the heat was oppressive. After a short walk, she returned to find *Stephen* in the same mood in which she left him.

"Are you hungry?"

"I'm always hungry."

His hot gaze spoke of his desire for more than food. Or was it her own creativity at work? She really needed to get control over her wild imaginings.

She prepared a light repast, and he insisted on feeding himself.

"Bring your bowl and sit with me. I do not like eating alone."

The arrogant knave.

When she just stared at him, he said, "Please."

Good Lord, she was a pushover. Procuring her own bowl and bread, she sat beside him on the chair she had become accustomed to since he had entered her home.

God, she was beautiful when she got her dander up. During his nap, she'd changed into a gown. True the thing had seen better days, and it hung loosely on her body. Earlier she had worn men's clothing, which reminded him there must have been a *Mr. Jennifer* at some point. She never mentioned her last name. Where was the bloody boor? Run off? Left her alone? Stephen's anger soared at the thought her husband snuck off, leaving her to survive alone.

Hardened by the land, she was not weak. This woman was the strongest female he'd ever had the pleasure to meet. She worked hard, her calloused hands were testament of that. She demonstrated a kind heart, for she had taken care of him without complaint. He could be harsh and unpleasant on a good day. Yet her gentle nature took a turn when her eyes sparked and her annoyance flared her temper.

Hit him right where he most liked to be struck—in his funny bone.

He liked the way the breeches molded her nice rounded bottom. But when she raised her arms over her head and tied her long sable tresses into a knot, the shirt shaped her curves, sending an ache to his gut. Watching her now, in her gown, the familiar itch returned.

"When are you going to tell me about your husband?"

The question took her by surprise. "I'm not."

Cool as a breeze across a moonlit deck, she did not even blink. "You are married?"

"My husband died."

So, there it was. Out in the open. Now he could deal with it.

"My condolences. How long ago?"

She stood ready to flee.

"Please," he said, his voice coaxed. "If I promise not to mention him, will you stay?"

She hesitated. Then, without speaking a single word, she sat back down.

He let out a breath. Temper flared quick with her. Stubborn too. Reminded him of his little sister, Kat. He liked Jennifer's company. Peculiar how ardently he fancied her presence. Unaccustomed to being vigilant with his words, he needed to be more careful, else his reckless tongue would chase her away.

He started to whistle, then changed his mind. "So, how's the weather?" Her smile freed the knot in his chest. "At least you aren't threatening to drag my sorry arse out the door."

She gave a full laugh. "Tell me, captain, a—"

"That is not my name." He feigned a growl.

"*Stephen*," she said with all the syrupy sweetness of a young debutante at her coming out ball.

"That's better." His tone hinted at anger, but he smiled with pleasure.

"Tell me, do you like sailing the seas?"

"What kind of question is that? I'm a captain. I would live forever on the sea, if I could."

A flicker of emotion crossed over her eyes. Envy? Distress?

"Seafaring's in my blood. A good sturdy ship and a durable wind can stir a man's soul. Sailing into the horizon brings a little bit of heaven here on earth."

"What about family? A home?"

"I have family. I have a sister who's a hoyden. But Katherine is growing up. My parents died in a carriage accident about eight years back. I took her to live with my aunt and uncle. Toughest thing I ever did in my life." He scooped a spoonful of food and slowly swirled it around in his mouth. He could move his jaw a bit, but he wasn't taking any chances with it healing.

"Katherine is your sister?"

"Yep. She's a handful. When I dropped her at my uncle's door, she met another hoyden, and the two of them think there's nothing they can't do. I knew my aunt would take her in hand and make Kat a lady."

"Kat?"

"One of my pet names for her."

Jennifer stared out the little window. He wondered if she saw anything, or if perhaps she was recalling a memory. Something captured her attention, and it was not anything visible. Giving her time to her private thoughts, he spooned more broth, the soaked bread dissolving to mush. He swallowed slithers of meat, small enough he did not need to chew them. Wasn't sure what kind, but it didn't matter. He could feel his strength returning. As soon as he could get out of this bloody bed, he would work on restoring his muscles.

⁓ℓℓ⁓

"What are you trying to do, woman? Scalp me? Give me that blade."

Stephen sounded like a grizzly bear, but she had grown accustomed to his gruff voice. Not that he railed with temper. The contrary. He simply boomed with his speech. She supposed it could be from shouting orders over crashing waves and sea winds. What was a normal tone of voice to him might seem boisterous to anyone who did not know him.

Did she know him? She sure was comfortable with him.

She drew back, boldly holding the razor out of reach. "You only have one good arm."

He held up his good arm. "I can manage with this one." Stephen's glare would terrify her, if she allowed it.

"This is not my first time shaving a man."

"It's the first time with me." Thunderclouds could not have appeared darker than his expression.

She knew he would not hurt her. He did not scare her in the least. "I will be more careful."

"I'll not be bled out by a bloody female," he roared.

"Oh, good Lord. Have it your way." She slapped the razor into his palm, and then placed the bowl of water on his lap. "I'll get bandages ready."

His vibrant laugh followed her through the door. Stubborn man. Let the fool cut his throat. What did she care?

Obscenities thundered from the other room making her wonder if he would massacre his face to preserve his pride.

"All right! Get in here!"

Smiling to herself, she cocked her head. He had not asked. He demanded. *Guess a ship's captain expected everyone to follow his orders.*

She peaked around the corner of the doorway. "You bellowed?"

"Being quiet is not a habit of mine." With a sheepish grin and a menacing frown, he looked anything but sorry.

A quick glance at his face and she saw blood. "What are you trying to do?" She hurried to his side. Blood oozed from a gash under his jaw. "I guess you would rather bleed out by your own hand."

His grin grew bigger.

"Men."

His grin was quickly replaced with a frown. "What's that supposed to mean?"

"Nothing." She wiped the spots of blood away, making sure the wounds were not deep.

"It must be something or you would not have said it," he barked.

"Shut up, or you will have another nick."

"You cannot group all men together."

"Oh, I can't?"

"No," he growled.

"I suggest you save your words for later if you want this job finished without any more mishaps."

His fingers curled around her wrist. "I'll save my words for later, if you promise I will still have a throat to speak with."

Warmth flowed from his hand smoldering her skin. Tingles of awareness attacked her senses. How long it had been since she had been touched by a man. Still, she'd never felt such heat, such burning intensity. Her response shook her.

"If you are unable to talk, it will be through no fault of mine." Not if she could control the trembling he stirred within her.

"You're a feisty one, aren't you?" He released her hand and leaned back. "I like that."

It took every ounce of will to concentrate on her task and not his words. The man leered at her. There was no other word for it. His eyes watched her every move. Trying her best to ignore him—which was near impossible—she carefully scraped the hair from his jaw. Determined not to meet his eyes, she willed her fingers to be steady and not scar the man for life. Although, he currently presented a great number of scars.

She held her breath, and then slowly released it after each scrape. Her chest hurt from nervous tension. Sending her mind elsewhere, she drew upon her memories of other times when she'd done this. Pretending Stephen was her husband only sent more heat to her center, so she halted that line of thinking immediately. The two men were as different as night and day.

A ship's captain. His size and his words hinted at the power he must have possessed, before he had been beaten and starved. Energy surrounded him as if he was a man who knew what he wanted and would stop at nothing to get it. Somehow, she did not think he would need to use brute force. His fierce scowl was intimidating enough.

His features were somewhat handsome, not pretty like the dandies in London. Yet she found him incomparable. His green eyes, sharp and daring, pierced, and captivated her on contact. A sense of command in his dangerous gaze, then his eyes had gone soft, and he managed what could pass for a charming smile, considering the split lip on his handsome, swollen mouth with full lips.

She mentally gave herself a good shake. Experience had taught her of men and their dominance over women. She may be attracted to his body, but she would never be vulnerable to a man again.

She managed to scrape his whiskers leaving his throat intact. She had no idea how she kept her fingers from trembling.

When she met his gaze, the devil's eyes twinkled. He knew his disturbing effect on her. *The scoundrel.*

"I'll empty this bowl and bring you fresh water for a bath."

"Now that sounds like a fine idea."

By his teasing expression, he must be thinking something wicked. She hurried from the room, conscious he was watching her. When she returned with a pail of water, his smirking grin was still in place.

She placed the pan within his reach. "You can wash yourself."

"How am I supposed to do that? My muscles are weak, and I am overwrought from having a shave. Never had a woman shear me before. Drained the energy right out of me."

She forced her lips not to smile. She would never admit, to him or herself, that the idea of running a cloth over his nude body sounded delectable.

"Very well." She gave a little huff to disguise her inner emotion. She wrung the cloth, lathered it with some soap, and started on his shoulder.

"You don't have to scrub the hide off me. I have very little left."

She softened her movements. Two could play at this game.

Unsure of her hasty decision, and ignoring any thought of changing her mind, she caressed his muscles as she drew the cloth in circles. She had never done anything so outrageous before. She had been tempted quite a lot where the captain was concerned. Her fingers slowed their movement as her hand slid across his chest, making sure she covered every devilish inch.

Again, she dipped the cloth in the pan of water and wrung the excess. Her eyes fastened on springy, auburn curls glistening with moisture. She tried to swallow. Realizing she stood there with a stupefied look on her face, she glanced up to meet his all-knowing gaze. Good Lord, she'd never had a man look at her so. His green eyes electrified her. As she stared into their depths, his irises darkened. The breath caught in her lungs. She dropped the cloth.

The sound of the light plop in the pan of water jerked her attention. "Oh." She quickly recovered, scolding herself. She needed to concentrate on the task at hand. She wrung the cloth again, and rinsed away any remaining soap on his mantle of fur. Recalling his early statement, and mindful of his ribs, she eased the cloth down his torso, and lower. Her eyes caught on the sheet just below his navel.

The linen lifted.

Chapter 7

His arousal grew, and there was not a damn thing he could do about it.

Nor did he want to. Seeing the flush spread over Jennifer's cheeks delighted him more than he could have imagined.

"Well? Are you going to wash the rest of me?"

Her gaze flew to his. "You can wash that part yourself."

"But I am so tired, and my arm hurts." He enjoyed this fun at her expense.

She grabbed the soap and lathered the rag with a vengeance.

He sucked in his breath. If she grabbed him vigorously, he would not be responsible for the consequences.

Instead of grabbing him *there*, where he wanted, the cloth landed on top of his thigh.

"You saving the best for last?"

"I am not going to . . . touch your . . . privates."

"But it needs to be washed. Dirt and grunge could develop some malady. What if it falls off?"

She gave an unladylike snort, but the pressure on his leg remained the same. "I have never heard anything so preposterous." She moved her hand to the inside, closer to his aching crotch. His manhood bounded to a full-blown salute, as if responding to a bugle's call-to-arms.

Her hand froze. Right between his legs. God, it felt wonderful. If his legs were in better shape, he would close them and trap her hand there. His manhood gave a jerk.

She nearly squealed, but closed her lips tight, not allowing her voice to escape. Her expression initiated a chuckle, but he swallowed before it could leave his throat.

Damn the woman was made of stern stuff. She resumed her duty and quickly washed the rest of his leg, and its partner. He nearly swallowed his tongue when her fingers slid the soft cloth between his toes. He would have to remember that and file it away the next time he made love to a woman.

For he was damned determine to get out of this God-forsaken bed. He had been a whole man. He would be again. And the next conquest on his list was the lovely widow.

When she turned to go, a hint of disappointment sprang in his chest. Only to be quickly replaced with anticipation. She was no bit of fluff. From his perception, this woman trooped like an ostrich. Long extended legs, and her head buried in the sand. He looked forward to ruffling her tail feathers. Anticipated extracting her head out of the sand and introducing her to pleasure. The kind a man stimulated in a woman.

❦

The sun's rays made their way through the sweltering air over the small farm. Jennifer suffered the humid haze blurring the country side as she dug in the dry soil. She wiped her face with the back of her wrist, smearing more dirt across her brow. Since she had been on her own, she did what she could to survive. Her meager vegetable garden helped to keep her fed.

For two weeks, she'd battled with a stubborn ox. The tenacious captain was slowly driving her out of her mind. He had demanded wood to make some sort of brace for each leg, then whistled while he carved the supply of sticks she'd chopped from the branch. He'd managed to fasten the device, a strap of leather below his knee and another around his thigh, preventing his feet from touching the ground, offsetting any pressure to his ankles. Then he fashioned a crude crutch, one for under each arm, adding several knobs at the bottom which resembled a spider with legs. Until he explained his reasoning, she thought his creation absurd. But he demonstrated the protrusions would help to balance each prop on its own weight.

How he managed to stay erect was beyond her imagining. But he did it—his peculiar appearance as ludicrous as his crazy idea. But it worked. He wobbled a lot at first, and she had expected to pick him up from the ground. The stubborn man battled the contraption until he conquered it. Now he sat in front of her little house, watching her.

"Why in God's name are you in this country?" His shout came out of nowhere. Startled, she turned to him in wonder.

"If you are going to grumble, you can go back inside." She returned to her digging.

"And miss this lovely day?"

She glanced over her shoulder. He'd requested a chair brought outside, then grumbled when she tried to help him. With his wood-caged feet propped upon a log, the uncanny picture would have been ludicrous, if not for the constant stare of those scorching green eyes.

"You are English. I would think fancy balls would be customary?"

Once. The reminder brought an ache to her chest. She shoved the irritant away and directed her vexation to heaving the shovel into the ground. "Have you forgotten where you are?"

"What of your hands? A woman's hands should be soft. Not calloused from doing man's work."

She spun around. "Do you see a man around here? You think I am incapable of taking care of myself?"

He stared at her. Hard. "I think you are an extraordinary woman."

His rugged voice managed to set her heart racing, more than the physical exertion of digging in the dirt.

"You have proven you can manage on your own. You cannot blame a man for wondering what an English lass is doing on the opposite side of the world."

She would never admit how much she hated her life. How her husband had brought her to this country and abandoned her. "What difference does it make? I am where I am."

"You still have not told me about your husband. Except that you do not have one."

Was the man clairvoyant? His question too close to her own weary deliberations. "You ask too many questions."

"All right." A thoughtful grin crossed his clean-shaven face.

How different he appeared. The bruising had faded making him look less sinister. Even with his menacing looks, the man was devastatingly attractive. More than likely, he'd left a trail of broken hearts in England, and in every port his ship had docked.

"What would you like to know about me?" His question took her by surprise.

"Absolutely nothing." She turned back to her digging.

"Come now. You must be curious. Isn't there something you would like to ask me?"

"Only when you will leave."

He laughed out loud. Motioning to his legs, he replied, "I think I may be here a while, yet. Are you tired of my company?"

No. She looked forward to every enlivening moment. She was no longer lonesome. No longer cut off from the world. If not a companion, she could pretend she had a friend.

"Come sit with me. Get something cool to drink."

More orders. But the idea sounded pleasant enough. She'd gone down to the stream early this morning for fresh, cool water.

Dragging another chair outside, she fetched two cups and retrieved the jug she'd left in the shade. Handing one cup to Stephen, she sat in the opposite chair.

After a few moments of silence, her tense muscles began to relax.

"You're a woman alone, and you have taken on quite a burden with me."

Of all the things she might have expected him to say, those words staggered her.

"I admire your strength," he went on. "I want you to know I appreciate what you've done for me. I will repay you."

"There is no need. I would have done the same for anyone." She took a sip of water, enjoying the refreshing rush in her throat.

"But you took care of *me*. I've not been beholden to any one—ever. I was in pretty bad shape."

She'd known how badly his injuries, and she had not expected him to live. "I thought you would die." Her voice caught. Without looking at him, she felt the heat of his gaze.

"I too, thought I was at my end. But as you can see, I do not give up easily."

No, he did not.

His voice stirred the nerves under her skin.

"You were . . ."

"No need to talk about it," he said with some force, but she heard his anguish.

They sat in silence.

After some time, he gave a heart-felt sigh. When he spoke, his words were low. "When I was a boy, a friend of my father owned a ship. He talked of life at sea. Spoke of his many voyages, which sounded like great adventures to me. I looked forward to his visits with relish. Of course, I wanted to experience adventures of my own." He stared into the distance.

She willed him to continue.

"My father had his own ideas. He raised me to follow in his footsteps, be a man of import. But I dreamed of the sea. Of being on a ship, with the wind in my hair. Seeking new lands. I even tossed around the whim of being a pirate." He gave a soft chuckle.

A pirate.

"At nineteen, I decided I needed to be on my own. The social order was not for me. Although I did enjoy the ladies, new exploits called. At the right time, too. My father's friend arrived for one of his visits, and I asked to sail with him."

"And he said yes," she added.

"He said yes." His voice sounded more depressed than excited.

She wondered what he was leaving out. "What did your father have to say?"

"He told me to follow my dreams. Which surprised me in a way. Then again, he always encouraged us to be independent. Kat and me.

"Kat. Your sister."

"Most times I call her Kitten."

"You sailed away and left your family behind." *Just like me.*

Stephen turned with indignation. "Who? My parents? My sister? A man needs to be a man. I had no other responsibilities. Nothing to hold me back. I sought my deepest desire."

"And you became a captain with your own ship?"

"Aye, I did." He settled back, and once again stared out into the distance. "The sea became my home. I visited my family when the wind blew me in their direction. After my parents died, my responsibility to Kat made me return home more frequently. But then, my love for my little sister is well-rooted, and has grown deeper since our parents' deaths."

"Your affection reflects in your voice when you speak of her."

"Do you have siblings?"

A hollow ache filled her chest at his question. How she wished she could see her family. How desperately she wanted to go home.

"A sister." She feared her voice would catch if she said more.

"Another as beautiful as you? The ton must have been on their ear with two exquisite beauties roaming about."

She flushed. He had known just what to say to keep her sentiments at bay.

"The dandies must have had apoplexy at your coming out. Not knowing which one to choose."

"Isabella is younger."

"That's worse. They took one look at you and knew what a beauty she would be. How did your father handle the constant parade at your door?"

What a rascal. Still, her heart lifted.

"There were no lines of suitors. I had made my choice."

"Ah yes. The husband. I am surprised your father allowed his daughter to live in a land such as this. And alone." His bushy brows drew together in a frown as he gave her an accusing glare. "Or does he know your husband has departed?"

"No, he does not," she said after a long hesitation.

"Of course he doesn't! What kind of father would allow his daughter to live the way you do?"

Her hackles rose. "I am doing just fine thank you."

He smiled. "You are at that."

Tension eased from her shoulders. Who could stay miffed with a smile that melted your bones?

"You are a strong woman, Mrs. Jennifer. What is your husband's surname?"

"What is the name of your ship?"

His face hardened and his eyes turned dark. "I have more than one."

That was a surprise. "How about the one you were on when you came to this country?"

He waited so long to answer, she thought he wouldn't. She had asked a question she doubtless should not have, and it was too late to take it back.

"*Serpent's Ghost*. She is a real ghost now. She lies at the bottom of the sea."

Regret washed through her. "I'm sorry. You said you had more."

"Ships can be replaced," he growled. "Men cannot."

The sky did not have to fall for her to figure out she'd trekked into forbidden territory. What happened to his crew? Had they suffered the same fate as him? No wonder he did not want to talk about his ship, or his crew. She had a million questions, but dare not ask any of them.

His face glowed harsh in the morning sun. She imagined him on a ship with the sun glimmering streaks of gold in his dark red hair. A full beard the same auburn would suit a captain. Arms crossed, feet apart, sprinkles of ginger curls on a bare, burnished-bronze chest. A current of awareness whizzed through her veins at the vision her mind created.

Heat suddenly infused her cheeks. She waved a hand to fan herself. What was wrong with her, having such thoughts about a man she barely knew? This simply would not do. She must stop imagining him with his clothes off.

Still, she could not help but wonder what it would be like to be touched by another man. To be held by Stephen, with his strong arms tight around her. And she was not immune to his attraction. She shook off her doldrums.

"You are welcome to stay here as long as you need." The time would come for him to leave soon enough. Until then, she must keep her mind on practical things. Like food, and . . . chores . . . and . . .

Warmth engulfed her. She glanced down to find his hand covering hers. He lifted her fingers to his lips. Her breath caught. She stared in awe—and anticipation.

"Thank you." His voice rasped.

Her eyes darted to his. Flurries swamped her stomach. Trapped, his gaze held her spellbound. Moments ticked by. For how long, she did not know. Did not care. She wished he would kiss her. Take her in his arms and kiss her on the mouth.

Her lips parted on a hopeful perception.

When he touched her, she realized he moved. The tip of his finger traced her lips.

"Soft. Like velvet. Full. So tempting. If I could reach you, I'd haul you onto my lap."

Like a bucket of water suddenly flung in her face, she snapped out of her irrational stupor, and jerked back.

"I need to fix dinner." She jumped from her chair like her seat was on fire. Spinning about, she scampered inside, embarrassed by her reaction—and her wishful thinking.

No sound came from the man outside. Maybe he did not find her humiliation amusing after all.

Chapter 8

Jennifer looked up at the thin man sitting on the grey steed with his elbow resting on the saddle-horn. Bright sun outlined his form. Strands of dark hair stuck out from under a well-worn hat. Close set eyes framed a crooked nose and the mustache above his lip barely hid the leering grin of even white teeth. The thought of him falling off his horse gave her a brief moment of satisfaction. If only she was a man, she would take pure delight in yanking him off and hurling him to the ground.

"Good morning to you, Mrs. Faircloth." His fingers tapped the brim of his hat.

"Mr. Barincott." She gave a nod, returning his greeting.

"What a lovely morning it is."

It was till you showed up.

When he shifted in the saddle, she held her breath praying he would not dismount. Not because she didn't like the way his evil gaze slid down her body, or because his sinister smile sent revolting chills down her spine. Frankly, it would not do for him to find an unexpected man in her house.

How in the world would she explain Stephen's presence? What if Barincott connected Stephen to the men who had tortured him? The fiends may be looking for him this very moment. Barincott knew too many people. Originally from England, he had made his home in India. By his own choosing, or if he had been run out of England, she had no idea. He always gave her the idea he'd done something wrong, and she should not let down her guard. She was not sure how long he had lived in this country, but he was well-known when she and Johnny arrived.

"What brings you here, Mr. Barincott?"

"Just being neighborly. Thought I would come by and pay a visit. See if you needed anything."

"No, sir. I am fine."

"Sir? That sounds so formal." This time when he shifted his weight, he threw one leg over and slid to the ground.

Her muscles tensed.

"Why don't you call me Abraham?"

"I'm sorry, Mr. Barincott. It would not be proper for a widow, still mourning her husband to be so familiar." She felt the need to remind him of her husband, putting as much distance between them as she could.

"I admire you for keeping to the English customs." He took a step toward her porch. "However—"

"I was on my way to the stream," she blurted out, quickly stepping to the ground. He absolutely could not come any closer. She prayed Stephen still slept. She scurried to the side of her little porch and quickly retrieved two buckets.

"Allow me to go with you."

"Oh, that is not necessary." Before she could further protest, he took the buckets from her with a guileless smile. Any more objections would make him suspicious.

"A lady should not have to carry heavy buckets when a gentleman is around."

Gentleman—could be disputable.

She should have thought of that. For now, he would certainly escort her back. She would deal with that later.

"Shall we?" He transferred the pail handles to his other hand holding the leading strap of his horse. Then he gestured in the direction of the water. She had no choice but to go with him.

"I am glad for this opportunity to speak with you, Mrs. Faircloth."

"It is such a fine day, Mr. Barincott. Could we not talk and simply enjoy the nature around us while we walk?"

The smile left his face, but he nodded in consent.

Thank goodness. She needed this time to think of a plan to get rid of him. She rubbed her palms on the sides of her breeches. Warmth spread across her thighs. Stephen flashed in her mind. A stroll with him would have definitely been more pleasing—in more ways than one.

Now why did the thought of him pop up the moment friction caressed her thighs? Her pace quickened.

"You must be in a hurry?"

"What?" How had she forgottten *him*? "Oh, I like a brisk walk."

Barincott lengthened his stride to keep up, his horse trailing behind.

When they reached the water's edge, she gave a sigh of thanks. Ignoring her outstretched hands, Barincott dropped the rein on his horse. He knelt on one knee and filled the buckets with water.

"Why don't we rest a spell?" Amazing how his grin did nothing for her—certainly not in the daunting manner as her houseguest. When Stephen grinned, her insides fluttered.

"I have to get back. I have chores to do."

"That is what I wish to speak with you about." Barincott's expression reminded her of her father when he was about to give a lecture.

Hands on her hips, she put a bland look on her face—one of confusion.

He removed a blanket tied to his saddle. "Let's sit, I have a proposition for you."

Uneasy at first, she hesitated to ask. But she would rather face a quandary than have a tricky situation sneak up on her later. "What kind of proposition?"

He spread the blanket on the ground. "Won't you sit down?"

"Mr. Barincott, I am a widow in mourning. Even if I were not, I am not the kind of lady who would participate in a tryst."

His eyes grew round. "Mrs. Faircloth, you misunderstand me."

Whether his countenance was one of offense, or one of glee that she had thought of him in those terms, she was not sure.

"I apologize for the confusion. If you sit there, I will sit on the grass. I only want to talk."

"You can speak while standing."

A flush filled his face. His nostrils flared. Uh oh. He was quick to anger. She needed to remember that. He took a deep breath, gaining control of his emotions. "Very well. I believe we got off on the wrong foot. I am not trying to have my way with you. I respect you."

"Thank you," she sniffed, letting him know he was not off the hook.

"I am very sorry for the loss of your husband. I would like to help you, if you will allow me."

"Help? What kind of help?" She asked in a calm voice, yet conveyed her suspicions.

"Please, Mrs. Faircloth. I have no ulterior motives."

And cows fly over the moon.

"You should not be doing chores that a man could do for you."

"Mr. Barincott. I can chop my own wood and—"

"That's man work. Not for a delicate young woman."

Barincott was much older. But she had never considered his age before. A touch of silver tinted his dark hair. Crinkles around his eyes did not take away from his handsome face. Only his glare lacked evidence of warmth. Yes, he most assuredly had ulterior motives.

"Delicate? I assure you I am not faint of heart, nor slight of muscle."

"I know you are strong. I admire that about you. But, a woman should not be alone. This is a different land. Things are not the same here. You have no family."

"My family is in England, as you are well aware. Are you offering to send me back to England?"

His shocked expression ascertained that idea had clearly not crossed his mind.

"If that is your wish." He gave a slight nod, then continued, "but, I would like you to know that you are not on your own. I am willing to help you. With your countenance, of course, I would like to take care of you."

What he meant by *take care of her* would probably involve a bed. And she had no hankering for that.

"What do you mean, take care of me?"

"I am an honorable man. I would offer you marriage. I would not think of disrespecting your honor."

"Mr. Barincott. Did you just propose marriage?" She added a touch of sweetness to her mock display of surprise.

"Uh, before I do that, I want you to consider the idea. I know you are still in mourning. We could not declare a betrothal at this time."

Of course not. You want to see if you can bed me first.

At her silence, he moved closer.

"Please." She took a step back and turned away. "I cannot."

"I won't rush you."

"I cannot even think of such a thing. Johnny . . ." She hiccupped on a sob for effect.

"I empathize," he said. "You loved your husband very much."

"Yes. Yes, I did," she lied. Her impulsive love for Johnny was a young girl's infatuation. She knew that now.

"Will you at least consider what I've said? A woman cannot live alone in this country. Anything can happen."

Which she knew all too well.

"Please. I am still in mourning." It was a daring move, but she turned her back on him, hoping he would think her distressed. "I must think."

"I never meant to upset you. I will see you to your home."

"No please. I cannot bear any more. Please go. I must think." He had unknowingly given her the perfect excuse to send him packing. "I must mourn my husband. Please. I need to be alone."

The sound of his harsh breathing retreated. She heard the creak of leather.

"Mr. Barincott. My husband has not been gone a year. I will not consider your intentions until the proper time." She had to throw him a bone. And still keep him at a distance.

"As you wish. But I will call from time to time, to be sure you are safe."

"Sir. I already told you I can take care of myself." She gave a hiccup and made her voice shaky for good measure.

"I know you would like to think so. You are a strong woman, Mrs. Faircloth. However, you are a woman living isolated. Unaccompanied. As a gentleman, safeguarding you is the respectable thing to do."

There was that word again. Gentleman. Debaucher, more like.

"Good day, Mrs. Faircloth." His horse snorted, he jerked the reins and rode away.

She crumpled in relief. Let him think her grief stricken. If truth be known, she had just escaped impending doom. His words may have sounded sincere, but he had a black heart, which showed in his eyes every time he looked at her. His gaze always sliding up and down her body, inspecting every inch, undressing her with his scrutiny. It was loathsome.

She feared she only evaded his presence for a short time.

"What did you think you were doing? Where are your crutches?"

Stephen hated his body's weakness. Being discovered face down in the middle of the floor rated right up there with humiliation. Although, he did not mind so much having a beautiful woman fawn over him. He could do without her anguished expression.

"I tripped," his voice irritable, embarrassed at being found in such a mortifying position. "It's about time I put these legs to some use."

Her fingers quickly checked his ankles. "At least you have them wrapped tight."

"Woman, I have lived on a ship for more years that you've been born. I have seen many mishaps, and doctored my share of broken bones."

"So, you are an old man *and* an old fool."

Damn the girl had sass. "I am not an old man."

"And, I am no child," She shot back. She helped him to a chair, then stepped back, frowning at him. "How old do you think I am?"

Old enough.

Her eyes flashed fire. Determined and loaded with fervor. He loved a woman with spirit. She was completely unaware of the picture she made with her hands on her hips and her divine bosom thrust forward. Her soft curves would feel delectable in his hands. She was all woman, he'd give her that. His mood lifted considerably.

"You musta been married out of the cradle."

"Ha. I'm not that much younger than you. I am two and twenty. And if I were a child, you would not look at me the way you do."

That got his attention. He quirked up a brow, catching her gaze.

"How do I look at you?"

Her cheeks flushed red.

"Come now, my lovely. Do not go all shy on me now."

She meant to pull away, but he was having none of it. He grasped her wrist and gave a tug. She bounced onto his lap. He quickly locked his arms around her while she wrestled to get free.

"Simmer down. I won't bite." He gave her a grin that had prompted many maids to eagerly jump onto his lap. "Unless you want me to."

"Of course, I do not want you to."

"Liar," he whispered, his lips close to her ear.

She wiggled again.

His loins stirred. This woman had a habit of making his manhood jump to life.

"Keep doing that and I'll do more than bite."

"You are no gentleman," she said crossly.

"You're right. I've been on a ship too long to sport gentlemanly ways. But I can be gentle. Let me show you."

His angel sat on his lap, not moving. Her breasts extended with each laboring breath, resembling a rabbit ready to run. Anxiety? Or anticipation? The woman was a widow. She knew the workings of a man's mind.

He leaned close enough for his breath to fleetingly sweep her neck. One hand stroked down her back while the other settled across her stomach, snugly on her hip, allowing her no escape. His fingers worked their magic, massaging, kneading, manipulating her, coaxing her to relax her inhibitions. Melt away her defenses.

Lifting a lock of her hair, he tugged her earlobe between his lips and gently drew in, with featherlike suction. Her eyes closed and her head drifted back. As light as a dove's wing, he blazed a trail of kisses down the vein in her delicate throat. She shuddered.

He slid his hand upward from her hip. Rising, gliding upward, over her rib cage to a swell of flesh. One finger slowly drew circles around her breast, each loop nearing closer and closer to its tip. A tiny sound escaped her lips when his finger finally touched her beaded nipple.

She was his. His for the taking.

He captured her cheek, and as she raised her face, he brought her mouth to his. "Ahhh. Sweet Jennifer." He brushed his lips over her warm, sweet ones. He added a bit of pressure under her jaw making her open her mouth. She sighed and he groaned in delight. Need drove him. He twisted and slipped his tongue inside, needing her taste. She gave a start of surprise, then quickly recovered, kissing him back with equal fervor.

His Jenny was a passionate sort. He slid a deft hand to unknot the upper ties of her shirt. Then he slipped his hand inside. Soft skin filled his palm as he cupped her breast. Damn she felt good.

She arched forward filling his hand, her body showing him she loved his bold caress.

And craved more.

She moaned, and he caught her soft cry in his mouth.

God Almighty, he wanted her. *Now!*

He wanted her pressed against him, naked, skin on skin. Her bare breasts rubbing his own unclothed flesh. Their hips pressed together as one.

His other hand slid down to her belly.

Damn man's breeches. Why didn't the woman wear a bloody skirt?

He kissed her thoroughly. Keeping her mind occupied, his hand slipped between her legs. The tips of his fingers pressed her center, stroking, creating a friction through her clothing.

She gripped his shoulders.

A thrill of delight cuffed his chest. Instead of pushing his hand away, she rocked her body as if seeking more of his stroking. He pressed harder, angled deeper for penetration. He would give her pleasure through her damn man breeches, just see if he didn't.

She lunged against his hand. He thought he would explode from the sheer pleasure of it.

Holy mother of —

He had to get the bloody breeches off. Or at least open them where he could get to her. Claim his prize. Give her what she begged for.

His fingers unknotted the rope. He kissed her passionately, using his tongue, seeking, laving every sweet angle of her mouth—and damned if she didn't respond just as madly. He drank in her sighs and moans, and pushed her down on his rapidly growing arousal.

"Stephen," she said in a throaty voice that drove him wild.

Tugging the constricting material out of his way, he found the slit in her drawers—and her delicious honeypot.

He gulped.

Dewy and warm. His eyes rolled back in his head. Sweet flesh, slick and moist. He glanced down to find her face awash with color. Her violet eyes glazed under a thick blanket of lashes.

"Jennifer," he breathed. And then kissed her with a fury that came from the depths of his soul.

With a flick of one finger he drove across her nubbin. She jerked and clutched him tighter.

His sweet little Jenny, full of passion, a woman responding to his every tormenting dream.

"Do you like this, Jenny?" he asked in a ragged whisper.

She did not answer, nor stay his hand. So he grew bolder.

He dragged her shirt off her shoulders, exposing her full breasts, and immediately sucked air between his teeth. Lovely, and beautiful, and so close to his mouth. Her bosom rose and fell in a tantalizing motion, creating a hunger he could not ignore. He leaned forward.

With his open mouth, he covered one breast. Her gasp rang vividly in his ears. He licked and nuzzled and feasted like a man consuming his last meal. She gripped his head and pressed her body closer. Her eager response exhilarated him. Made him want to give her more, more of everything. When he scrapped her nipple with his teeth, she squirmed scooting her pretty little bottom harder against his groin. God Almighty, his cock reared for glory. Blood raced to his temples.

He drew her flesh deeper into his mouth. The more he sucked, the more she ground against him.

She needed release. And so did he.

He slipped one finger into her moist cavern.

A husky groan escaped from low in her throat.

The sound flaming his desire higher. Blood pounded in his ears.

He inserted a second finger, her juices flowed so freely he dove into her with a frenzy. His mouth ravaged hers, his tongue mimicking the thrust of his fingers. She nearly gyrated off his lap. She bucked and grew wild in his arms.

The turbulent squall intensified to a raging storm. Arching with uncontrolled passion, she suddenly cried out. Shudders racked her body while spasms convulsed around his fingers. He pressed his thumb to her nubbin, adding pressure to prolong her release.

What a beautiful sight. Pleasure, pain, gratification, bliss—her face expressed every sentiment while she experienced each emotion. His chest filled with pleasure, and pride. He had given sweet Jenny her release. He had given her pleasure. And damned if he didn't feel like an peacock, wanting to strut and fan out his feathers.

He drank in the sweet aroma of her release.

God, he could scarcely wait to fill her. Feel himself in her.

Why did he hesitate? Normally he would toss up a woman's skirts and finish the deed. Normally, she would not have on any skirts. She'd be as naked as he. Which reminded him painfully that he was fully clothed.

Her head dropped to his shoulder. She fit right in the curve of his arm, and his chest. As though she had been poured from a mold to fit his body.

A sense of peace filled him. The first since his journey to India began. Lord knew he'd suffered the last several months. His satisfaction could wait.

This moment was for her. Right at this instant, he cared more for this woman than any basic need. Funny how he'd never cared before. Still, he had always given a woman pleasure. What kind of selfish man thought of his pleasure and did not allow a woman her own?

Moments passed before his sweet Jenny stirred. She gave him a look of such shocking awe, he would swear the woman had never experienced an orgasm before. Which delighted him beyond measure. *Good God!* Why should he care if it was her first? Of course, his pride rose a few more notches—like any man who had just given a woman her first taste of passion.

Her reaction and her cries of need rocked him to his toes. Kissing Jennifer came as natural as breathing. He'd built a sweet fire within her. Having tasted her passion, he burned for his angel. And he coveted a bit of heaven right here on earth.

Other emotions filled him with confusion. Like how wonderful she felt in his arms, where no other woman had fit so perfect. Like how her lips tasted sweeter than any he'd ever supped. Like how her breasts begged for his caress. Even now, his fingers molded her softness.

Still, he felt a bit unsettled. He couldn't explain it. All he knew was spending the last few weeks with Jennifer had inflamed his every nerve. He was a healthy man. With a healthy appetite for a delectable body. In every harbor he'd sailed into, there was a woman waiting to greet him with open arms. Jennifer was not the sort of woman to open her arms to just any man.

She worked too hard. A bit thin, which more than likely was a result of her labor. But she had ample curves in all the right places—which enticed him to touch her body, taste her sweetness. And now he behaved in a manner not to his liking. He was a man of strength and confidence. He had no tolerance for bewilderment.

He glared down to find Jennifer staring at him.

A frown graced her elegant brow. The trusting hero worship in her eyes soured to anger. The warmth in his arms grew frigid.

What the devil had changed? His frown etched deeper, then he realized his expression must have alarmed her.

He gave a smile.

Which only seemed to incite her further.

Did embarrassment motivate her anger? Was she angry over her release? Angry that he had seduced her? Or that she'd allowed him to seduce her?

It was a little late to yell fire after the building had already burned to the ground.

Chapter 9

An enormous full moon glowed against the midnight sky, providing the only illumination across the countryside. The group turned north and hastened across the moonlit opening. One look and anyone would know they were not tradesmen. Giles had promised to find Stephen, the brother of his best friend's wife. Every muscle in his body was taut and on alert.

His hands fisted tighter with every gallop. Strained until they reached the other side of the clearing where their horses would blend with the darkness. Stephen had fallen into some sort of trouble. Splinters from an English ship littered an inlet, which lead Giles and his men to a stronghold where a Rajput Chief resided. From what Elmes gathered when he'd sneaked inside, this particular prince resented the British Empire, and when the captain's ship crashed, the chief captured the crew. A man fitting Stephen's description had escaped with a bunch of rebels.

After several more miles, the group dismounted. Creeping through the brush only increased his apprehension. Giles held up his hand. From the information they'd been given, this must be the place. Yet, the Rebel leader and his companions were nowhere to be found.

Piers stepped beside him. "Where are they?"

"Hiding, no doubt." Giles narrowed his eyes, his instincts more vigilant in the darkness.

"Those peasants may have been afraid of the prince, but I think they are protecting the rebels. If the rebels think we're in cahoots with the prince, this could be bad for us."

Giles agreed. Not much he could do about it at the moment. "The men are tired."

"We all know the importance of this mission."

"Until we find Katherine's brother, we must push on." The longer it took to find the rebels, the more his sense of foreboding. Danger signals ignited in the back of his brain.

"Tis a great place for an ambush," Piers said. "Just pray we have time to announce ourselves and offer a truce before the rebels kill us."

Elmes stepped up beside them. "We are being watched." He pulled a wad of tobacco from his pocket and bit off the end.

The hair on Giles neck tingled. His colleagues never understood how he remained calm in critical situations, but he needed a clear head to make good decisions. Anger and fear lead to anxious choices, which most times resulted in disaster. His reserved manner had a nervous energy running underneath—not from nerves, more from excitement. His composure came as second nature to him. And if luck was on his side, he would live to see another day.

Men trickled from the brush, their weapons gleaming in the moonlight.

"Saints be," Piers exclaimed in a harsh breath.

"Hold," Giles quickly ordered in a harsh voice barely above a whisper. "Keep your heads."

One man came forward from the group. Two others trailed a short distance behind. By the first man's confident stride, he must be their leader. Hair hung into his eyes, a day's growth of beard covered his face. Even in the dark of night, his body portrayed strength and confidence.

Giles took a tentative step forward hoping his life would not end abruptly.

The man gave a slow movement of his hand, gesturing to his men forming a circle. "As you can see, you are surrounded."

Giles took a deep breath, concentrating on the air going into his lungs, and willed his muscles to relax. "We are not your enemies," Giles said.

"Ah. English."

"Yes. We are looking for another Englishman."

The leader's eyes narrowed. "What is this Englishman to you?"

"A friend."

The man shrugged. "Many claim to be friends when they are truly an enemy."

"The man we are looking for is the captain of a ship named *Serpent's Ghost*. He is the brother of my closest friend." Well, his wife anyway. But that would take more explaining. Too much explanation would make him sound desperate, and less truthful.

The leader may have meant to hide his expression, but his eyes gave him away. Giles was an expert at reading a man's body language, and an excellent judge of character as well. He would bet his life this was the man who took Stephen from that hellhole.

"My name is Giles. My men follow my instructions. We are not here to cause anyone harm. You have my word."

"Your word?"

The leader studied Giles as if he were a bug under a micro-scope. Damned uncomfortable, but he stood with the self-confidence of a man speaking the absolute truth. He suspected the rebel leader was a good judge of character, as well. That was most likely why he had helped Stephen.

"My name is Tarak. And my men, also, are loyal to me."

"You must be the leader we heard about."

"You have heard of me?" Tarak spoke with the calm and poise of a man in charge. His cool exterior portrayed his self-assurance and certainty that he had the upper hand.

"Of a rebel leader who escaped a prison, and took our friend with him. If you are he, you are a fair man. I am obliging to you."

Tarak seemed to consider his words. "You came here looking for me?"

"I would do anything to find my friend. If you are the one who rescued him, then yes. I have come a long way to find him. Since a certain prince may also be looking for him, and I hear he does not take kindly to Englishmen, then time is of the essence."

Tarak took several more moments to study him. After making an assumption, whether or not Giles could be trusted, he gave a slow nod. "Your captain withstood more than a man can bear. He was near death when we escaped."

Fury ate at the bile churning in Giles' stomach. Hating his next thought, Stephen had died, he prayed it was not so. He could not deliver news to Katherine that her brother was dead.

"Where is he?" Giles grated through his teeth.

"I don't know."

Giles blinked to clear his mind. Surely, he had not heard the man right. Then his instincts kicked in and rage replaced his momentary grief.

"What the bloody hell do you mean you don't know?"

Armor clicked and feet shuffled as the rebels aimed their rifles. Tarak held up one hand. "You forget where you are, Englishman."

Giles cursed under his breath at his loss of control. Holding back his emotions, Giles flexed his hands. "I forget nothing. But, you must explain your earlier statement."

"I am the man who took your friend. He needed medical attention. I found a couple with healing herbs and such. We put your friend in their care. We fabricated a trail in the opposite direction for anyone who followed."

Giles' chest eased a bit. At least another trail to follow instead of a grave.

"I am apologetic, Englishman. I do not know if he lived. But if any man could live after what he went through, it is your friend. He survived far longer than I expected. Still, he was weak. And lost a lot of blood. You must prepare—"

"The only thing I must prepare for is another journey," Giles interrupted. "I am a man of facts, Tarak."

"Then you should remember it is quite possible the prince is also looking for your friend."

"I will remember. I will not give up. Tell me what you know."

Chapter 10

S tephen did not like it. Not one bloody bit. The woman left
before sunrise, and it was now dark. Even so, he glanced out
the window again. Pitch black. Couldn't see a blasted thing. He
paced, if one could call the fumbling gait he managed a straight
line.

Turning, he bumped his toe. "Christ." The damn thing
throbbed like the very devil. Ridiculous really, when he'd survived much worse. He needed some footwear. Boots preferably.
But where the devil would he get them out here?

He needed some decent clothes too. Good thing Jennifer
knew how to use needle and thread. She had added cloth to a
pair of her husband's breeches so Stephen could cover himself
and not shock her female sensibilities.

He gave a chuckle. She'd had ample opportunity to examine
every inch of his marred skin. More than likely, she had removed
his rags under the cover of a sheet. He laughed out loud at the
possibility.

Bloody hell.

This prolonged malady muddled his sanity. He needed
something to do. He needed action. As if he hadn't had enough
turbulence in his life over the last few months. But then, he
could not be blamed for his fragile state.

Thanks to his angel, his body had healed. Mostly.

Where was she?

He settled his weight in the wooden chair and leaned his arms on the table. Waiting without certitude, living without purpose agitated his mind. Days with nothing to do. Boredom he could not stomach. He stared at the glowing embers of the fire.

A noise drew his attention. Stephen sprang from his seat, a string of oaths flying from his mouth. He nearly landed on the floor again. His ankles reminded him of his rash movement. The door to the little cabin opened. The imprisoned pain in his chest—the one he had not realized grew with each agitated moment of her absence—vanished.

He filled his eyes with her, quickly affirming she had come to no harm. At least the willful woman had on a gown.

His peace of mind rapidly changed to anger. "Where the bloody hell have you been?"

With the tranquility of a saint, she slowly closed the door. When she turned, he saw she carried a bundle. She placed her items on the table, then removed the wrapping from her head.

Ready to spit nails, he flexed his hands to keep from strangling her. Then she raised her head, lavender pools glaring at him.

"Excuse me. I did not realize I had to get your permission for my movements. My actions are my own, *Captain Radbourn*. I will thank you to remember that."

"You were gone before dawn." He spoke as though his reasoning should excuse his outburst.

"If you must know, I went to market."

His brows shot to his hairline. "There's a market around here?"

"Some distance away. I had to leave early."

"You went alone." He drew his brows together and his voice lowered.

"I remind you, I have adapted to taking care of myself."

Still, it did not sit well with him. He woke to find her gone. After their lovemaking yesterday, he thought he had scared her off. Or she was angry with him and had left in a tiff. Hell, he'd imagined all sorts of things.

She unwrapped her bundle.

"It took a while to find suitable shoes for a man of your size. Plus, avoid suspicion as to why a widow would be buying man's clothing."

"You found me some boots?"

She held up her purchase. A leather pelt rolled into a ball. It was a boot alright. Not one resembling anything he'd seen before, but would serve its purpose.

He rubbed his fingers over the soft rawhide. Spinning the chair around, he dropped onto its wooden surface. Working the covering over his ankle, he pulled the soft leather over his calf.

"I thought these would be better for your ankles."

He glanced up to find she held a second shoe. He felt like an arse. With a humble 'thank you', he pulled on the second boot. Then, he wiggled his toes and flattened the hard soles on the floor. The tough undersides would protect the bottom of his feet from stones. The tightness around his ankles would help support any movement there.

Snugfit.

Perfect.

"I am not a thoughtless man, Jennifer. I'm used to my ways." He lifted his head to meet her eyes. "You were gone before sunup, and I was a mite worried. I'm sorry for my tone. Thank you for thinking of my needs."

Being indebted galled. This woman had been taking care of him for weeks. The fact that he had shown his unwarranted temper irritated him, rubbed him raw like a horse chafed a bare backside. He needed to pull his own weight. He'd never been in someone else's debt. Damn, it ate at his craw.

But where would he be without her? She did not deserve to be on the receiving end of his nasty temper.

The man could show his gratitude with a bit more enthusiasm. Would a kind word be too much to ask? After all, she had walked miles for him. After last night, Jennifer worried how she would react when she faced Stephen again. Remembering their intimacy, excitement and shame filled her. With every step she took, the image of him burned brighter in her mind. Green eyes smoldering with promise. His mouth on her bare flesh. She recalled how she had clutched him to her breast and gone mad while his fingers . . . Heat flushed her cheeks. She had to think of something else. Anything to avoid the memory flashing in her mind.

What a relief to be home. She was tired and hungry and . . . She sniffed the air.

"You prepared supper?"

"Only a joint of meat and some boiled carrots."

She forgot her aching legs as the aroma of stew floated to her nostrils. Joy filled her at the realization she could relax, and would not have to cook food.

Stephen ushered her to the table. "Sit," he said while he pulled the chair back for her.

He hobbled to the fire, a plate in one hand. Her mouth watered as she watched him dip a ladle into the pot. Even with a limp, and possibly because of his sluggish movement, he looked more attractive than any man she had ever encountered.

"I cannot believe you did this."

"Why not?"

She shook her head.

"You think I am unable to cook a meal? A man of my size—my former size—needs to know a thing or two on how to prepare food. I like to eat." He wiggled his brows. "Or maybe you think that I believe it is woman's work."

"This is exceedingly kind of you," she spoke softly. "But your ankles. You should be resting."

"I'm no invalid."

"No. You are a very strong man."

"Later I will rub your feet."

She straightened in her chair. A strange heat flared in her belly. Tearing off a piece of bread, she decided not to think about his hands on her feet. "Thank you . . . for the meal."

His shoulders lifted in a shrug. "It is your food."

"I was really hungry. It was very thoughtful of you, having it ready." She glanced over her shoulder. "You've already eaten?"

"No."He dipped another plate for himself.

"You waited for me?" Her voice filled with wonder. She felt like a child in awe, seeing a falling star for the first time. The feeling staggered her. How long since anyone had considered *her*? She had forgotten what it felt like for someone to take care of her.

How ridiculous. She'd been alone for so long, Stephen's gesture honestly caught her unaware. That was all. Sentiment was an emotion she could not afford. Stephen did not care for her. He was a stranger.

But he cared enough to fix supper.

She toyed with the carrot on her plate. "May I ask you something?"

He shot her a warm glance under hooded eyes. With a mouth full of bread, he nodded.

She took a deep breath. "Do you . . . um . . . have a . . ."

"Do I have a what?"

She simply could not ask him what she yearned. Who cared if he had kissed a dozen women in London? Maybe if she still lived there, she would have been on his list of many. Those green eyes blazed with mischief. The man was too handsome for words.

"Do not be shy. If you want to know something, do not let your sweet disposition hold you back."

"I am neither reticent, nor sweet tempered."

He gave a bark of laughter. "No, you are one of the most resilient women I have ever met. What is it you want to know?"

"I simply wanted to make conversation."

He stabbed his meat with his fork and held it aloft while his eyes singed hers. "Ask me anything."

She tried for nonchalance. "Is there a special woman at home? Or in some port?"

"One or several?" His grin split his face. Enjoying himself entirely too much.

"It is no matter to me if you have a hundred strumpets." She regretted her rash outburst. His eyes gleamed in amusement, the handsome devil, and he took his sweet time answering.

"I like women. I think all women are beautiful. I have no wife, and no intended. The only family I have are my sister, and my aunt and uncle." He plunged the meat into his mouth and chewed.

Last night she had made the mistake of letting down her guard. But was it a mistake? His touch burned her body, thrilling her to her very core. Her curiosity demanded she ask another question. Did she dare?

"Why did you . . . you know . . . last evening?" She fluttered her hand about quickly changing her mind. "Never mind. Do not answer."

"You do not want me to answer, or you do not want to know?" His gaze grew hotter.

How would she ever find out if she allowed this moment to slip through her fingers? She carefully placed her fork on the table, and met his stare. "I want to know."

An ironic smile touched his lips. If he laughed at her she would slug him. He must have sensed how close she was to temper, for his hand covered her fist.

"You are a fine woman, Jennifer. Beautiful, in fact. And I am a man. Your lips are full and invite a man's kisses. You tasted just as sweet as I knew you would. Once I tasted your sweetness, when you responded to my kisses, well, you fit well in my arms, and you inflamed my passion."

The bulge poking her bottom had made it perfectly clear she had aroused him.

"Um. . . I know you . . . that is, I felt . . ."

"You felt my rabid lust. Ah, you blush so prettily." His warm fingers rubbed her knuckles. "How are we going to have this *conversation* if your tongue hides behind your pretty teeth?"

He pulled her, coaxing her to rise, then held her hand, tugging her around the table and onto his lap. He cupped her jaw, his gaze locking on her lips. The magnetic pull intense. She lifted her hands and pressed against his shoulders.

"You seduced me into kissing you last night. I will not allow you to do so again." *No matter how much I want you to.*

"Then why did you bring up the subject of what happened while you were sitting on my lap last evening?"

Motivated by anger, and embarrassment, she struggled to rise—but he held her firm in his grip.

"Now settle down." His voice low and husky. "You like being here just as much as I like having you in my arms. I'm lonely too."

"I am not . . ." Why try to deny it? Sometimes the solitary confinement of her home made her feel abandoned. There were days when she had been so forlorn she had been desperate for another human being. Someone to talk to. Someone to eat with, walk with, share things.

Someone to hold her.

Until he brushed her cheek with his thumb, she did not know a tear escaped. With his urging, she leaned her head on his shoulder. Her own vulnerability made her nuzzle into his neck. Soap wafted, but the essence of Stephen assaulted her senses. His very own scent. Stephen the man.

His hands roamed her back with soothing caresses, sending tingling warmth throughout her body. She leaned into his comfort, her muscles relaxing as she slipped into tranquility. Her chest rose and fell in a deep sigh.

Heaven.

A land of dreams.

A dream where he could be her husband. He would keep her safe. Protected. Loved.

A heated kiss on her breast brought her from her doldrums. My Lord, when had he unbuttoned her dress? As the previous evening, the sight of his head against her bare flesh exhilarated her. Oh, how she wanted to enjoy the same sensation he had awakened in her last night. She was a loose woman. Wicked, indeed.

When she felt a bulge brush her hip, she pushed out of his arms, scooting off his lap. Breathing heavily, she darted out of reach.

"I'm sorry," she said.

"No need to apologize."

"I. . ." She heard a shuffle and realized he stood. Before he could touch her, she bid a hasty goodnight and hurried through the door to her little room. Two weeks ago, he had insisted she return to her bed while he made a pallet on the floor in the main room. As she pulled down the coverlet, she pictured him in her mind. She saw Stephen sprawled upon the sheet. And secretly yearned for him to join her.

What would it be like to make love with him? Johnny may have been her husband, but he was a boy compared to Stephen. Goosebumps covered her flesh just thinking about the man in the next room. She wondered what he had looked like before he'd been tortured. Before he came to her home. A ship's captain, strong, tall, commanding. Ribbed muscles covering his chest, his arms, his thighs. He must have been a large man once. Judging from the day the sheet stood up, his man-thing was big too.

She jumped into bed, still in her smock, and pulled the covers to her chin. She cursed her weakness and her wayward thoughts. Johnny had made promises, and then he deserted her. She would not fall victim to another man.

She could take care of herself.

Chapter 11

S tephen watched Jennifer swipe an errant curl behind her ear. Her attempt to confine her long tresses into a knot only drew his attention to the mass of raven waves gleaming in the sunlight. He swallowed, leaning his shoulder against the rough wood, one knee propped at an angle on her tiny porch. Normally, he rose every morning at the crack of dawn. He loved watching the sunrise, red and gold hovering on the horizon. Now he had another reason to get up early.

Jennifer.

He looked forward to her soft voice. Her flashing eyes. Every time he saw her, he wanted to run his fingers through her silky strands, caress her bold curves, and lose himself in her softness. She should be like any other woman. But damned if she didn't put him on edge.

Heaven knows he'd had his share of enticing women. Some had tried every wile imaginable. Even though the land had made Jennifer tough, she had an air of natural grace. He'd grown more than fond of her, and felt a bond of sorts budding between them. Her beauty and responsiveness distracted him.

She'd slapped a crude covering on her head, and now she starred off into the distance. Her facial expression gave nothing away. But he wondered if she thought about their intimacy. Having her in his arms, giving her pleasure was a constant in his own mind. He continued to observe her, without her knowledge. Long sooty lashes adorned her sun bronzed cheeks. A peculiar hitch stirred in his chest. No matter how much he tried to shrug it off as lust, he knew the feeling went much deeper.

He shuffled over to lean against the rail of the fence. "Good Morning."

"Morning," she replied.

"You're out early." He stared ahead, same as she.

"I am no slugabed."

"So I've noticed," he said with a smile.

Quiet surrounded them.

"You are much stronger," she said.

"Is that your subtle attempt to tell me I have outstayed my welcome?"

Jennifer spun around. "No. I—" She stopped when she saw his grin.

"Glad to hear it."

She turned from him and gazed in the direction she had earlier.

Stephen filled his lungs with fresh air. No matter what country in which one resided, being outdoors sustained the soul. He looked toward the clear blue sky, a cloud of white here and there. Amazing how much more he appreciated the beauty of nature since death had looked him in the eye. The grass seemed greener, the trees swayed with the wind, displaying they too were a creation of life. Things everyone took for granted.

Each day he pushed his muscles to their limits. Who knew being able to stand on his own two legs would be so gratifying? And having a beautiful woman cling to him so sweetly, be so appeasing.

"Thought maybe you were avoiding me."

"No, Captain, I am not avoiding you."

"Captain, is it? You must be upset with me, then."

"No Stephen, I am not upset with you." She gave a little sigh.

"Then would you mind telling me what's on your mind?" The silence stretched between them.

"May I ask you something?"

"Ask away."

"Why did you come to India?"

Bloody hell.

Where had that come from? He was silent so long, she continued.

"Johnny followed rainbows. Blinded by dreams, he believed the rumors India was a place to make his fortune. Instead of jewels, he foolishly found his way to a bottle."

Stephen had convinced himself he needed adventure. Had he been any different? He risked the lives of his crew the moment his affiliate unwrapped a glowing jewel the size of an egg.

"I did not come here to find a fortune."

Her shoulders dropped with a heavy sigh. "I do not want to pry, and you may not want to talk about it."

"My ship was headed to India's English trading dock. A storm hit us pretty hard. I told you true when I said we were knocked off course. We were sailing along the coast line when another ship came out of nowhere firing cannons. We also took fire from the beach. My crew had to abandon ship, and when we got to shore, men with guns were waiting for us."

He could not—would not—give her more details. His men in chains, shot before his eyes. She already knew he had been tortured.

"I do not believe those men were rebels," she said. "There are others who refuse to accept the British influence."

"I know. Found out the hard way. The leader was a Rajput prince. He believed that I encroached on his private beach."

"He did this to you?"

Anguish filled her eyes. What a woman of compassion. She did not know him, yet she hurt for him.

"The prince would not accept my word that I found the cove by accident."

"What of your crew?"

Stephen turned away in torment. This voyage was to be an adventure. When all he'd done was condemn them to their deaths.

The bloody Rajput prince.

"He killed them." Stephen's hands tightened on the fence to the point his knuckles turned white. He curled his fingers into the wood, wishing he had the bastard's neck within his palms.

"No." Jennifer grasped his arm and pressed her cheek to his sleeve. "I'm so sorry."

This woman melted his resolve. Melted his heart. He put his arm around her and drew her close. "You know the rest. An angel of mercy nursed me back to health."

They stood in silence, her snug against him. With a knuckle under her chin, he lifted her face. He glowered down at her, transfixed at how lovely she was. Uncertainty showed in her eyes. Damn, he did not want to hurt her.

He brushed his thumb over her bottom lip, sucking in his breath when her tongue touched the tip. He should release her. But the pull she had on him was too strong. Sweet Jenny did not know it, but she had cast a spell on his sanity. He could not stop himself from leaning down, and pressing his lips to hers.

Angel.

Heaven sent.

He held her with tenderness and warmth. Then he eased his tongue over her lips seeking entrance. She opened to him like a flower opening for a bee, surrendering its nectar.

Sweet. The sweetest woman he'd ever tasted. She yielded. He drank greedily. A moan tore from her throat enticing him to the point of delirium.

His heart thundered. He wanted her here—now.

Lost in his desire, he pressed her back into the fence.

Her soft cry pierced his ardor. Good God, he'd injured her. He quickly released her, and fumbled, "I'm sorry."

"I'm alright." She breathed heavily unaware of the desperation in her voice.

Collecting himself from his near loss of restraint, he stepped back, emotions clawing through him. Shaking off his frustration, he gave her a rakish smile.

"That is some good morning, Jenny."

The devil was pure temptation. Stephen proved perilous, and he grew more dangerous every day. Denying her desire last night had been deceptive. A false illusion. An attempt at doing the appropriate thing.

But when had she ever made the reasonable choice?

Her alarm mounted. Not at his attentions, but at her own wanton thoughts. Desire swamped her belly. He created a passion in her she never knew existed. She hungered for more. More of his kisses. More of his caresses. And she would surely burn in hell for she craved to know what it would be like to make love with him.

Stephen was a real man. There would be no fumbling under the sheets. No quick entry that left her empty with longing. For she now knew what she'd been longing for. She now knew what ecstasy meant. Stephen's caresses had been tender but with a burning need, as though he truly craved her. What a boon to her woman's self-esteem. He made her feel beautiful. He made her feel desirable. Her heart skipped a beat at the thought of him taking her to bed.

She glanced down at her body clad in her husband's clothes and immediately thought of the lovely blue gown packed away in her chest.

Her gaze leaped to his. Even wearing breeches, he wanted her. Her confusion must have mirrored in her eyes, for his clouded, and a frown etched his brow.

"What's wrong?"

"Nothing. I was merely thinking."

"Of what?"

She shook her head. "How in the world can I appeal to you looking like this?"

He laughed. "Ah, sweet Jenny. You have no idea how beautiful you are."

Jenny. She loved the way he said her name. When he reached for her, she quickly stepped around him. "You must be hungry."

"Ravished." The curve of his rakish smile deepened.

"Come inside then, and I'll feed you."

"I hope that is a promise." His brows jumped vigorously with excitement.

She had the feeling he did not mean food. She loved his playful bantering, now that she'd gotten to know him. "You will get pork and bread."

"Ah, Jenny. Have a heart." He placed his palm over his chest in a dramatic gesture.

Ignoring him, she linked her arm with his. "Why Captain, have I not shared my lodging with you? Have I not treated your wounds? I believe I have shown you, in several ways, that a heart does indeed beat within my chest."

"Tis true. For I was just a shell of a man when I landed on your doorstep. I will accept your offer of food, woman, for you never know when I may need my strength." He wiggled those bushy red brows again.

With one leg propped out, Stephen sat at the small table. His elbow braced on the corner, he studied Jennifer's backside. A perfectly rounded bottom in a pair of man's breeches. More fetching, possibly, than in women's finery. She placed a steaming bowl of stew on the table and took a seat across from him. Her well-curved breasts filled out her shirt quite nicely.

Blinking, he took a bite and chewed, spices trickled across his tongue. His jaw still tender, at least now he could eat solid food. He never knew how much joy could be found in chewing.

With hooded eyes, he hid the fact he watched her. When she spoke, he listened with half a mind. The other half wondered how fast he could get her out of her clothes.

Hang it all. He ogled her boldly. When she turned to him her eyes flew wide. For a second, she resembled a frightened hare. But then, she latched onto his glare with blatant interest, and then her mouth fell slightly open. His gaze dropped to her full lips, then lowered to her swan-like neck. She swallowed. His breathing thickened—along with another part of his anatomy.

Tin clattered against glass, sounding like a crack of thunder in the still room.

She jumped.

He liked the effect he had on her. A grin sprang to his lips.

"You may remove that leering smirk from your face."

"Leering, am I? Why I'll have you know I was enjoying my food."

"Humph." She grabbed her fork.

"What an unladylike sound."

He regretted his words as soon as they left his mouth. Jenny looked down at her shabby clothes and the light went right out of her eyes. She placed her fork carefully beside her plate, then folded her hands in her lap.

"You must think I am quite plain."

Conscience-stricken, he hurried to lift her spirits. "Fishing for compliments, Jenny?"

She glared in surprise, then a smile flitted across her lips, and danced right up to her eyes.

"Want to know what I'm thinkin'?" He looked at Jenny, thinking he wanted to pick up where they left off. "Sweet, passionate—"

"Do you think of anything else?"

Brazen. His Jenny had come out of her shell and given him tit for tat.

"I am a man. Men crave women, no matter what they be wearing."

Her mouth fell open.

Even if the thought of bedding a woman was a constant in his mind, no need to concede the fact.

Stephen dried the last plate and hung the cloth over the wooden peg. With the meal finished, he had offered to clear the table so Jenny could rest, or carry out some womanly thing, like knit or whatever she did in this tiny cabin. He had to do something to drag his thoughts away from ravishing her.

For all the good it did.

She'd carted in a huge tub for bathing. Ignoring her protests, he insisted he carry the water to fill it. Now his imagination ran rampant with visions of the blasted woman in her bath. Long silky legs, lathered with soap. Voluptuous breasts with beads of water on her puckered nipples. *Christ!* How was he to remain sane?

He thrust his hand through his wild locks and forced images of naked limbs from his mind. He glared at the lighted lamp, watching the flame create shadows on the bare wall. How the hell she lived in this shack astounded him to no end. Being alone would drive him to seek companionship of some sort, even if it was with a bloody bear. Good God. How could she stand it? Day after long aimless day. In a country not her own.

She had come close to getting under his skin.

Face it man, she already has.

He shook his head at the thought. He had not even toppled her, for God's sake.

A rustle sounded from behind. He shifted in that direction.

The breath left his lungs.

There in the doorway stood the loveliest bit of fluff that ever tempted a man's eye.

Jennifer.

Dressed in a creation of sparkling blue satin. Jeweled combs held back the sides of her ebony waves. Strands fell forward resting on a generous amount of exposed flesh above her bodice.

After feasting his eyes on her full bosom, his gaze dropped to the curve of her waist. His fingers flexed. The blue evening gown draped over round hips and slithered in a dainty cascade to the rough floor.

Every drop of moisture left his throat at his attempt to swallow.

Jennifer boggled his mind. She did not do any of the predictable things a woman did to entice a man. He thought to close his eyes and open them again in case he was dreaming.

Fearing she would disappear, he doused the idea. Speechless, he stared, devouring every luscious inch of her curves.

His hunger grew leaps and bounds.

"Will you please say something?" Her voice so soft he might have imagined it.

Gathering any sense he might have left, Stephen cleared his throat. "You are exquisite."

"You do not need to use flattery. Just talk to me."

"There are no words to describe how lovely you are." He took a step closer.

"When I left England, I brought my favorite ball gown with me. Irrational, I suppose. But it gave me some security. I have not had a chance to wear it."

Her voice came out soft, she was unsure of herself. How could she not know of her beauty? Married, yet her innocence showed her vulnerability. Awe and appreciation combined into an alien emotion unknown to him.

"You put on this dress for me."

"Yes", she replied, taking a step toward him. Her chest rose as she took a deep breath. "I wore this for you."

Her deed pleased him more than it ought. In her own naïve way, she dallied with him.

No! She did not dalley.

This was a widow who knew nothing of seducing a scoundrel.

Nervously, she chewed on her lower lip. His attention snagged on the movement. His gaze slid down her slender throat, then dropped lower to her alluring cleavage. When she gripped her hands together, her breasts bounced. He damn near swallowed his tongue. The rod in his breeches lurched in torment.

He took the crucial step that closed the distance between them. An erotic fragrance teased the air compelling him to inhale deeper. A mystical scent of the orient. Seemingly, it too, was worn only for special occasions.

Tonight.

A special occasion.

Tonight, for him.

She had suddenly become the one thing he must have.

Chapter 12

"Jennifer."

Stephen spoke her name so adoringly she wanted to weep.

His gaze swept her hungrily, then he pulled her into his arms and held her. Surely, he'd had women well-versed in seduction. What if he found her lacking? If he rejected her, she would just die. She took a deep breath and tried to calm her racing heart.

A woman of character would push him away.

She angled her head in self-doubt, fighting down the surge of excitement. She loosened her hold, placing one hand on his chest ready to withdraw. He caught it with his own.

"There is no shame in desire," he murmured huskily.

Every nerve she had stood to attention.

His green eyes glowed with passion sending a tiny thrill through her veins. He lowered his head and placed the gentlest of kisses on her neck. A touch so soft it could have been a whisper of butterfly wings.

Warmth exploded in her center and she hissed a sharp breath.

He dragged one finger down her throat into the valley between her breasts. His eyes followed the movement, burning her skin as he trailed a path along the edge of her bodice. At some point she stopped breathing. Suddenly, he entwined both hands in her hair and held her fast while his mouth devoured hers. Straining against him, she returned his kiss with equal fervor.

They broke apart. His breathing rugged, his eyes glittering with passion. He looked as dazed as she felt. He nipped her earlobe, then kissed a path down her neck. Her head fell back, and her fingers dug into the sinews of his shoulders. All thought left her, all she could do was feel. A wanton heat settled low in her belly as he pushed her gown off one shoulder. She willed him not to stop. Lips and tongue followed, leaving open mouth kisses upon her bare skin.

She heaved a shaky breath and dug her fingers deeper into his shoulders.

He slid an arm about her shoulders, tilting her backward, and continued his assault on her upper bosom. Her body's response was strong and swift. Tingles raced over her skin. Heat scorched her everywhere he touched, and her mind screamed *more*.

He nuzzled one puckered nipple through her gown while his hand plucked the other. Her belly clenched. The ache between her legs grew. He squeezed and massaged her until she moaned low in her throat. Her breasts felt heavy. She burned with longing. When he raised his head, she saw the raw need burning in his eyes.

His leg slipped between hers and he pulled her core against his arousal. The desire she had been ignoring all day flared to life, consuming every part of her body. She whimpered with need. He angled his hips, pressing his hardness into her.

Instincts she'd never known existed took over. Hungering to feel his skin against hers, she slid her hands under his shirt. Sparks tingled the tips of her fingers, warmth speared her hands. She caressed his skin, slid over rough lesions, and twined her fingers in his springy curls. He groaned, and it thrilled her. He arched into her hands.

Suddenly he straightened. Grabbing the bottom of his shirt, he quickly drew the linen over his head. Fire blazed in his eyes while a slow, sexy smile grew on the very lips that had set her heart to pounding.

Her gaze dropped lower.

"Don't look, Jenny. My body's not a pretty sight to see."

Oh how wrong you are. You are wonderful, perfect to me.

She fingered a scar across his breastbone, close to his heart. Three more connected across his ribs. "I have already seen the scars on your body. I have already touched them." She lifted her gaze to meet the reservation in his.

"You are a man. With a man's body. These markings only map your journey in life. Your strength. Your métier. Your intensity. Your depth."

"There are many. And they are ugly."

"They are you, Stephen." She opened her fingers, spreading her palm against his furry chest, rippled with scars. Emotion overwhelmed her. His large hand covered hers in a caress of understanding. Then, his eyes held hers hostage as he raised her fingers to his lips and kissed the tip of each one.

Her knees grew weak. Her pulse leaped. Sparks of need tingled through her belly. She leaned in for him to kiss her again. He gladly gave her what she wished. Standing on her toes, she tangled her fingers in his hair, sweeping the skin at his nape.

Suddenly her feet left the floor. She tore her mouth away.

"No, Stephen. You mustn't. You will hurt—"

"Dammit woman, you just told me I'm a man. Do not make a eunuch of me now."

Her heart near to bursting, she burrowed into his neck. His groan sent a flitter of delight racing through her. Yes, she sighed. Her Stephen was definitely a man. He carried her to the bed and gently, as if she were the most precious thing on earth, lowered her to the feather mattress.

"I've never had a man carry me before," she whispered.

His russet brows shot up, hidden by his falling locks. "Never? Well, my angel. Tonight may be a night of firsts."

He tugged the fabric down her arms and lower, leaving a trail of warm kisses on her bare skin as he did. Humility gone, sensual craving in its place, she lifted her hips and helped him remove her clothing. When she lay naked and panting, he sank onto the bed and stretched out beside her. Resting his weight on one elbow, his other hand stroked her skin.

He seemed to be in no hurry to remove the rest of his clothes. She wanted to see *all* of him.

She closed her eyes tight. Such wicked thoughts. She was a fallen woman. But, how delightful the naughty anticipation thrilled her.

"You have on far too many clothes," she whispered.

He broke away. She lifted her head to watch. His fingers drew the leather ties at his waist. Unable to tear her gaze away, she stared at the bulge in his trousers. Waiting. Silently begging him to hurry. Her eyes widened with fascination when he revealed himself. Her mouth dropped open with awe and his manhood grew even more.

Sensations ripped through her.

Stephen stood there, tall and proud, allowing her to look her fill. Glory be, how could a man look so magnificent? Or look at her as though she were the most glorious thing on earth?

He climbed onto the bed, comparable to a panther slowing prowling, pursuing his prey. His fingers dove into her hair and he took her lips in a heated kiss. When she could no longer hold her breath, he drew back and searched her eyes, giving her time, silently asking her permission. Her answer was to show him with her yearning body.

Fraught with need, she pulled him to her, and nestled into him getting as close as possible. His hands roamed, creating an ache within her that built into a raging desire. His thumb rubbed her already hard, sensitive nipple. His mouth licked and sucked one breast while his palm molded and pressed the other. It was as though he needed to keep touching her. And she loved it.

Stephen kissed his way down to her stomach. She thought she heard him mumble something about *another first*. When he gripped her knees and spread her thighs, she felt exposed and reacted by clamping her legs closed.

"Trust me, Angel." He gave her another bone-melting kiss while his lower body shifted between her thighs. His hand covered her mound, and then one long finger slipped inside.

Her breath caught. She kissed him with everything in her, showing him how much she craved him.

His fingers worked their magic. Every caress left her weak with longing. Every stroke deepened her desire. Again, he slid down to the indentation of her navel, his tongue darted out and pierced her. Butterflies attacked her stomach. His wet tongue tickled.

Then he moved lower.

"You're going to enjoy this." His deep voice vibrated in her gut, and then—

His open mouth covered her. *There.*

She jerked in surprise. His mouth was so hot her blood hummed. He kissed her mons, and then he flicked his tongue. Good Lord, he was driving her crazy.

He pressed her down and held her firm as his darting tongue speared in and out of her. Bolts of fire shot to her core.

She'd never known anything so sinfully delicious. Her head dug into the pillow while her hands gripped his hair, holding him—there. He nipped and bit and sucked hard. The bewildering pressure grew to a powerful force, and abruptly she spiraled out of control. An explosion of shock waves propelled through her body, hurling her over a cliff.

She was falling—falling—falling.

When the world righted itself, she found she could not move. She never—in her wildest imaginings—had never thought such bliss existed. Twice, Stephen had given her pleasure. The other night when she'd experienced the overwhelming emotion—the experience new to her—she wondered if she would ever delight in such ecstasy again.

And then tonight ...

Slowly she drifted back to reality, thinking of the man who created such sensations within her body. He made her lose all reason. All rational thought. She had nearly lost her mind to his powerful ministrations.

The man was lethal.

He shifted, stirring her back to consciousness. She opened her eyes to find him hovering over her. A gratified glint in his eyes, and a satisfied smile on those devilish lips.

She flushed with embarrassment.

"Another first?" His pleased grin turned to a confident smile bordering cocky. "There's no shame in enjoying your pleasure. And we are not through."

Not through?

Her blood still thrummed from her eruption.

Before she could recover from his unnerving words, his weight bore her down into the softness of the feather mattress. He feasted on her breasts again, laving, teasing until her hands once more clutched his hair in desperate need, relentless to hold on to the electrifying power that swamped her. He slipped his hand between them just as he raised his head and gave her a bone-melting kiss. She tasted her own essence, which excited her and drove her into a frenzy.

His hardness, probed, and found entrance. She wiggled, trying to rush him along, force him deeper. He held, not moving. Teasing, provoking, inflaming her senses. Her body arched up to greet him. And finally, with one last nudge, one smooth thrust, he filled her.

So full.

So achingly wonderful.

He moved, just a bit. She clutched his shoulders not knowing what she feared. Knowing only that he was where she wanted him, and she must hold him forever.

When he pulled back she gasped, but he quickly filled her again. "I am not going anywhere," he rasped.

With his arms holding his weight, he withdrew and entered her again, and again, moving deeper, and deeper. Friction built, plunging her higher and higher until there was a roaring in her ears. The world disappeared. There was only blazing fever.

Her body coiled.

"That's it, Angel. Give it to me."

His strokes quickened.

Her body splintered, shudders racking her body.

Stephen gave a hoarse shout, and pulled out. Hot liquid shot onto her belly.

Chapter 13

Jennifer's fingers clutched her shawl tighter as she stared into the flames of the burning fire. Her stomach felt as hollow as an empty well. Embarrassment crowded her chest.

She had been used. She had allowed Stephen to use her body. He'd spilled his seed on her. She had never been so humiliated in her life.

The most wonderful feeling she'd ever known, and then reality crashed down on her, the shame of her actions hitting her square in the face. A tear slipped down the side of her cheek.

He'd embraced her, said sweet words. But the shock of what he had done—after—mortified her. She did not understand. Oh, she knew a man's seed created a baby, but to witness . . . to have his actual . . . on her skin . . . was humiliating. Evidently, while he held her, and made her lose her mind, he had kept his wits about him, calculating how he would not leave her with child. She, of course, had been so obsessed with his lovemaking, she'd completely lost her faculties.

At first she thought something was wrong with her. Maybe he had not wanted to finish with her. But he curled up with her in his arms, and fell asleep. She did not understand.

What did she know of love-making anyway? Her husband had been her only lover. Stephen did things, and made her feel things . . .

How foolish. She had stars in her eyes. A handsome man—a lonely woman. A lonely defenseless woman. She really could not be faulted for her weakness. A captain. A man of the world. He had taken advantage.

Really, Jennifer? Stop feeling sorry for yourself. He nearly died. And you are not weak.

Since her husband's death, she'd survived quite well. She had a home, she had a garden. She had even managed to outfox her neighbor, when she would really like to trounce the beleaguering man. Pride had given her self-confidence, and granted her freedom. Of course, being stubborn as a mule had a lot to do with her independence. If a goal was to be achieved, determination held the key. Her father had taught her that. She was strong. Had been strong—until *he* came along.

How could she have let down her guard? How could she have allowed a complete stranger into her bed?

Sweet words. Sweet disposition. And a soft heart for an injured animal. Did her pity bring about her fall from grace?

Pity was far from the emotion she felt for him. Empathy for Stephen never entered her mind when his lips tantalized her body.

She covered her face with her hands and hung her head.

Oh God. What am I to do?

"Jenny? Sweetheart?"

Using the shawl, she scrubbed her eyes. "What are you doing up?"

"I missed you."

"Oh. I, ah, stoked the fire."

"Come back to bed. I'll keep you warm."

His throaty voice warmed her as much as his suggestion. Will-power deserted her. Oh, how her body craved his touch.

Warmth caressed her neck. He placed his other hand on the side of her face. Heaven help her, she leaned up for his kiss, and melted when his lips brushed hers. His strength and scent enveloped her as he lifted her from the rocker. With a will of their own, her arms wrapped around his neck.

Tomorrow would arrive soon enough. Until then, she would relish being in her lover's arms.

———ele———

Stephen stood beside the bed looking down on Jennifer in peaceful slumber. His angel made love with zealous abandon. He wondered at the hot-blooded creature. From a purring kitten to a spirited tiger, she had surprised him. The way she reacted to his touch, like a new born babe coming to life, taking a first breath of air. Every caress seemed new. She responded with a passion that had been locked away and suddenly set free. Her reaction encouraged him, made him bolder. Thrilled him beyond any experience he'd ever had.

He tied the bits of leather holding up his breeches. With a deep breath, he thrust his hands through his hair as if that would clear his mind. The woman was too bloody winsome.

He closed the door softly behind him.

Flames no longer blazed in the hearth. Coarse wood scraped the soles of his feet as he shuffled to the stack of timber. He hated the devils who had done this to him. Marred his body. Taken the lives of his crew. Sunk his ship. Agony pierced his chest while guilt flooded his soul. He would return to England alone.

When on his ship, he typically enjoyed the quiet of the night. Sailing was rooted deep in his bones. He longed to stand at the helm of his ship, have the rocking sea beneath his booted feet—wind in his hair, fresh salty air, he could truly be free.

Only the ocean could heal his spirit. Memories would haunt him forever. Someday he hoped to forgive himself.

He shook his head in frustration. Revenge. He swore he would have the Rajput prince's head.

A few embers still glowed within the pit. He stirred the ashes, added a few logs and soon he had a fire blazing within the stone-barrier. Rising, he made his way to the rocker. Sparks danced to the tune of crackling bursts. He stared into the blue flames.

He'd be dead if not for the kind-heartedness of a brave woman. A caretaker who'd nursed him back to health, and he appreciated her generosity. But the woman was sheer invitation to sin, and she was not even aware of it. His own reaction alarmed him. Maybe he should not have taken things so far. Hell, he was a man, for God's sake. And Jennifer would temp a saint.

Not only was the woman beautiful, but she had pluck. More daring than any woman he'd met. She'd adapted to the land without her husband, made a life for herself. Her actions more courageous beyond anything he would have expected of any woman.

And she had given herself to him.

Not that Jenny was innocent. Not that he deserved or wanted her forgiveness. For that would mean he'd wronged her. He did what any man would have done when faced with a beautiful woman. Whether or not she admitted it, she had wanted him. Why else would she have worn that bloody gown if not for seduction?

A rush of guilt bit at his conscious.

The woman had tended him. She sang to him. She brought color and light back into his own private darkness when he could have gone mad.

He leaned back, the bottom of his skull barely met the top of the rocker. He closed his eyes to the memory of sweet bliss.

He had no idea how long he'd sat there before the first ray of sunlight glimmered through the small window. A new day. Since Jennifer made a habit of rising at dawn, he expected to hear her footsteps any moment. He had to be careful, for already he recognized the signs that he was headed for trouble. Despite the fact he had spent the early hours pondering his predicament, he had no answer regarding his disturbing state of mind.

The creak of the door alerted him the day had begun.

Jennifer had no idea how to greet Stephen. After their love-making, she had been exhausted. She slept a bit later than the hour she normally rose. After their first coupling, and her moment of disquiet, he had carried her back to bed. To her complete accord, he'd been demanding most of the night.

A tingle coursed through her body. She supposed she should have been less enthusiastic. But then, Stephen stood a strapping man. Even so, she had not meant to appear so wanton.

She took a deep breath and opened the door to find him sitting in her rocker before the fire.

Apprehension rooted her feet to the floor. His frame alone caused her heart to lurch. Seeing the firelight dance over his fetching features took her breath. Especially when she remembered the acts performed only a short time ago. Heat swamped her body. The idea of his touch scorched her skin more than the flames of any fire. She drew her shawl tighter.

Stephen turned in her direction. His fierce gleam told her he too remembered their passion.

Good Lord. Her knees wobbled.

She thrust out her chin and held her head higher, refusing to cower because she had behaved so wickedly. She hoped her traitorous body would perform her morning chores and resist the compelling magnetism pouring out of this man. Without another glance in his direction, she headed for the bucket of water. For she knew it would only take one look and she would succumb—most willingly.

"Good morning." She failed at the attempt to make her voice sound strong.

"Good morning."

Until Stephen spoke, she did not realize that she expected *Angel* to fall from his lips. The sentiment had become almost a second name to her. He had called her *Angel* throughout the night. She loved hearing it, although the term certainly did not describe her. But as an endearment from Stephen's lips, her soul had swelled with contentment.

Stephen turned back to the fire, giving her a chance to gather her composure. When nervous she oft times chattered. Her nerves reared now.

"I will stoke the fire. No, I see you already have. Would you like something to drink? Water. I need water for tea. I should . . ." Words spilled from her throat, hopefully keeping her mind too busy to think.

It did not work.

He remained in her rocker, his gaze on the fire. She did not need to be a sorcerer to see this did not bode well. His silence instigated errant thoughts racing through her head. Was he ashamed of her behavior? Did he think her a wanton? Maybe he was just tired. After all, he had kept her awake most of the night. He could have stayed in bed. Slept the day away. No. There must be something else. But what?

Unable to stand it any longer, she asked, "Stephen? Why are you staring into the fire? Is something wrong?"

He flinched. If she had not been watching, she would not have seen it.

"No. Nothing is wrong with me. How about you?"

Me?

"What do you mean?"

His body grew stronger each day. His movements more sure. He shoved from the chair with a smooth motion, making her think of his swaying on his ship. "There is nothing wrong. I simply asked you the same question."

"Oh." She rubbed her hands on her shift. "It's just ... you were quiet."

"Would you rather I prattle nonsense in the early hours?" His low voice seemed harsh and weary.

Was he insinuating that is what she had done? "Suit yourself. Go back to your dark perusing. I will leave you alone." The man infuriated her. She spun around to march back into the bedroom.

"What's got you so wound up this morning?"

She stilled. Took a deep breath, and turned to face him. Before she opened her mouth, he continued.

"Usually the morning after, a woman purrs. But you." He shoved his hands through his long waving hair. "You are different from any bloody woman I have ever encountered."

She fisted her hands at her sides. "Purr? You expect me to purr?"

"Usually, a woman is a lot more gentle after a long night of—"

"Stop right there," she said holding up one hand. "How can you speak so coldly of . . . of . . ."

"Of what we did?" He braced his hands on his hips. "Go on. You can say it."

Her faced flamed. Blast the arrogant man. "How can you be so callous? So unfeeling? Have you no shame?"

"Shame is it?"

Her head spun. She was not exactly ashamed of what she had done. But she could not speak so freely as if it were an everyday occurrence.

"What's wrong woman? What did I do other than give you what you wanted?"

She gaped at him, hardly able to believe the words falling from his lips. Tears pooled in her throat. Curse him for the dog he was. Determined not to let him see how he'd hurt her, she summoned her anger to be her shield. Before tears could spill out and betray her, she turned away—fury in her heart. Darned if she would let him intimidate her. "You were gentle. You desired me."

"I wanted you my sweet," he mocked. "Nothing else."

She thought he shared some of the same warm feelings. Now, his hateful words proved him a scoundrel. Life had dealt her harsh blows. This was just one more. The strong survived, and she had survived worse.

She marched over to the window, bracing her arms on the little table, next to the wall. She would not regret her decision. She had willingly given her body. She had found ecstasy in his arms, even if only for one night. Her own foolishness was believing he felt some emotion. How wrong she had been.

How could he touch her and bring her body to life without feeling something for her? True, he was a skilled lover, and she had no experience—other than her husband—but she knew what she felt. She could still hear his sighs at her touch, his coaxing and delight at her responses. What about his words? His endearments?

Such an idea was ludicrous. She swiped at an imaginary tear.

"Using your own words, I believe you have outstayed your welcome." She turned again, facing the tall demon who had unexpectedly spouted horns. She glanced up, meeting his glaring eyes. "You have healed. It is time for you to leave."

"You are putting me out? Because you are frightened?"

"What you mistake for fright is fury." She shoved her hair out of her face. "You have repaid my hospitality with arrogance and insults."

"Insults?" He jerked her against his chest, his arms tightened against her struggles. A look of chagrin crossed his face. "I may have behaved a bit boorishly, but no insult was ever intended."

His husky words flowed over her like honey seeping over a hotcake. Her body betrayed her. She did not want to need him. But she did just the same.

"You wanted me. Admit it." Stephen spoke between kisses he nibbled along her neck. "As much as I wanted you. No harm in that." He dropped another kiss, again and again. "You are so beautiful. I cannot keep my hands off you, my lovely angel."

Lord forgive her. Anger melted at his touch. Fury transformed to desire when he called her *Angel*. Her bones turned to liquid. She wrapped her arms around him, her fingers tangling in his hair. He bent down and slipped one arm under her knees, lifting her against his chest. His lips came down on hers with a passion that would not be denied. By either of them.

As he carried her to the bed, she wondered if they could spend all their days locked in each other's arms.

Chapter 14

"**I** told you before. The answer is no."

The big oaf laughed. "You will change your mind."

Jennifer swallowed and tried not to insult her neighbor, of sorts. Barincott was the last man on earth she wanted to marry. Not only did he think himself the greatest catch—which she supposed he was entitled to some consequence since he did own most of the land in the area—but, his leering grin depicted he expected women to fall at his feet. He did not attract her in the least.

Especially since Stephen.

How could she possibly compare the two men? They were as different as night and day. Where Barincott's hair was dark, Stephen's hair blazed redder than the sunset. More like the fox her father allowed her to chase on one of their hunts with the hounds. When Stephen entered her life, he'd had a beard. She shivered remembering the grimy mass and how quickly she had washed him, to find a full flowing beard the same russet color of his magnificent hair. A mustache hid Barincott's upper lip, but did not hide the slant of his ogling smile.

And their bodies? Stephen had gained some weight over the last several weeks. Enough where his skin did not hang on his bones. And with clothes that fit, he looked remarkable. She dare not think of his touch.

Barincott spoke and she nearly missed his words. She tilted her head back, her eyes lifted to his smirk. If he were on the ground instead of being up on his horse, maybe he would not appear as intimidating.

"No, Mr. Barincott. I will not leave. This is my home."

"Mrs. Faircloth. This is *vara* season. You barely made it through the last flood. And you had a husband then."

Jennifer bit her tongue to hold back the heated reply. Yes, she'd had a husband. Worthless creature that he was. She refused to fall victim to another man. Especially an unpleasant buck-fitch like Barincott. True her husband had pursued his dreams. Chasing rainbows which always seemed to be waiting around the next bend. Well, he was gone. And she would never completely blot away the stain on her conscience, she owed her husband that much. After all, she had chosen him instead of her family. But she was a fighter. She would survive without him.

Barincott. Another Englishman who'd pooled his resources in England, then trekked to a new land to make his fortune. Her lip curled down. She did not trust him.

"Out here in the middle of nowhere," Barincott spread his arms in a wide gesture, "is no place for a woman. This country does not accept a woman's independence. You cannot stay here alone."

He did not need to remind her she dwelled in a foreign land. "I can take care of myself."

The gelding shifted. Barincott leaned forward bracing one arm across the saddle. "You'll get lonely."

Not that lonely.

Saints save her. If she married the likes of him, she would cut her own throat. "I will manage." The pain in her fingers made her aware of the grip she had on the rake. The thunderous beating of her heart caused her chest to hurt. If he decided to use force, she would be at his mercy. She would be completely vulnerable.

Anger ripped through her at the memory of Johnny's foolishness, and her own ignorance.

"You need protection."

"She has protection," came the steely voice from behind.

Oh Lord.

When Barincott's head jerked to the sound of the new voice, she cursed Stephen for his reckless appearance. Why couldn't he stay hidden?

The smile faded from Barincott's lips. His eyes hardened and his teeth, still showing, ground together. Knowing what she would find if she glanced back, she struggled not to turn around. She lost. At the front of her abode, Stephen stood with his arms crossed, lazily leaning against the wall at the open doorway. She gave her best glare, but he stared right past her to the man still sitting on his horse.

She braced herself.

"Well now, Mrs. Faircloth. It would appear you are not alone after all." Barincott straightened in his saddle, his voice held a rigid edge of steel. "Abraham Thaddeus Barincott. And who might you be?"

"Stephen McArthur Radbourn."

Damn. And double damn.

Barincott studied Stephen for some time. "What business do you have with Mrs. Faircloth?"

Stephen stepped from the shadows into the light. "Jenny and I are old friends."

The gleam in Barincott's eyes turned to hatred. "Is that so, *Jennifer?*"

Dear Lord. What kind of impression did Stephen think he'd given by addressing her so personally? And now Barincott used her Christian name, too. "Yes . . . yes," she said with a surprisingly composed voice. She looked up to meet Barincott's gaze. "Stephen is a friend of my family." How easily the lie flowed from her lips.

Barincott leaned back in the saddle as his horse shifted. "No one from your family has visited the entire time you have been here."

Before she could think of a reply, Stephen saved her.

"I bring news from Jenny's family."

Jenny.

Barincott's jaw tightened at the nickname and the way it rolled off Stephen's tongue. She hoped she would not have to split the two men up from a fight. Each had the look of a rooster ready to strut for his hen.

"Oh? What news?" Barincott leveled his gaze on Stephen.

"That's personal." Stephen took a step, and once again acquired the familiar stance with his arms crossed over his chest. His expression hard and unyielding.

"I do not mean to pry. I am a concerned neighbor. I've been keeping an eye on Jennifer since her husband's death. Merely curious if the news came from Jennifer's family, or perhaps, her husband's."

If he meant to get a rise out of Stephen, it did not work. He knew she'd had a husband.

"We are the same family. Johnny was my cousin. Parents on both sides of the family are concerned for Jenny's welfare."

Oh, Stephen was a master. Even she began to believe his nonsense.

Barincott seemed to consider this new information. It was obvious he did not like it. But he could not dispute it. He glanced around the house and lifted his chin. "How did you get here? There's no horse."

Her fingers tightened on the rake. She refused to look at Barincott for fear he would see the fear and guilt about to devour her.

"I have a wagon. My driver will be back by dark."

She blinked her eyes in relief. It seemed her houseguest happened to be a proficient liar. What had she been worried about? Her gaze zipped from Stephen to Barincott, waiting for his reaction. She bit her lip to keep her mouth shut.

Barincott looked ready to explode. He held his tongue. A long time passed between them as the two men stared each other down. Barincott gave a nod to Stephen, his fingers touched the brim of his hat. Then he gave her a nod. "If you need anything . . . *anything* . . . I am only a short distance away." He glanced once again to Stephen and his voice lowered with aggression. "Good day. Until next time, Mr. Radbourn." His horse danced, and with a kick to his ribs, he spirited away.

Jennifer let out the breath she'd been holding while dizziness clouded her vision.

She swayed holding on to her rake.

The ground came up to meet her.

Stephen watched the man ride away. His teeth clenched, his jaw ached up to his temple. The urge to hurl the man to the ground and throttle the fop took every ounce of his self-control. A seaman's life was hard, and their survival required a tough hide. Being the captain, he had kept strict discipline among his crew. He allowed no quarter, earning him the reputation of being ruthless. Months ago, he would have tied the man to a rope and swung him overboard. But then Jenny might not take too kindly to her neighbor being keelhauled, even if he did deserve it.

His gaze swung to Jennifer. He nearly swallowed his teeth when she hit the ground. He ran to her side with a clumsy gait.

"Jenny? Jenny, my love." *Where the hell did that come from?* He brushed a raven lock from her face.

Heat exhaustion? Stubborn woman. How long had she been out in this heat, anyway?

Uncurling her limp form, he lifted her up and carried her into the little house. Fear gripping his chest, he headed straight for the bed. Once he placed her on the quilt, he hurried to the bucket and dipped a cloth in the cool water, then rushed back to her side. Careful, he sat next to her on the side of the bed, wiping her face, hoping to cool her flushed cheeks.

From what Jennifer had told him, her neighbor intended to replace her husband.

Over his dead body.

Her husband might be dead, but Stephen was very much alive. Thanks to Jennifer.

He thought of earlier, when he had heard voices. Peeking outside, he'd seen a man giving Jennifer a moderately hard time. He figured the man was her neighbor, but when the man looked ready to dismount, he decided to make his presence known. When he stepped through the doorway, Barincott, his attention on Jennifer, never noticed. So, Stephen had stood there—waiting. When Barincott insisted she needed protection, Stephen refused to remain silent any longer.

"Ohhh." Jennifer's lids fluttered open. Gradually her gaze focused on him. Pools of soft velvet. Indigo eyes that suddenly narrowed and lit up with fire. "What the blazes did you think you were doing?" She pushed him away and scooted to the end of the bed. She jumped up waving her arms about. "I have never been so scared in my life."

"You," he replied slack-jawed. He stood with the cloth still in his hand. Quick to anger, his temper flared. "How do you think I felt when you toppled to the ground? Damn Jenny. You scared ten years off my life."

"Why didn't you stay hidden?" She paced as she shouted.

Stephen gave a shrug. "I did not like the way he looked at you. And he was not taking no for your answer."

"I can handle Barincott."

She stood with her hands braced on her hips, determination in her beautiful, furious eyes. God, she was pretty. She probably *could* handle the bloody man. "Well, now you won't have to."

"What is that supposed to mean?"

He stepped to the dresser and placed the cloth on its surface. "He will leave you alone now that he knows there is a man around. And you will not need to put up with his constant pestering."

"You have made things worse."

"The devil you say!"

"You do not know him." Her eyes pleaded while she held her hands out to him. "He will dig until he finds out who you are. What if he locates the men who are after you?"

Her words gave him a jolt. His gut revolted. Revenge. But not the shape he was in now. He needed to be stronger. And he could not risk Jennifer being in the clutches of the Rajput prince.

"Those men would have found me by now."

"You don't know that."

True. He didn't. But it had been months. From their conversations, he had traveled some distance before landing at her door. And the men who helped him escape would have covered their tracks.

"Let's just hope they are a long way from here and your neighbor does not run into them. I have a feeling they travel in different circles."

"How can you joke about this?" She spun around and strutted into the open room.

"Believe me, I am not joking," he said grimly. "The Rajput prince was nothing to joke about. He terrorized people, tortured them, murdering—"

"This is serious. Barincott will cause trouble. I know it." A frown marred her pretty forehead. "He did not like the idea of you being here with me."

"If I were interested in becoming your next husband, I wouldn't like it a bit that another man was in your house."

She gave him a confusing look making him wonder if he'd just insulted her. What the hell had he said?

"He will poke around. If he doesn't find out what he wants to know, he will do something else." She picked up her pacing. "Barincott will not let this go. He will . . . he will . . . I don't know what he will do."

Stephen stepped in front of her bringing her to a sudden halt. "Don't worry your pretty little head . . ." He reached for her.

"Is that all you think about? Getting me into bed?" Her eyes flashed fire.

He paused, his hands immobile, very near where her long dark hair curved around one breast. "Now that you mention it . . ."

"No." She spun around. "You need to see reason. Barincott can be dangerous. He will be back."

"If he comes back, I will deal with him." His voice rose as his irritation grew. Did she have any faith in him?

"What if he brings men and they take you? What if . . .?"

"Shhhhh." He slipped his arms around her and pulled her back to his chest. "Come here." He placed his chin in the curve of her neck and cradled her in his arms. Even though he had to bend down, Jennifer fit so perfectly. He inhaled her sweet scent. She'd worn it since the night she'd dressed in her beautiful gown. A hint of the orient. God, he loved holding his angel like this.

Suddenly, she spun around and threw her arms around his neck, burying her face in his chest. "Stephen. I'm scared."

"Hey, now. I've got you." He held her tight with one arm while the other caressed her silken hair. The curve of her head fit in the palm of his hand. His fingers grazed her neck through the long, fine strands. She clutched him as if she would never let him go. A thrill shot to the center of his chest, creating a feeling like none he'd ever known.

His ears prickled.

Riders.

"Jenny."

She must have heard it too, for she jerked back, her eyes locked with his.

"He's back."

"You go in there and shut the door." He gave a nod toward the little room with the bed.

She glared back at him refusing to move—just like he knew she would. He did not have the time or the patience.

"I said go." He shoved her inside giving her a threatening look, she dare not disobey.

He slipped to the window. Men on horses. Barincott was nowhere in sight. A little too soon for him to take action, anyway.

Stephen wished he had a weapon of some kind. He glanced over his shoulder to the closed door. For once the female best listen.

Might as well get this over with.

He opened the door cautiously, and stepped outside.

Chapter 15

Stephen counted five men on horseback. Not more than he could handle, were he at full strength. Restless animals pranced. Nostrils flared and heavy breathing indicated the lot had been ridden hard. Ears back and eyes splayed wide, one horse jerked at his reins. The rider steadied the beast with gentle strokes and soothing words. The steed snorted and pawed one hoof on the ground.

He studied the group, assessing each man one by one. No sudden movements or threats of any kind. By the look of their clothes, they could be Englishmen. But in his experience, he knew not to judge by looks. Although he did trust his instincts. And right now, his gut did not forewarn danger.

Still he had to tread carefully. He would present himself much stronger than he actually felt. Hell, he'd just gotten back on his feet.

"We are not here to cause trouble." The man in front spoke, evidently the leader of the group. "We are looking for a friend."

"Friend's not here." Stephen didn't know who these men were, but when a group of men used the term friend, typically the opposite rang true.

"In fact, our friend looks a lot like you."

Bloody hell. Every nerve stood to attention.

"He is about your height. Same color hair. Although you are a lot thinner than I'd imagined."

Another rider spit a stream of juice to the ground. Stephen kept his gaze on the man speaking.

"Course if our friend had a run-in with a certain Rajput chief, he more than likely lost some muscle. Would you be Captain Radbourn?"

Confusion crowded Stephen's mind. But he could not let down his guard. "Who wants to know?"

"Don't tell them who you are," came a whisper from behind.

Damn woman. He knew he should have locked her in.

"Katherine sent us."

A blow hit his gut just as sure as if the man had punched him. How the deuced hell did they know his sister?

Or a lucky guess?

"I know you have a lot of questions." The leader spoke in a persuading voice, as if he knew he presented a threat. "You don't need to worry. If you are Stephen, I've got a lot to tell you." He leaned one arm on his saddle-horn, letting his words sink in.

Mentioning Katherine, and then his own name, could not be coincidence. That, and being good at taking a man's measure, Stephen decided these men presented no danger. He decided to listen. With the odds stacked against him, he didn't have much choice.

"We found the rebels who helped you escape. We are not your enemy. Katherine is worried, and she has convinced Lord Whetherford you might be in trouble. Your uncle contemplated the same idea. We are here to rescue you."

Katherine. If he knew his sister, she'd raised a ruckus until someone listened to her. Then she convinced Lord Whetherford, whoever the hell he was, to look for her brother. And his uncle? Where did he fit in all this? Stephen rolled his shoulders and released a heavy sigh.

"You've found me. We can offer food and rest. There's water close by for the horses."

"Thank you." The leader nodded to the others and the men dismounted.

While Stephen observed the men, Jennifer slipped beside him.

"I am Giles. This is Piers, Elms, Paddy." He turned to his left. "And this is Nathaniel." Each man gave a nod as his name was mentioned.

"As you have guessed, I am Stephen. This is Jennifer . . ." He hesitated while remembering Barincott had called her Mrs. Faircloth. ". . . Faircloth."

"Miss Faircloth. Pleased to make your acquaintance," Giles said as he put his fingers to the brim of his hat.

"If you are truly friends, then you are welcome in my home," Jennifer said.

Jennifer did not correct him. Then there was no husband about.

"Much obliged, ma'am," Nathaniel said, and gave her a blinding smile.

"There is a path to the river, that way." She gestured with her arm.

"There's a fenced area in the back," Stephen said. "A small space for your gear. When you're ready, come inside."

Giles handed Elms the reins to his horse. When Jennifer stepped inside her home, Stephen indicated for the leader to follow. He glanced over his shoulder watching, as the rest of the riders disappeared around the side of the house.

Stephen closed the door and faced the man equivalent to his towering height. "Now, Giles. Why don't you tell me how you know my sister?"

"Stephen, if the man is here to rescue you, you should be more gracious."

Stephen crossed his arms over his chest, while Giles' gaze flicked from Jennifer to him. "Rescue me?"

"Our mission was to find you, and rescue you if necessary," Giles said.

"You still haven't said how you know my sister."

His lips curved in a smile. "That's a long story."

"Make it short," Stephen said gruffly.

"Might take some doing. May I have some water?"

"Of course." Jennifer dipped from the bucket she'd brought from the stream earlier.

"Thank you." Giles drank, then wiped his mouth with the back of his hand. "Before Morgan became the Earl of Whetherford, he and I traveled from one country to the next on special assignments. You know how gossip sweeps through the ton. Rumormongers spread word of Morgan's past. Your sister heard the gossip and approached Whetherford asking for his help—to find you. He sent me. Is that short enough?"

"Devil take her." Stephen spouted. "Just like Kat to do something so foolish. And what of my uncle?"

"I met with him. He assigned me the job."

"Then I shall thank my uncle for his intervention."

"I assured him I would find you." A frown crossed his brow. "My only regret is that I did not discover your circumstances or your whereabouts sooner."

Stephen's instincts told him that Giles knew about the torture. "No one knew I was in trouble."

"Your sister did."

"Kat." Of course, she would know. When he hadn't come home, she must have guessed. She knew he would never stay away from her for long. Just how long had it been? He had lost track of time in hell's pit.

"Please, Mr. . . ." Jennifer hesitated.

"Giles, ma'am."

"Mr. Giles. Please have a seat."

He gave a smile of admiration to Jennifer causing Stephen to narrow his eyes. He pulled out the opposite chair and lowered his frame.

"How did you know where I'd gone?"

"Thornton has some very influential friends. And I have my own contacts. My former . . . occupation . . . instilled a dedicated set of skills. I've not had much occasion to use them of late, but I have not forgotten what I learned."

Nor had he lived a life of constant peril, either, if Stephen had his guess. By his speech, Giles had been educated. Sounded like a blue-blood.

"When the rebels told us . . ." Giles glanced at Jennifer in her rocker, ". . . what happened, we were not sure we'd find you alive."

"I'm stubborn."

A choking sound caused both men to look at Jennifer. When she recovered, she glared at him. "Well, you are."

Damn feisty woman. He loved her spunk.

When he glanced back to Giles', the man's eyes glowed with appreciation and his lips turned up at the corners. Stephen wanted to wipe the approving grin right off his face. Preferably with his fist.

"He nearly did die. And when we heard horses, I thought . . ." Jennifer faltered. She twisted her hands in her lap.

Her words reminded him of another threat. "Barincott."

"He could still come back." Anxiety bounced off her.

Giles eyes grew hard and his jaw tightened. "What does she mean?"

"Her blasted neighbor," Stephen grunted and slapped his hand on his thigh. "He left a short while ago."

"My neighbor has been . . . uh . . ."

"The man wants her. He saw me here, and Jennifer is afraid he'll cause trouble. She thinks he will connect me with the prince."

"She may be right. The prince most likely has his scouts scouring the land, looking for information."

Jennifer's gasp ripped through him.

"They nearly killed him. If the Rajput prince finds him, he will finish what he started."

"Then time is of the essence." With an abrupt movement, Giles stood. "We should leave. Now."

Stephen liked the man's instincts. "I agree. Jennifer, pack some food." He placed both hands on the table and rose.

She grabbed a linen sac and raced to the corner, filling it with supplies. All he had was the clothes on his back, so he gathered any items he thought essential for the journey. Footsteps outside signaled the men had returned. Giles slipped out, making his men aware of their situation.

Jennifer handed Stephen the bag. Her head down, she trembled.

"Hey." He placed the sack on the table, and when he pulled her, she came willingly into his arms. She snuggled into the curve of his neck. He buried his face in her soft, silky hair.

Mmmm. Sweet.

"I've got you, Angel. You have nothing to fear." His hands caressed her back, his fingers pressed into her flesh while he drew her tighter against his body. Awareness plucked his inner recesses. He'd wanted to console her, but one moment in his arms and he hungered for more than her kisses. Good God, he wanted to ravish her.

"Let's get going. We do not want to be here when Barincott comes back."

"I am not going."

He curled a finger under her chin and wrenched her gaze to his. He searched her eyes. "What did you say?"

"I said, I . . . I'm not going."

"Jennifer. You must come with me. I will not leave you here alone."

"I have been on my own for quite some time."

"Are you daft, woman? Barincott will not rest until he finds out who I am. Then he'll be back."

"I can handle him."

"Blast it, woman. If Barincott returns with the prince's men, they will take you. He is a cruel man. There is no way in hell I'll let that bloody bastard get his hands on you."

"You are not in charge of me. I will remind you, Stephan, that I was the one who took care of you when you were weak and helpless. I can take care of myself. I will deal with him."

Stephen bent down, his nose nearly touching hers. "No you will not, because you will be gone."

"Now just a minute." Her hands on his chest, she pushed away.

"Bloody hell, woman." His hands tightened, refusing to let her go. "If I have to throw you over my shoulder and carry you every step, you will go with me."

"I will not." She stamped her foot. This time, when she shoved, she broke free.

How she reminded him of his little sister. Bottom lip distended in a stubborn pout. Hands on her hips like she wielded a weapon. Fire shooting from her eyes.

He took a threatening step and heard snickers from behind.

"Looks like you got your hands full there, Captain Radbourn. If what you say about this Barincott is true, we best not waste any time."

"See, Stephen? You must go."

"I will not be repeating myself." The muscles in his cheeks tightened with each word, so much so, he thought his jaw would snap. "Pack, or leave everything behind. That is the only choice I will give you."

When she opened her mouth, he'd had enough.

"That's it."

He lunged, but she quickly darted out of his reach. He stomped after her, mindful of the pain shooting through his ankles and up his legs. His steps slowed and his gait lightened, but he continued until he caught her, pinning her arms within his iron grip.

"All right, all right." She struggled unsuccessfully, to free herself. "Let me gather my things."

"Make it few. We travel light. And if you give me any grief . . ." his nose nearly touching hers with only a breath between them, he growled, "you will be riding up-side-down with only the clothes on your back."

"You have made your point quite clear. Now get out of my way."

He graciously stepped back, and with a swing of his arm, he gallantly waved her forward, like any gentlemanly swain taking a knee at an elaborate ball.

"We should leave before dark. The cover of night will aid in our ship not being seen. But first, we have to get there." A grim line formed on Giles' mouth.

The resonance of his voice triggered something in Stephen's brain. More of a quality, actually. Giles may be the leader of this bunch—and he definitely looked the part of a nomad—but his words and actions hinted in the region of autocratic, and not in the tyrannical sense. Giles had a certain air about him, an essence of power. Authority yes, but respectability as well.

A man's rightful claim to being a gentleman was not something one could inherit like a title.

His father's words. But Stephen's dealings with the gentry instilled enough to know a gentleman of the upper-crust when he saw one. He also recognized a man who'd traveled down the devil's road. Giles hid secrets. Since both images seem to fit him, Stephen had to wonder what hand fate had dealt the man.

They were destined to spend the next few months on board a ship together. His curiosity demanded he find out correctly which, or maybe both, were the true Giles. Disturbing as it was, assuming anything without facts would be unjust. Besides, he needed answers to more than the man's character. And there was the mystery concerning his sister. For without a doubt, the fellow knew more than he declared.

Chapter 16

With his arms crossed and his feet braced, Stephen stood alone on the deck of the *Sea Sorceress,* his gaze following the water lapping at the cliff's edge. Few clouds drifted while a soft breeze wafted blowing his red mane. He breathed deep of the salty, sea air. *Home.* A ship had always been more of a home than any dwelling or land, even English soil. It never ceased to amaze him, the deep gratification that sluiced over his core every time he stood just like this, immersed in the quietude around him.

A glorious star filled sky. Gentle flapping of sails caught the north wind. He lifted his head higher, welcoming each gust as his skin tingled in anticipation. His body rocked with the rough waters of the cape allowing the current to soothe his soul. Closing his eyes, he gloried in the moment. Not too long ago, he had thought never to be on the ocean again, let alone a ship headed for England. Never would he take life for granted again, or the gift of being at sea. Not that he had before, but he never thought his days on the ocean would come to an end—an end not of his choosing.

It pained him, the loss of the *Serpent's Ghost.* But the loss of her crew had nearly broken him. He, alone, would return home, but the memory of their lifeless bodies would haunt him to his dying day. When he'd hired his crew, he took on men who had no wives or family, hoping to avoid any attachments that would hinder the sailors or take them away from family responsibilities. He had thought his men would be sailing home with him—with great riches.

He had given most of his life to the sea. Only his duty to Kat, had made him return home as frequently as he did. But then, his love for his little sister had grown stronger since their parents' deaths. If not for the rebel leader, he would have rotted away, his family never knowing of his demise. Unwilling to allow the monster prince to destroy him, he had somehow managed to stay alive.

His family.

Taught muscles stretched. Stephen rubbed his stubbled chin. Soon his beard would grow back. For now, he would return to his family. He strode to the stern, resting his arms on the rail. A full moon reflected off the water's surface. He gazed at the white-capped waves of the swelling sea. The ship edged away from the cove under the dark of night, quiet as death. He silently cursed when a pang of guilt hit him anew.

Serpent's Ghost.

His crew had not deserved their cruel ending. He would always carry the memories. If it took the rest of his life, he vowed to avenge their deaths.

"Would you like me to leave you alone to your thoughts?"

Stephen gave a slight jerk. He hadn't heard Giles come up behind him. Given time, Stephen hoped his instincts would function as acutely as they once had.

"A change of thought would be appreciated," he replied.

"Reflecting on your crew? I understand. Believe me." Giles propped his elbows on the wood and stared at the coastline.

"You understand," Stephen grumbled.

"Talking helps. I too lost men, and wondered why I lived."

A sense of camaraderie developed between them. "Guessed you'd been down this road before."

"Not too long ago I lived on the edge." Giles words held no emotion. He spoke as if he were simply spinning a fable. "I dodged more bullets than those that found their mark, made my opinion of myself grow. I didn't care. Danger meant nothing more than a challenge. The riskier the better. I had no regard for my own life. Seems like another lifetime."

"Yet, here you are," Stephen said.

"Yes. Finding you, following your trail, has brought it all back." Giles turned to face him. "Give it time. Your wounds will heal. You will still carry the scars in your heart and the demons in your mind, but you will manage to go on."

"Maybe you did. But I will have my revenge." Anger boiled inside at the words. He meant them with every fiber of his being. His knuckles ached from his grip on the rail.

"You are lucky to be alive. Let this go."

"Let it go?" Stephen roared. "Those bastards slaughtered my crew. For no other reason than we were in the wrong place. We found his cove by accident, for God's sake."

"You're in a foreign land. Things are different here." Giles' tone grew stronger.

"By God, do not preach to me. This land or any other, *his* kind of cruelty makes a man lose his mind. Rips his soul right out of his chest. I cannot overlook such a vile man. I will have my revenge. The Rajput prince will die." He spun on his heel to leave.

"Wait. Don't you have something else to live for?" When Stephen hesitated, Giles continued. "She saved your hide."

The first thought in Stephen's mind had been Kat. Then he realized Giles spoke of Jennifer. Yes, she had saved his neck, his skin, and his sanity. He owed her a great deal. But she had nothing to do with the subject at hand. He owed a reckoning for his men, to honor them. To avenge their brutal deaths.

"Do you know what that Rajput did to me? Not just to my body. He made me watch while he tortured and killed my crew. I would have told him anything, done anything to save them. But the heartless bastard refused to believe me, and I did not know what lies would save them. He broke every bone in my body, and a few I didn't know I had." Stephen's weak attempt at humor helped him to remember the cutthroats had not killed his spirit.

"Somewhere in the back of your mind, you wanted to survive. And you did," Giles pointed out. "Remember that inkling and focus on living. You've got a long way to go. Get your strength back. While your body recovers, so will your mind."

Stephen met his stare. "You give the impression you know what you are talking about."

"Like I said," Giles turned his gaze back to the shore. "I have been there."

Stephen shoved the hair out of his face and stepped beside Giles, facing the wind. "All the time in the world will not make me forget."

"No. But you can find a corner where you can bury the darkness. It will surface on occasion. You can allow the grief to swallow you whole, or you can stroke it, and then bury it again. The choice becomes more tolerable as time passes."

"This worked for you?"

Giles gave a nod of assent. "Although, I did not have someone who cared for me while time healed my remorse."

"Jennifer has nothing to do with this."

"Oh, no? Didn't look that way to me. Sparks were flying between you two."

"I could not leave her behind." Stephen hit the wood with his fist. "If the prince caught up with her . . ."

"No sense traveling down a line of thought where it does not exist." Giles placed one hand on Stephen's shoulder. "Take joy in the fact she is safe. And here with you."

"If you're trying to change my mind by changing the subject to a more agreeable one, it won't work."

"I merely mention there is a beautiful woman aboard this ship who seems a bit taken with you." Giles spread his hands and gave a slight shrug.

Stephen narrowed his eyes, and gave a threatening look that he had used on many men with every intention to intimidate. Since the blasted man neared his own height, the task grew difficult of staring down his nose with a lofty glare. "Just why are you thinking about Jennifer being beautiful?"

"Good God, man. I have eyes."

"I will be thanking you to keep your bloody eyes in their sockets. Or you might be sporting a black one or two."

The crafty grin flourishing on Giles face suggested he was not worried in the least. Stephen could like this man. Giles would make a good comrade. He gave a two-finger salute. "We've got some hard sailing ahead of us if we are to avoid any ships that might come after us." He turned and strode to the quarterdeck addressing the captain at the wheel.

Leaning his hip against the wooden rail, Stephen scrutinized the two in conversation. Why had Giles risked his hide? And what about his friend, the earl? Nothing Stephen could do until he arrived in England—going directly to the source of the problem. And find out just what his headstrong sister had been up to.

Kat would have to wait. For now, he had another woman who needed his immediate attention. A magnificent creature. One he desired. He could not blot out the beauty crowding his mind, nor control the stimulation of his wayward body.

Ahh, Jennifer. What was he to do now?

A small lantern made it easier for Jennifer to see as her eyes scanned her surroundings. Since the cabin seemed large, she supposed it belonged to the captain. The first thing she spotted was the bed. A bit large for a cabin on a ship, but then this room happened to be quite large. She glanced to the heavy wooden table bolted in the middle of the floor. On the surface, she saw a bowl of apples. However, her stomach revolted at the thought of food.

Once again, she had fled her home leaving all her belongings behind. True the items in her small house did not compare to the abundance of belongings in the bedchamber of her parents dwelling. Stephen, in his haste, had allowed her even less. The things she'd brought with her when she had run away with Johnny, she'd had to leave behind. Except for her blue gown. The one true surety that buoyed her during her trials.

Glancing around she saw a bench braced against the wall at the foot of the bed. A large trunk rested in the corner. She chewed on the end of her finger. Any second she feared the prince or his men would find them. Every moment of waiting increased her worry. She placed her fingers at each side of her temples, hoping to rub away some of the painful pressure. She needed something to do to keep anxiety from attacking her skull.

The rocking of the ship confirmed they were exiting the cove. Bitter sweet relief washed over her. Glad, knowing they would soon sail in open waters—frightened they could yet be captured.

She took a deep breath. No sense in hopeless speculation.

Shadows flickered on the door. The longer she stared, the more she fretted. Where was Stephen? She spotted a set of carved doors, high in the wall on the other side of the cabin. If she counted her shortcomings, curiosity ranked top on her list. If she remained idle, she would go mad. She opened one door. Objects, she supposed, used for direction or navigating filled the shelf. The second door contained several maps, papers and some books. She selected one and was just about to open it when there was a rap on the door.

She stood in the middle of the cabin and watched the latch on the door lift. A wave of relief swamped her when she saw Stephen. A light entered his eyes and he smiled as though he too, was glad to see her. The band around her chest eased.

"We are well on our way." He stepped inside and closed the cabin door.

"Thank God." One affliction gone, and another took its place. Her first impulse was to rush into his arms. Beg him to kiss her senseless. Drive every menacing thought from her mind.

Her feet stayed rooted to the wooden planks.

"Are you still mad at me?"

His hair wild and free, whiskers grazed his chin, a probing glint in his eyes—her heart raced. *Mad?* She blinked, completely taken back by his question.

"I could not leave you behind."

Heaven forbid. He thought her cross with him. "I am glad you didn't," she whispered.

He opened his arms. Her heart in her throat, she ran to him. He crushed her in his embrace.

"Angel." He bent his head to nuzzle the tender spot just below her ear.

She grasped his shoulders and wiggled as close as she could get without liquefying and becoming one with him. His breathing thickened.

Safe.

The emotion hit her with a blow to her senses. Yes. Safe. She could not remember ever feeling so secure, or so protected as she did this moment. A tiny alarm flashed in her brain, warning her, she should not allow a man such control over her feelings. Locked in his arms, contentment thrust any forewarning away. This man, Stephen, made all the difference in the world.

"You rouse my blood," he muttered.

She snuggled closer. Mmmm. How she wanted him. How she longed for his comfort, his embrace, his kisses. And more. His passion had created a wanton in her soul. He had made her a woman. Those urges rose inside of her once more. Her skin tingled at the open mouth kiss on her neck. Shivers of delight and desire raced down her spine. He pressed his hardness against her belly, and the bottom dropped out of her stomach.

"Good God, woman you feel good." He gave her a hard squeeze. "I must stop."

"Why?" She hugged him tighter.

He gave a soft chuckle. "Because, with you in my arms, you are irresistible."

She did not want him to stop.

"It's dark. You should rest. I will not take advantage of the harrowing day we've had." He pulled away. "Do you require anything?"

Only you.

"Do you think we will be followed," she asked.

He skimmed his hands up and down her arms, creating warmth with his touch. "The captain is sure to put plenty of distance between us and any threat. You are not to worry your pretty head."

"And Giles? What is his part in this?"

"Appears he came to India looking for me." At her confusion, he continued. "My family sent him to find me. I have been gone a long time."

"From England?"

He took a heavy sigh. "My sister, Katherine. She is the only reason I go back there. Ever since our parents' deaths, I feel responsible for her."

"Responsible?"

He gave a chest jarring sigh. "More than responsible. She has always hung on my coattails. But, years passing, we have grown closer. She is my little sister. She pulls at my heart strings with just her eyes. What do you think she is like when she really tries to have her way?"

A faint chuckle left her lips at the thought of Stephen's scowl turning to helplessness while being confronted by a young girl with a pouting lip and the same color hair as her handsome sea captain.

"I visit when I can." He shoved his hands through his windswept mane. "I've lost track of time, but near as I can guess it's been about two years since I've seen her. She is a spitfire. A wonder my uncle isn't deranged."

"You love her."

The corner of his tempting lip rose in an endearing smile. "You would like her. She would like you."

"Why do you say that? She does not even know me. She might resent you bringing another woman home."

"Another woman!" He quirked a brow. "She's my bloody sister."

"If she's as possessive as you describe, she may not want another female anywhere near you. For any reason."

"Not possessive. Protective. Like I said, we are close. We only have each other. My aunt and uncle do not count. Sure, they are blood. But Kat was devastated when our parents died." His voice dropped. "And she was worse when *I* left her."

Jennifer could not stand to see his grief-stricken eyes. Leaning her head on his chest, she slid her arms around his waist. Their conversation brought back images of her own sister. And how much she longed to see her family again.

Even if they might not be as eager to see her.

Chapter 17

The first hint of dawn lit the morning sky with the sun's rays streaking her golden glow across the horizon. Even the breeze embraced the beginning of a new day. Stephen filled his lungs with tangy salt air. With the wind blowing his unruly mane and the sun kissing his wind burned cheeks, he relished knowing he was alive. His senses had sharpened. The sun seemed brighter. The wind more brisk. The air held more oxygen.

For the first time in a series of months, he breathed without trepidation. Without the devil lurking over his shoulder hounding his days. Without pain from inflicted torture, or worry of the next day's happenings. Being back on a ship, he had achieved some sense of normalcy. His male ego needed a healthy dose of self-assurance. The crew accepted his intrusions, mindful he had once captained his own ship. The loss of his men weighed heavy on his conscious, but he scorned pity.

Last night, he'd slept on deck, under a clear balmy night sky dripping diamonds. He missed long weeks and quiet nights on *Serpent's Ghost*. Neither the creak of timbers, nor the slap of waves against the seasoned hull lulled him to sleep. For the stars kept forming an angel's face with gemstones for a pair of eyes. When he left Jennifer's cabin, his limit had been stretched tighter than a rope tethering a sail. Lust had him ready to change his mind, stay with the beauty who kept his body in a state of arousal. The ache for her consumed him. Drowning in her lavender eyes, inhaling the scent that was hers alone, he'd called on every fragment of strength he possessed to turn his back and walk away.

He had no doubt, she would not have refused him if he'd asked to spend the night with her. Hell, her eyes had begged him to stay. Her curves were generous enough to stir a man to recklessness. But with a will he didn't know he possessed, he used the head on his shoulders to make the correct decision. On a ship, discretion sailed away with the tide. He would not embarrass her or give the crew fodder for conversation.

He strode to the quarterdeck with purpose. Giles stood with his back to the wind, speaking to the first mate at the wheel. When he noticed Stephen advancing in his direction, Giles broke away and stepped forward.

"Fine trail wind this morning."

"I'd like to finish a conversation, slipped my mind last night." Only because Stephen watched, he saw Giles eyes grow guarded.

"You have my attention."

"You've got some explaining to do. Regarding my sister."

"Very well. I will answer all of your questions. How about we have our discussion over a bottle of brandy," he said with a brash grin.

Stephen could feel his mouth slavering. "Now you're speaking my language." He followed Giles below deck. When he stepped into Giles cabin, a whistle escaped his teeth.

"I thought Jennifer occupied the captain's cabin. This one is more lavish."

"She does. This one is mine." Giles stepped to a cabinet housing an array of glass. "I enjoy traveling in comfort." He removed a bottle of amber liquid and held it toward the light coming through the porthole.

"Or would you prefer port?"

"Been a while since I've downed anything harder than water."

A massive desk with detailed carving sat to one side, with two leather upholstered chairs placed in front and one of the same quality next to the wall. Giles gestured to the chairs in front. Stephen sat down and inhaled the scent of fine leather. Placing two glasses on the shiny wooden surface, Giles poured a measure of brandy and took the seat beside him.

On any given occasion, Stephen could drink a man under the table, and keep his wits about him. He stared at the brown-gold liquid. His stomach had been empty for so long, he wondered if the blend would burn a hole right through it. He took a swig and relished the embittered honey taste before he swallowed.

"Some think a well-honed wine makes a bitter pill easier to swallow." He stared at the contents of his glass while he spoke.

"Some men simply enjoy a pleasing drink over an exchange of opinions." Giles said with a hint of mirth.

Stephen met his gaze. "You will have my opinion without reservation."

"I do not doubt it. However, let me assure you I have the utmost respect for your family. Katherine is a lovely young woman. She is very worried about you."

"I know my impetuous sister."

A corner of Giles mouth lifted. "Ask your questions?"

"I suggest you start at the beginning." Stephen leveled a harsh glare. "And leave nothing out."

No emotion crossed the man's face. Devilish calm, not a concern in the world. Probably honed his skills to cover his thinking. He drank from his glass, then made a grand gesture when he swallowed. Black eyes bore into his. "It appears your sister overheard your aunt and uncle discussing the longevity of your absence."

"Another bad habit which has gotten her into mischief."

Giles smile grew wider. "During their conversation, Thornton mentioned he'd asked a Captain Danvers to gather information, and as coincidences happen, his ship had docked that day. Katherine, if I may, slipped out of the house early the next morning and went to the docks in search of the captain. Before she found him, two sailors found her."

Stephen's hands fisted in anger. He emptied his glass and pointed to the bottle for Giles to pour him another.

Glass clinked, and then Giles poured another for himself. "A good friend, and honorable man, Morgan Langston, Earl of Whetherford went to London in search of a thief. He happened upon the two sailors beleaguering your sister. He fought them, but he was stabbed. Due to blood loss, he lost consciousness."

"Must not be much of a man if he let two galoots manhandle my sister. I would have killed the bloody bastards."

"He did."

Stephen's arm stopped midway. The bold statement surprised him. He might need to change his opinion. "Good. And Katherine? She was not harmed?"

"No. She was not." Giles turned up his glass, downing his brandy. He filled his glass again.

When he offered Stephen more, he shook his head in refusal. Already his stomach burned.

"Your sister bears a remarkable likeness to another woman. A thief Morgan was searching for in England. When Lord Whetherford's men found him, they assumed Katherine to be that woman. They took her to Whetherford Manor."

"I have a hard time believing she went with these men willingly," Stephen growled.

"These are honorable men. They would not hurt a woman. But they did lock her up in one of the bedchambers. When

Morgan recovered, he rectified their mistake. He offered marriage."

"So, my sister is betrothed to Whetherford."

"No, she is not."

"Don't tell me the stubborn chit refused!"

Giles shifted in his chair. "At first. But then Morgan convinced her."

"She is or is not going to marry Whetherford?"

Giles drew a deep breath before he answered. "She is not."

"There is something you're not telling me." Stephen slid forward and propped his arm on the wooden table. His gut told him there was more—much more—to this tale. But then, his willful sister could be pigheaded at times. "What happened? What did Katherine do to sever the engagement?"

"Actually, Thornton sorted it out."

"My uncle?" His brows rose in surprise.

"Katherine's disappearance was kept secret. Thornton spread the story Katherine visited her friend Viscountess Roxborough thinking no one would question the Viscount. And no one did. Thornton released Lord Whetherford from his promise. Morgan accepted on the stipulation that Katherine agreed that she did not want marriage."

"The betrothal was dissolved."

"Yes."

Kat didn't know what was good for her. She'd been spoiled for far too long. That would change as soon as he got home. Stephen lifted his glass, then decided he better not risk burning a hole clear through his belly. "Continue."

"When I mentioned, before, about accepting risky missions," Giles met Stephen's gaze with a solemn look. "Morgan risked his neck with me."

The way Giles skipped from the man's name to his title, Stephen had a hard time keeping up. It took a minute for the name to register. If Morgan and Giles were together in treacherous situations, did neither man give a farthing for human life? Missions which possibly were slayings?

"So, the two of you play at being nobles while you sneak off in secret to do your spying and unlawful acts?

Finally, a reaction. Anger steamed off Giles. A white line formed around his mouth with the tightening of his jaw.

"We play at nothing. He is an earl. I am a duke."

Stephen pounded his fist on the oak. "I knew it. I knew in my bones you were a bloody aristocrat. A damned duke." Stephen rose to his feet.

"No one knows of my title, and I'd like to keep it that way." Giles eyes glared. His gaze questioning, yet to some extent—a warning.

"Rest at ease. I have no reason to announce your nobility."

"My past is a different life."

Stephen crossed his arms and looked down his nose. "Seems more current than former to me."

"I am here only because of my friend and your sister."

"Thought my uncle sent you."

"I'd already been abreast of the matter. Your sister approached Whetherford, and asked him to find you."

"This tale you're spinning has more manacles than a ship's anchor." He leaned closer, absorbed with intense curiosity. "Now, why would Kat go to an earl, one who held her captive, no less? You did say he locked her up."

"His men. But she was well cared for."

"And, he seems very forgiving. What else are you not telling me? Why did she go to him?" Anger boiled in the pit of his stomach. The more he heard, the more fire fueled his temper.

"You know how gossip flows in the ton. When Whetherford Manor's earl finally returned to accept his inheritance, stories—mostly made up from outrageously creative minds—were spread about his absence. His dark past, dark deeds, fanciful tales making him mysterious. Katherine surmised the Earl of Whetherford could help her find you."

"Women." All the more reason he needed to get home. He glanced at the empty chair, deciding he may as well sit for the rest of this account. "How did she manage to get the earl's cooperation without my uncle knowing of her scheme?" Did he really need to ask? The little minx had a knack for twisting everyone around her little finger.

"That, I do not know."

Stephen waved a hand. "Never mind. Why did the earl . . . Morgan accept?"

Giles coughed to clear his throat. "I believe he is infatuated with Katherine."

Infatuated?

"What did he ask for payment?" Stephen growled, not liking the impression.

"Morgan is a gentleman," Giles answered in a tone of resentment. "No money exchanged hands. No deals were made. However, he did ask me to locate her brother. He hoped it might put him, shall we say, in her good graces."

Stephen shoved out of his chair and charged, like a cannonball exploding from a cannon. He grabbed Giles by the throat. "Are you telling me a bloody assassin, who fled his title in disgrace, a man who thought no more of his life than a fart in the wind, has designs on keeping company with my sister?"

"Calm down. Nothing inappropriate was intended," Giles said in a rasping voice.

Stephen squeezed. Before he could say another word, Giles knocked his hands away and Stephen found himself on the floor. Pain seared his left leg. *Damn.* "If I were at full strength, you'd never best me."

"I do not want to fight you." Giles shrugged, a corner of his mouth tilted in a smug grin. "But I cannot let you kill me before I deliver you to your family."

"Fair enough. You will have to show me how you did that. Tis a maneuver I may need to know, since I am half my normal size." When Giles offered a hand to help him up, he accepted. Stephen rubbed his aching thigh. "I may have lost some of my bulk, but my resolve is true. Friend or no, I will kill the blimey bastard if he has harmed Kat in *any* way. You aiding me now will make no difference."

"You have my word," said Giles.

"I do not know you, man. You came looking for me. You are taking me home. I'm obliged to you. But Kat is blood. She's my little sister, for God's sake."

"Morgan is an honorable man. He would not take advantage of her."

"An honorable man becomes downright shameful when his willy is involved. If I find the man has disrespected my sister in any way, I will tear his limbs from his body. Starting with his most private one."

Chapter 18

Jennifer placed her hand on her chest to calm her racing heart.

Stephen slammed the cabin door behind him. Eyes blazing, he thrust his hands through his bushy lot of hair. "A duke. A bloody duke. I knew it."

After the jolt he'd just given her, she could barely speak. "What?"

"Giles is a bloody duke."

He glared at her like she knew what he was talking about.

"London aristocracy is one reason I preferred my ship. The *ton* and their vanities. With their self-importance and self-centeredness."

"Giles is a duke? You're not making any sense." She thought maybe she misheard.

Stephen leveled his steely gaze on her. "A duke. The aristocracy in full form."

Giles did not look anything like a duke. He certainly did not act like one.

When she realized Stephen waited for her answer, she plunged forward. "Surely a duke would never hire himself out on retainer to go searching for a missing person, let alone put his life in peril."

That seemed to take some of the gale out of Stephen's sails. The lines on his brow cleared, but confusion lingered in his gaze.

"I knew from his speech." He turned and smacked a fist into his palm causing her to jump. "As sure as my gut suggested, I recognized the signs. Giles moves with imposing authority. Not just as a leader, but with the assurance of a nobleman. Expecting his orders to be followed without question."

Like you?

"Um, Stephen . . . doesn't a captain also expect his orders to be followed?"

His eyes flew wide. "Of course. But his manner. I have seen enough blue-bloods to spot one. Giles' actions betrayed him."

"But a nobleman? How can you be sure?"

"Other than his admission?"

Her gasp sounded like an explosion in the cabin.

"Yes, my dear Jenny," his voice low and persuading. "A high-born. Not arrogance most titled men deem their entitlement. No, Giles is an exacting individual. Difficult to surmise at first. The man is crafty—lithe movements, keen skills of a particular sort."

Stephen paced about the small space. She heard the sound of his words, but at the moment nothing penetrated except the fact that, apparently, Stephen hated the nobility. She had expected this to be difficult—she'd had no idea he felt so strongly.

Jennifer chewed on her fingernail. How would he react when she told him? Guilt assailed her.

"Stephen. Is not your family of the aristocracy?"

He turned and glared as if she had suddenly grown a new head. "There are others in my distant family. Enough of the male gender to stand in line for a title. I have never cared for the dull life of Parliament."

She must tell him.

He gathered her in his arms and rubbed his jaw against the side of her head, caressing her hair. "Ahh, sweet Jenny. I merely came to see how you fare and bid you goodnight."

A familiar ache centered in her belly. How could she say anything, think anything, when he held her like this? Of their own accord, her arms lifted, and her fingers slipped under his hair, seeking the skin at the back of his neck. She loved the feel of him. She loved his reaction to her ministrations.

After a few idyllic moments, he pulled back. Enclosing her fingers within his own, he kissed the back of her knuckles. His gaze held hers while his thumb stroked the back of her hand, sending tingles dancing down the center of her spine. And his grin? How could a girl not melt with a handsome rogue bestowing the gleam of a devil's invitation?

A mane of tousled hair as red as the fiery sun setting in an evening sky. A rough voice that gentled to husky softness. Sea green eyes that glittered, and sent her tumbling right over the edge of wickedness. Full lips and mind blowing kisses that still burned on her memory. A tingle of awareness chased through her body.

Revealing her secret would only spoil this moment with him.

There was always tomorrow.

Leaning on the wooden rail, Stephen jutted his head into the wind, mindful of the morning sun edging above the horizon. His mind twisted with errant thoughts and irrational ideas. Jenny took up too much of his contemplation. Even now he examined his feelings too closely.

Feelings?

There were no *feelings*. He'd been around the woman too damn long. Generally, his life consisted of sailing the wide span of ocean, more often than not, a new wench in a new port when it suited his fancy. Circumstances had delayed his normal way of life—drinking and wenching. Pleasure would be his first objective. Pay a visit to a tavern and find himself a woman. A woman with blue eyes or brown, no matter. With luscious curves and bright colored hair. A tavern maid was just what he needed. If for no other reason than to prove Jenny had no hold over him. Being the only female in close proximity, of course he lusted after her. Saint's blood, he *was* a man.

And so was every member of this ship. A stab of unknown fervor, very much like jealously, sliced his chest. As quickly as the thought came to his mind, he cursed himself for allowing it access. He searched the deck. Sailors went about their normal duties. How would he know if one was missing?

Good God. Had he lost his mind? With a certainty, his reaction must stem from protection. Looking out for her well-being. But the little twinge in his chest refused to be discharged. The sensation burrowed and dug, and settled like sentiment. Love? Not bloody likely.

He hooked his thumbs in his belt. Thank God, some of Giles apparel fit. Amazing what a proper set of clothes could do for a man's dignity. Creaking wenches, flustering sails, raucous sailors—harmonious sounds restoring his soul. He hated being weak. His body would heal. The only thing he needed to concentrate on now was going home.

Tinkling notes of Jennifer's voice floated across the breeze and hovered like music to Stephen's ears. Lifting his gaze, the object of his thoughts strolled toward him—on the arm of the bloody duke. A strange little pressure grabbed his heart. Damn the man's sorry aristocratic hide. Judging from his dress, no one would guess the man a titled lord, let alone one so high in the nobility.

The wind tugged a few feathery locks away from Jenny's face. Her head tilted, she shielded her eyes while she scanned the masts. She radiated with beauty. Her enthusiasm only heightened her desirability.

Then she saw him. Her blinding smile landed a blow in the center of his gut.

"Good morning, Stephen. His Grace—"

"Please, Mrs. Faircloth," Giles interrupted. "We discussed this. Giles, please."

"Your rank has prominence. Yet you continue to address *me* formally."

"I stand ceremoniously." He gave a slight bow.

"*Giles*," Jennifer said with a nod to Giles, "was showing me everything on the ship. How impressive." Her eyes twinkled with glee.

She wanted to see a damned ship, he could show her a damned ship.

"Surely you have been on a ship before?" Stephen's voice came out cold, showing his irritation.

"Not like this one. And I have a personal escort." She gazed at Giles bestowing her admiration.

Stephen glared through a red haze. At the first sign of a squall he would throw the damned duke overboard.

"If you will excuse me, Mrs. Faircloth, I see the captain signaling me." Giles engaged a conspiratorial smile. "Perhaps Stephen will finish your tour. He is familiar with everything on a ship. After all, he is a captain."

"I would be honored." Keeping one eye on Giles, Stephen held out an arm. Contrary to what some believed, he had been raised with manners.

Giles' smile grew bigger. He gave a slight bow and headed to the stern.

Cocky devil.

"You're up early." Stephen took Jenny's hand, placed it in the crook of his arm, and led her around the deck. Just her nearness was enough to send his blood humming.

"I am an early riser."

"The circles under your eyes tell me you did not sleep." He shoved a curving shock of hair away from his forehead.

"Tossing and turning will do that. Even the rocking of the ship did not lull me to slumber." She raised her gaze to his. Violet amethysts sparkled with intensity. "I missed you."

His heart stopped. At least his breathing did. Her plump lips begged for his kiss. The knee-jerk reaction made him lose his footing. Could he blame the stumble on his weak ankles? Maybe his bones had healed, but being immobile was not an easy acceptance for a man with his impatience.

"Good God, Jenny. You cannot say that to me."

"Why not?" She faced the wind as though she had merely mentioned the time of day, and then continued with her stride.

"Because, knowing you want me makes me want you all the more."

Her bottom lip formed a pout and her pert little nose lifted in the morning air. "You leave me alone each night."

"By all that's holy," he gritted through clenched teeth. He spun on his booted heel, steering her to the door under the quarterdeck. His steps quickened as he towed her to the cabin, then jerked her inside, slammed the door, and pinned her against the wood.

His tongue demanded entry and took it. His sweet Jenny kissed him back, long and deep and hard. Tongues thrust and parried, until their lungs near to exploding, they broke apart, each gasping for air.

"My God, woman. You will be the death of me. This is why I leave you each night. This is why I cannot stay. For if I did, there would be no denying my hunger."

Her eyes beseeched him. She pulled his head down for another kiss.

Lost in mind-numbing elation, he kissed her with a yearning, a craving so great, only she could appease the fire burning within. He kissed a path across her cheek and left a damp trail down her throat, over her collar bone and down to the sweet sensuous swell of her bosom. Keenly aware of every sensual breath, every intimate sound she made, his groin surged with need.

A ragged breath escaped her, and then she arched against him. His arms instinctively tightened around her. In a moment of insanity he bent, slipped one arm under her knees, and carried her to the bed. His body demanding he take her, gratify his longing, grant his body, and hers, ecstasy.

When he placed her upon the covers, reality crashed, replacing his crazed madness. He dwelled on a ship with fifty men hovering about. His chest heaved. Blood propelled through his veins. His manhood throbbed. When her eyes glazed over, he nearly swallowed his tongue. Swollen lips pouted, insisting to be kissed. Air hissed through his teeth, her arms reaching for him, his will at an end.

He shoved his hands vehemently through his mane, wanting to tear his hair out by the roots. He flung himself from the bed. "God's blood, Jenny. Have you no shame?"

Her eyes flashed and their glorious warmth turned cold. "What . . . how dare . . . ?"

He'd wounded her. He crumpled to the spot beside her, then jumped up again as if the comforter was on fire. He dare not touch her. He flexed his fists in frustration.

"Forgive me, sweet Jenny. I have lost control of what little wits remain. Have no doubt of my need for you. But I will not take you on board this ship with a lusty crew watching our every move. I'll not give ammunition to a loaded gun, and that is what we would be doing."

She scampered off the bed and readjusted her bodice. "Shame? I have no thoughts when you touch me. My body takes over and I am unable to think."

"Jenny, please. I'm sorry. The blow was aimed at myself. Not at you."

"It makes no difference." The glint in her eyes grew soft. "I know you were thinking of me. Wanting to protect me."

A ragged breath escaped and he cursed. "Well, I did not do a very good job of it. I bloody well massacred the principled notion." He took a step nearer. "Bloody hell, Jenny. This is new to me. I have never been so twisted, nor felt like my gut was being wrenched from my body."

Oh, hell? What had he just admitted?

"I mean, I'm not in the habit of curbing my lust . . ." Her eyes shot fire and he stumbled over his words. "I mean . . ." Fear of revealing too much—of what, he still wasn't sure—he had said the wrong thing. He'd been as tactful as a bloody jackass.

"Put your tongue back in your mouth," she huffed as she twisted her gown to cover her bosom. "I understand."

He gaped in shock. How the hell could she understand when he could not even comprehend his own actions?

Chapter 19

J ennifer feared more what she needed to tell him, than his panicky attempt of explaining himself. For now, Stephen controlled his desires out of respect. After she revealed her secret, he might rebuff her altogether. Dread swamped her belly.

"I think it best we go no further until we talk," she said.

"Talk," he repeated in a deadened tone.

"Stephen. I need to tell you something." Her voice faltered, weakened with apprehension.

His gaze took on a mistrustful attentiveness.

Good Lord, she could not look him in the eyes. "I think you should sit down."

He crossed his arms and took the familiar stance she'd seen so often of late. How handsome he looked with his hard chin hoisted and his legs braced ready for battle. A thrill crashed through her insecurities, overriding her apprehensiveness. Power radiated from him, attacking her woman's center, sharpening her need. God, the man was too handsome for her own good.

"What do you have to tell me?" His eyes bore into hers.

She slipped to the table and took a seat. "Please, Stephen. Sit with me."

With a grunt, he dropped to the opposite chair, his back as stiff as when he'd stood. How could she speak when he glared at her like that?

"Alright. I'm sittin'."

She grasped her fingers to keep her hands from shaking. She glanced to her lap, and then forced her gaze back up. His eyes resembled dark thunder clouds over a green stormy sea.

"Well?"

She jumped. "You do not need to shout."

"If you do not want me to shout, then you best be telling me what has got you so worked up."

She swallowed. "I need to tell you about my family." She held her breath, waiting for a response. When he said nothing, she hesitated, searching for words. "Um . . ."

He leaned one arm on the table between them. "Just spit it out."

Blast, the man.

"I am trying. If you would not glare at me like a hungry bear, maybe I would not be so nervous."

He blinked. The lines creasing his brow eased. He reached for her hand and covered her fingers with his own. "All right. Tell me."

His eyes engulfed her. Tenderness and concern filled their depths, giving her the encouragement she needed. "My family may not be too happy to see me."

"Is that's what's got you worried? Of course, they will. After all, it has been a long time."

"But, the way I left . . ."

"You ran off. Surely, they would not condemn you for wanting to begin a new life with your husband? That is what a wife does. She follows her husband."

"But, you see? It . . . it just is not done. Not in my family." Her tongue hid behind her teeth. Summoning strength, she took a deep breath and tried again. "My father . . . is . . . well . . ."

"What are you trying to tell me?" He brought his other hand forward, now both engulfed hers. His tenderness jeopardized her control. "Is your father a murderer? Is your mother in New-gate? Because it does not matter."

No. It's worse.

Just spit it out.

"My father is of noble birth."

There. She said it.

Nothing.

No shouting. He still held her hand.

"You know my married name," she continued in a strained voice. "You do not know the name of my family. Or maybe you do." She bit her bottom lip. "Before I married my husband, I was Jennifer Louisa Gascoyne." She searched his face for any sign of recognition.

One brow arched in question. "You say the name as if it has some significance."

"How about Salisbury?"

"As in the . . ." His breath caught on what he had been about to say. Then his eyes narrowed and glittered.

She plunged on. "My father is Marquis of Salisbury."

"The British conservative statesman?"

Jennifer bobbed her head.

Stephen's jaw grew taut. He jerked back. "He's The Prime Minister, for God's sake."

Unable to watch his face change again, Jennifer hung her head. "Yes."

"*He* is your father?"

She nodded again, without looking up. A brusque whistle stung her ears.

"You are a Marquis's daughter."

Fear choking her, she raised her gaze to meet his. What was to happen now? She held her breath, dying to know his thoughts. She swallowed, searching for something to say. Something that would relieve his mind regarding her father's title. She tried for a laugh, unfortunately the sound came out like an awkward croak. "He is just a man, like any other."

"Like any other. Hmmm." He leaned back, propped one boot on his opposite knee. His arm rested on the table between them. "This is what you were afraid to tell me? Why?"

"You have this aversion to nobility."

"What? Where did you get that idea?"

Her mouth fell open in shock. "You have mentioned the aristocracy several times with . . . with repulsion. What was I supposed to think?"

"If you are referring to the duke, I do not like being tricked, or lied to. His was one of omission, not that we asked, but I knew he did not present the whole picture. There had to be more, and he was not forthcoming. You must admit, his current status—the one he bestows—is far from a titled lord."

"But, Giles explained he did not want the other sailors to know."

"I imagine some already do. The way the man carries himself reveals a lot." When she opened her mouth, he shrugged. "I know what he said. I will keep his confidence. But I never said I did not like the aristocracy."

All she could do was stare. Stephen had her at sixes and sevens.

"Do not worry your pretty head, Jenny. I have a temper and a way of speaking my mind. Living on the sea for long periods of time, I've not had to curb my tongue. My voice matches my size. Which of late, I am lacking a bit of meat on my bones."

"Then you agree my father is just a man?"

"A very important man." His eyes narrowed as he looked down his nose.

"Then you should understand my apprehension."

He straightened, dropped his booted foot to the floor, and once again gathered her fingers within his own. "Jenny. You are his daughter. He will welcome you with open arms. Might even bring a tear to his eye."

"Ha. A fat lot you know." She pulled her hand free. "He disowned me."

"How do you know that?"

She sniffed. "Because he is a most infuriating, unreasonable man. Or at least I once thought so. He was right, of course."

"Right about what?" His deep voice softened.

"Right about Johnny." Her shoulders dropped with her sigh. "He was weak. I suppose I should have been smart enough to realize my father tried to protect me. I should have trusted him."

"You were a young lass with stars in her eyes." His reassurance melted her heart.

"You are wrong about one thing, though. I'm not sure he will welcome me with open arms. You see, I did not just leave my home. I ran away. I disgraced my father. A second son was not marriage material for his esteemed daughter. He did not decline Johnny's suit—he would not even consider it." She glanced down to her clasped hands in her lap. "I disobeyed him. I committed a cardinal sin."

"I cannot believe a man would turn away his daughter. He had to be worried."

A tear slipped from her eye and she hastily wiped it away.

"Jenny, look at me." He slipped a finger under her chin and lifted her gaze to his. "He is your father. He loves you. How could he not? Think of a father's love for his little girl, not knowing if she is alive or dead . . . in all probability, all he thought about *was* your coming home. Trust me on this."

She lunged from her chair, and landed smack on his lap. He cradled her in his big caring arms. Clinging to him like a frightened child clung to their life-saving parent, she buried her face in his neck, wishing she could stay—just so—for all eternity.

"Now, now, Jenny. I've got you."

After soaking his shirt with her tears, she decided she had wallowed in self-pity long enough. "I'm sorry," she sniffed.

"Nothing to be sorry about. I will always be here for you—as your friend."

Chapter 20

Cold dread shivered down her spine.

Bile threatened to choke her.

She forced the queasiness in her stomach to calm and hoped Stephen's words did not mean what she suspected. "Friend?"

"I want to be your friend. I would never vanish from your life without a word. I will always be here if you need me. I promise you that."

"As my friend." Her voice sounded defeated to her own ears.

"Do you not want me for a friend?"

She balled up her fist and clonked him on the head. If she had something breakable within reach, she would clonk him with that too. She shoved from his lap, anger pumping through every vein.

"No I do not want you for a friend. Blazes, you are a stubborn man. Is that all I am to you?"

"What are you getting all riled up about?"

"Friend," she spat. "How dare you. How dare you!" She marched across the short space to the little hole for a window. "Damn you, Stephen. Are you such a coward?"

That got his gourd. "I am no bloody coward, you raving madcap. What are you bleating about?"

She would not cry again. Not over this. She whirled to face him. "You stubborn, arrogant pig."

"Calling me a pig, are you? What the bloody hell's gotten into you?"

She whirled around placing her hands on her hips. "Not five minutes ago you had your tongue down my throat. You had me panting and ready to give myself to you. You wanted me. You cannot deny it. Is that the action of friends?"

Surely that was not guilt that crossed his face.

"How can I refute what we both want? But I won't . . ." he halted.

"Won't what? Call it by the name it is?"

His face turned as red as his wild mane of hair. "Just what name would *you* be giving it? I warn you before you speak. Do not sully what was between us." His anger intoned in every word he spoke.

Was?

Her mouth dropped open. "Then what would you call it?"

"Desire." He stood. "A man's uncontrollable desire for a beautiful woman. A woman he did not give the chance to say no." He took a step closer. "A woman he cherished enough to take her with him to paradise." He gritted every word through his teeth, but pain lurked in his eyes.

"I did not want to say no. You did give me the chance, and for my answer I willingly and eagerly gave you my body."

He flinched. An unfamiliar expression flickered in his gaze just before it vanished. What had she said to cause a second of vague suffering? She wondered at which statement. Her body—did he want her heart? Every word she'd said had the ring of total honesty. If he wanted her heart, why was the stubborn man throwing the word friend at her?

"Your actions conveyed affection," she said.

"Never doubt this. I care for you." His voice lowered to a growl.

"How much?" There. She had given him no quarter.

"What bloody nonsense is this? You are wanting me to put a measure on our . . . friendship?" He grew more angry. His cheeks puffed as he bellowed.

"All right. Never mind. Answer me this. Where do we go from here?"

His eyes grew wide with confusion. "What do you mean? We go back to England. I will escort you home."

She pushed further. "And then what?"

His eyes narrowed. He rested his fists on his hips. "Then I leave you in the care of your fine father. You may think he does not want you, but he does."

"And then?"

"And then you live a happy life as a Marquis's daughter," he shouted.

"That's what I thought." No matter how much she wished it otherwise, his blunt comment told her exactly what she wanted to know. He was leaving her. Dropping her in her father's lap and she would never hear from him again.

No. She would not allow him to just walk out of her life.

She swung her hair over her shoulder. "And you will go to your home?"

"I will go to my uncle's house. I need to see what mischief my sister has created."

The mention of his sister gave her the idea to try another approach. "I have a sister, too. Would you like to meet her?"

"I suppose, if she is there when I take you home I will exchange pleasantries, but I doubt I will meet your family. They will be too busy welcoming you back to care who brought you home."

"I care."

Silence.

"Will you come to visit me?" She bit her lip. "Will you call on me?"

"I have more mending to do." His gaze softened. "I imagine once my aunt gets her hands on me, I'll be holed up for a spell. I'll have to mollify her." His expression turned solemn, almost angry. "Then I'll be back to sailing. You will forget me."

He spoke as though he needed to convince himself.

"Is that what you want?"

"I love the sea, I told you that," his voice gruff again. "The sea holds my heart."

And he will never give his heart to me.

"As you said, you need to heal and gather your strength before you take to a ship again."

"All right." He placed a hand on each hip. "I am a man of plain speaking. So I will not discredit you for your intelligence, and I will not degrade you by lying. You are a Marquis's daughter. You've already had one dispute with your father over an unsuitable match. I will not be responsible for another."

When she opened her mouth, he held up his hand. "You asked, let me finish. I do not have a lofty title, and I damn sure do not adhere to society. I am a captain. A battle and bruised one at the moment. I have scars, Jenny. Scars on the inside that may not heal."

"Let me help you." She took a step forward. When he glared, she stopped in her tracks.

"I will give an allotted time for my bones and wounds to heal properly. Then I plan to sail back to India."

Her gasp echoed and bounced off the cabin walls. "You can't. You cannot mean to go back."

"I do, and I will."

"Revenge!" she spat.

"Yes, revenge." He clenched his fists.

She thought he had been angry before? But, at this instant pure rage crossed his features. He harbored such fury, his body shook with it.

"Stephen, you cannot." She closed the distance between them. "Please, I beg you. No."

So many emotions crossed his face, she knew he battled countless demons. How could she allow him to sail back to India when he could very well meet the same fate—or worse? And she would not be there to save him. Several moments passed while she waited, her heart in her throat. She prayed he would see reason.

"Please, do not push me away." Tears filled her eyes. God help her, but she wanted him, needed him. She cared for him, more than she dared allow herself to admit.

Finally, his fingers opened, and his body slackened. Tight lines on his brow relaxed to smooth his features.

He pulled her close. "All right, Jenny. Don't worry. Let's get home. Think of our families, for now."

After some time, he released his hold and leaned back. "Your life is very different from mine. You will attend parties and balls . . . you will be so busy you won't even miss me."

If Jenny had learned anything the last few years, one thing was to save an argument for another day when the battle could be won. She would not give up. Why couldn't the lout just admit he cared for her?

Stephen may not know it yet, but he would not leave her. She would see to it.

⸻ ℓℓ ⸻

Stephen lost himself in the soothing motion of the ship, rocking to the sway of the sea. Overhead, a half-moon guided their direction. This was the time he liked best. When the waves were calm, the night was black, and the only sounds were the waves smacking against the hull.

He faced the winds that carried him closer to home. Farther away from the hellish nightmare that had been all too real. He closed his eyes allowing the night to swallow him. For a brief moment, he could almost relax. For a few seconds, he could almost forget the despair that had nearly destroyed him.

He took a deep breath, tasting the salt on his tongue.

He had believed he would never sail the seas again. He had succumbed to the belief he would die in that hell hole. Almost did. How had he gone from one bloody mess to another?

The bloody Prime Minister.

It would appear he'd lost his intuitions along with his good sense. Another aristocrat.

"You don't look too happy."

Stephen shook the troubled thoughts from his mind. "Women."

Giles slapped him on the back of one shoulder. "The complexity of their gender is the agony of man's existence. But we need the female species for our survival."

"Need?" With one brow raised, Stephen faced Giles.

"Reproduction," Giles clarified.

"Oh." Stephen stared at the white caps rippling across the ocean under the moon's reflection. "Damned unreasonable."

"You have a disagreement with our lady passenger?" By the smirk on his face, he already knew the answer.

"You mean the Marquis's daughter?"

Giles whistled through his teeth. "I take it you had no idea."

"Of course, not. A woman living alone in a shack on the other side of the world? Would you have guessed?"

"No, I suppose not. But what does that have to do with anything?"

Stephen spun in anger. "The woman is a bloody aristocrat. A matriarch, for God's sake."

"Who is she," Giles asked completely bewildered.

"The Marquis of Salisbury," He said on a sigh, and rested his arms back on the rail.

"Hmmm." Giles faced changed with recognition. "I see your point. But, at the risk of repeating myself, what does that have to do with anything?"

"Of course, you would say that. You're a bloody duke."

"Why would her father's position be a problem?"

Stephen turned to face Giles. "Her father is a very important member of the aristocracy. When we get back to England, Jennifer will be a member of the aristocracy. Every blueblood will be knocking at her door."

"Is that what has you worried? All you need do is set the gentlemen straight. Tell the dandies she is spoken for."

"I am a captain. I sail the seas. Or at least I did. How can I compete with nobility?"

"You are not a man one can ignore. Jennifer seems quite taken with you. I dare say your station will not matter."

"It will bloody well matter to her father. He did not approve of her first husband, who was a second son. I have no lofty title."

"Your uncle is also an important man."

Stephen leaned his forearms on the rail, again. "That life is not me."

Giles leaned on the rail beside him. "I understand your apprehension. I can't help but wonder if you place obstacles where there are none. The two of you may have had a quarrel, but I doubt she has the same concerns. She has been living on her own. From what I see, she is more than capable of making her own decisions."

"Oh, she is more than capable. And that is not what we argued about." Stephen fisted his hands. "She does not understand."

Giles laughed out loud. "It is the nature of the beast. Men think differently." Giles shifted. "What does she not understand?"

By avoiding Giles' question, Stephen also evaded his own guilt.

Guilt? Bah. Why should he be uneasy over a female's point of view?

"She should empathize. Anyone would fathom a man's need for retribution."

"Ahhh. You plan to retaliate?"

Stephen stood to his full height. "The Rajput prince will pay for his horrendous deeds. He's a monster."

"In this case, I must side with the lady," Giles said with a sigh.

"The hell you say."

"I did not save you so I would have to come looking for you all over again."

"So, you have no faith in me either." Stephen turned away in disgust.

"Must I remind you of your sister?"

He had taken three steps when Giles words stopped him cold. Stephen slowly turned, abhorrence biting at his insides. "You use Katherine as your weapon? To excuse your jumping into Jennifer's camp?"

"Not a weapon. Motivation. If you refuse to be reasonable, I will use whatever means necessary." Giles straightened, matching Stephen's height.

"You have no reason to be so concerned with my affairs."

"I have several," his voice deepened with conviction.

"Pray, list them." He did not have to like what Giles said, but he would listen.

"All right." Giles leaned his hip against the wood. "One. You have a beautiful woman who seems to like you in your skin. Two. The obvious. You barely escaped with your life. You were tortured, your men killed. The same could happen again. Nothing to do with your strength, your cunning, or your skills. Or the number of men you take with you. Life is a game of chance. And the odds are not in your favor."

Stephen flexed his hands. Then braced his feet and crossed his arms. He may not intimidate the man, but the accustomed stance gave notable comfort.

"Three. You have a family waiting for you. I do not think Katherine will be too happy if her brother returns to the same shark infested waters. Especially after moving heaven and earth to come find you."

"Do not waste your breath. You don't know what that . . . bloody pig did to me. To my men," Stephen snarled.

"I have a pretty good idea." Giles shoved the hair from his face as he took a step forward. "You are alive. Go live your life."

Stephen's gaze followed Giles across the moonlit deck. How easy for him to give advice. Which wasn't exactly fair on Stephen's part. He knew the man had, at some point in his life, experienced his own adversity.

Once more, Stephen leaned his forearms on the rail and gazed into the night. Glittering stars lit the dark sky. How he had longed for a swaying ship under his feet again, for the pitching sea to carry him across the endless ocean. Longed for peace and tranquility to fill his soul. But there would be no peace, no comfort until the dog paid for his offence.

The Rajput prince would burn in Hell.

Chapter 21

A feeling of déjà vu gripped Jennifer as she clung to the ship's rail. The last time she'd seen the same commotion, she had been on a ship with her new husband, ready to leave her home. A lifetime ago. She looked down at the boisterous activity going on around her. The ship had docked early this morning. The sleepy-eyed town came alive with street vendors putting out their wares. The crew welcomed the early morning chill while they struggled with ropes as big as their arms, pulling and tugging. Men carried crates and unloaded cargo while passengers disembarked and were welcomed by their families.

Jennifer's heart lurched. Family. Eager reunions took place on the dock below her. If she were meeting her family, would the reactions be similar. She placed her hands on the rail to keep them from shaking. She feared not.

As everyone else went about their business, Jennifer tried desperately to control her fear. Stephen, confident in his explanations, thought her family would welcome her with open arms. Even with his positive assurance, she could not help but feel powerless and vulnerable. She stared at the plank with dread. Ropes tied for balance, temptation urged her to jump. Since courage failed her, maybe someone would chuck her in the river. Wishful thinking.

What was to become of her? She would try to be strong. Really, she would. She must. She could not hide like a scared rabbit. She had survived the voyage. She was not about to turn coward now. Besides, she had nowhere else to go.

After much thinking, she reached the conclusion that she would endure this reunion and go through the motions that were expected. If her family threw her out, she would deal with that when it happened. She could not help but wonder when, not if. For there was slim hope they would accept her back into their perfectly knit, unblemished household.

Untarnished, until she had committed an unforgivable sin.

She squared her drooping shoulders, and for a second time decided to meet her fate head on. Now, if she could just squash the choking sensation, and find the courage to follow through.

Jennifer surveyed the crowd looking for Stephen. He had departed to find transport and make preparations, any last-minute arrangements. Only a few minutes passed before she spotted him. Taller than the others, his auburn hair stood out among the crowd. Her heart leaped at the sight of him. Then his eyes met hers. His searing gaze fired her blood, striking her numb. Her lungs were in desperate need of air.

Friend.

How could he even suggest such a thing? His stare devoured her. Most times he looked at her as if she wore no clothes. A heat began in her belly and flowed through her limbs. She wondered if he knew her thoughts. If her own eyes might reflect her inner turmoil. He broke eye contact and bounded up the roped boards. She inhaled a deep breath and released it just as he approached.

"Are you ready?"

"As ready as I will ever be."

He placed a hand at her elbow. "Come on."

Stephen lifted Jennifer into the waiting carriage, then climbed inside to the seat across from her. He rapped on the roof of the coach, then sat back and stared at her in sufferable silence. She smoothed her skirts, adjusted her new bonnet, and then placed her hands firmly in her lap. Two seconds later she shifted her skirt, tapped her fingers on her knee, then played with the ribbon on her bonnet.

A cocky grin lifted a corner of his devilish mouth.

"I am not a brainless nitwit." She tilted her head toward the window. "I cannot help but be anxious."

"You may fidget all you like."

She looked up to see a smirk of arrogance on his face. He sat there with his arms crossed looking relaxed as the coach swayed back and forth.

"Easy for you."

"Not so easy for me. I have demons still alive in my skull. I choose not to let them control my actions."

"What a liar you are."

He dropped his hands to his knees and glared. "I beg your pardon."

"You plan to sail back to India. If that is not allowing your emotions control—"

"Bad choice of words," his hard voice interrupted. "However, my actions in the distant future is not relevant to the here and now. I will not discuss it. Choose another topic to speak of."

Good Lord, he looked ferocious. If it were possible, his glare would bore holes right through her. Had she not known him, she would scuttle in fear. She sat straighter and clutched her skirt to keep her fingers still. It was maddening being confined to the carriage, considering the fact that every circle of the carriage wheel brought her closer to her fear.

"Do not look so alarmed."

"Would you rather I shout in glee. 'I'm home'," she said in a raised voice. "I'm going to see my devoted parents and my adoring sister." She gave him a look to match her sarcasm. "Is that better?"

"No." His frown showed his displeasure.

"What do you expect? I am terrified."

He shifted in his seat and she thought he meant to join her. But he stayed where he was, clearly uncomfortable. He ran a hand through his maze of glorious hair.

"You are not a man to sugar coat your words. We are going to have a very long ride, if you do not speak your mind. 'Spit it out', as I have heard you say."

"Damn. You try a man's patience."

"So, you have told me before," she replied curtly.

"You have nothing to fear, Jennifer. You are wrong. Your parents will fall all over you with hugs and kisses. If it makes you feel any better, in case they don't, I will not leave you standing on their doorstep. I will stay with you until you find the truth of my words for your own stubborn self."

"Stubborn?" Her hackles rose. "I am not being stubborn by being realistic."

"Realistic? Or skeptical?"

"Don't you think I have reason to be?"

"Jennifer." He leaned forward and took her hand. "I admire your courage. The number of instances boggle my mind. The most recent one—you are about to face your family for the first time in years. True, you left under covert circumstances. But I dare say, your family loves you." His gaze consumed her features from her hair to her eyes, to her nose, her chin—as if he committed every molecule to memory. "How could they not," he said in a breathless whisper.

Her heart lurched against her ribcage. Her breath caught in her throat. When his scrutiny dropped again to her lips, she felt herself leaning forward, caught in a spell of timeless wonder.

"You tempt me beyond my ability, and I have no care to resist." He closed the distance.

Fire exploded when their lips touched. She pressed with urgency, seeking more. His hands gripped her upper arms and she landed in his lap, right where she wanted to be. His arms tightened like bands of steel. His tongue teased her mouth open and he thrust inside. Oh God, how wonderful. How delicious.

She plunged her fingers into his hair and pulled his head as close as their bones would allow. A satisfied groan reached her ears giving her such joy she wanted to kiss him forever. His fingers glided up her arm, his thumb brushing over the tip of her breast. Her breath quickened and she ached for more. She yearned for his hand to boldly caress her. Instead, he dropped a warm kiss on the exposed flesh of her bosom.

This was exciting and harrowing at the same time. His tongue slipped out dancing a lazy pirouette. She held his head, relishing the teasing tickle, while her fingers delved in his glorious hair. When his teeth nibbled and leisurely traced the contours of her feverish skin, delectable shivers shot through her. She twirled strands of his silken hair around her fingers and clutched his head, enjoying every moist kiss, every wet skid of his tongue. He delivered sweet torture.

His fingers slid down her thigh. She grew excited, for what was to come. She closed her eyes and waited with anticipation. He searched, found the hem of her gown, and blazed a trail up her calf, behind her ticklish knee, and on to her thigh. His hand was hot enough to burn. When he stroked the inside, she instinctively opened her legs wider.

Dear God, she had become a wanton.

His roving hand came to rest possessively on her mound. A feeling rushed to her chest, pressing down hard. She held her breath. A stray finger prodded into her moist heat, making the pressure in her chest tighten. She writhed beneath his slow, flicking finger, feeling consumed by the urge to rise against him. Willing him to plunge within, or better yet, have the boldness of his manhood fill her aching void.

Soon all thought was forgotten, by the unbearable lance of pleasure when he inserted two fingers inside her. He swallowed her gasp and gave a groan of satisfaction. His fingers worked their magic, and she could not be still. Close to the point of oblivion, she ground her hips against him. Seeking more. Teetering precariously on the brink.

And then it happened. Glorious, breathtaking, most spectacular of wonders. The tingling that made her heart stop, and her body take flight.

She held him tight. She would never let him go.

The carriage stopped in front of a large manor house with several extensive wings. Stephen barely had time to take in the impressive dwelling before the groom opened the carriage door. Stephen stepped out, studying the stone structure from the ground up to the third story windows. Mindful of Jennifer behind him, he extended his hand and helped her from the carriage, securing her hand in the crook of his elbow. He ushered her up the steps and through the front door, where the butler greeted them.

He watched as Jennifer's gaze focused on the set of double doors to the left, then darted to the grand staircase. Her eyes large with apprehension, her hand squeezed his arm. He covered her shaking fingers. To look at her she appeared calm. But the elegant lady beside him trembled in fear. He had done his best to sooth her, to prepare her for this moment. He even escorted her to a clothier for the latest fashionable ladies' clothes. Of course, she'd protested in earnest of him paying for her apparel, but he could not allow her to show up on her father's doorstep in rags. Compared to her father's lofty station, the gown she wore on the ship would have been considered thus.

"Please inform the Marquis his daughter has arrived."

If the butler suffered shock from the announcement, he hid it well. Showing no sign of surprise, he said, "This way, my lord."

Uncaring to correct his mistake, Stephen gave a nod. As if her feet were stuck to the floor, Jennifer stayed rooted to the spot. He gave a slight tug, she tripped, then righted herself, still holding onto his arm. The butler opened the set of double doors and stood to the side. Stephen led Jennifer into what appeared to be a drawing room. Everything was done in bold colors of dark pink and forest green. A long sofa with wooden arms shaped into paws with a pair of matching wooden feet. On each side a set of identical mahogany tables glowed with polish.

Jennifer looked as if she were headed to the gallows.

"Are you all right," he asked.

She squeaked in alarm, her gaze flying to his.

He took both of her hands and caressed her gloved fingers. "I am right here."

"Stephen, you cannot imagine what I am going through. Everything looks the same. As if I left for an hour of shopping and returned the same afternoon." Slipping her hands free, she moved farther into the room.

She stepped to the large stone hearth, a fire already burning. Running her fingers along the top, she stared at a silver frame. From where he stood, the photograph appeared to be an image of two females.

"Your sister?"

"What?" She started. "Oh yes. Isabella and me."

"Jennifer?" A shaky voice echoed from behind.

Startled, she spun around, her eyes wide. Stephen turned to find a slightly plump woman, her hair ribboned with grey, holding her hand to her throat. Jenny's mother?

Suddenly, tears trailed down her cheeks and she opened her arms. A blur streamed from the side of his vision, then Jennifer was enveloped in the woman's arms. A huge weight lifted from his chest.

Thank God.

Sure, he'd done a lot of talking. Bravado mostly. The entire time he tried persuading Jennifer her family would welcome her home, he had devoutly prayed it would be so. Seeing their reunion, his worries vanished.

Now. How was he to get out of here? He felt like an intruder on their moment.

She had forgotten he was there.

Chapter 22

"Eeeek! It is you. You're home!"

A young woman with bouncing curls, the same dark color as Jennifer's, came running, and nearly crashed into the other two women. Screeching at the top of her lungs, her arms flew around Jennifer, then she too was crying. Evidently the sister.

Good God. A room full of weeping women. They reminded him of what was sure to await him at his uncle's house. He cringed thinking of Kat and Aunt Elizabeth making the same sounds. Where the hell was her father?

A booming voice echoed off the walls. Hell fire. He must have conjured the man up.

Stephen wasn't sure what he expected, but the short bald man was not it. For his size, the man packed a wallop of a voice.

"Here now! What's all this caterwauling?"

The women quieted and Jennifer's head jerked up, her eyes wide with distress.

"Daughter. Come here."

At least the man recognized his daughter. His resounding voice commanded her to come to him. Stephen held his breath. Everyone else in the room may deny his existence, but if her father dared to raise a hand to her, he would make his presence known—rather quickly. And forcefully, if necessary.

Jennifer dragged her feet as she stepped forward. When the man opened his arms, surprise etched her features. Then she ran.

Stephen sent another prayer of thanks toward heaven as her father gathered his daughter against his chest. He could not swear if the man shed a tear, but his body shook.

Well, that's that. Time to go.

Without drawing attention, he stepped close to Isabella. At least he assumed the girl was Jennifer's sister. He tried stepping around her to get to the doorway. "Excuse me."

"Oh." She whirled around. "Forgive us. We are so glad to have Jennifer home. I am Isabella."

"It is a pleasure to meet you. Stephen Radbourn." He gave a slight bow.

Jennifer's mother stepped toward him with an outstretched hand. "Welcome to my home. And thank you for bringing our daughter to us."

"You are welcome, Lady Gascoyne. It was my pleasure."

"We are so grateful." She swiped a tear from her cheek.

"Now, now. What must your gentleman friend think of us?" Jennifer's father gave a loud sound of clearing his throat. "Introduce us."

Hell. He had almost made it out. All teary eyed, and still the most beautiful creature he'd ever seen, Jennifer met his gaze. When she smiled, his heart turned over.

"Father, I want you to meet Captain Stephen Radbourn. Captain Radbourn, this is my father, Marquis of Salisbury."

Stephen's tongue tripped over her use of his surname from Jennifer's lips. But then her father need not know how close the couple had become. He quickly recovered. Giving the appropriated leg, he said, "My Lord Marquis."

"Captain Radbourn, no need for all of that. Please accept my sincere thanks." He grabbed Stephen's hand and shook with the strength of a drowning man securing a life line.

"No thanks necessary, Your Lordship. Your daughter saved my life."

"I would like to hear about everything. But for now, I want to speak with my daughter."

"I understand. My family awaits my arrival. Please forgive me if I do not stay. With your permission, I shall take my leave."

"Of course, Captain. I will send my man around, and you will let him know when it is convenient. I look forward to your rendering."

"Your Lordship." He gave a nod, then stepped to Jennifer's mother. "Marchioness."

"Thank you, Captain." Her blue eyes glowed with gratitude.

"I will see you out," Jennifer said.

He froze. She had just been reunited with her family, and she dared to leave the room with him? Before he could ponder further, she twirled and led the way. He swallowed the lump in his throat, straightened to his full height, and followed.

Once in the foyer, reality hit Jennifer square in the face.

Oh my God. Stephen is walking out of my life.

She did not want to lose Stephen. It was too soon. He'd been correct in his assumption of her parents' acceptance, but she could not let him walk out that door. For if he did, she had the sinking feeling, she would never see him again. He would be gone from her life. And she would never get him back.

She wanted to cry, beg, plead, *Please don't go. Take me with you. What about me? Don't you care?*

She could see it now. The disgrace she would bring to her family again, as he pried her fingers from his shirt, while she clung to him yelling at the top of her lungs *I Love You*.

Instead, she drew on any shred of sensibility she possessed, cocked her head and said, "You were right."

"Right? About what?"

"My family." She raised tear filled eyes to meet his.

Understanding came over his face. "I'm happy for you. There is nothing like a parent's love."

"Thank you."

"It is I who should thank you. You saved my life. I will never forget."

There he went. Talking as if this was the end. Would she never see him again? Oh God. How would she stand the pain? He took her hand and barely brushed his lips over her fingers.

"Goodbye."

She could not speak. Tears clogged her throat. Her wayward heart gave a thud of despair.

He dragged his fingers through his hair, clearly uncomfortable. Then he conveyed with his eyes what he could not put into words.

All too soon—he was gone.

She watched through tears, until the carriage was only a small dot in the distance.

"Come child." Martha Gascoyne put her arms around her daughter and led her back inside. Father stood with Isabella while Mother aimed her toward the sofa. "Darling, you must be exhausted. Let's get you upstairs. Marie will unpack for you. After a nice nap, you can tell us all about your adventure."

Jennifer opened her mouth to speak, but no words came out. Her mother patted her on the shoulder.

"Doesn't a nap sound like just the thing, dear?"

"I'll take her up, Mother." Isabella hurried to Jennifer's side. "We have so much to catch up on."

Arm in arm, Jennifer went with her sister out the set of doors and up the grand staircase. She put one foot in front of the other, one step at a time. With each stride a large stone settled in her stomach. Another step, another stone. The end of her world suddenly seemed within sight.

In the twinkling of an eye, she would have traded her homecoming for a life with Stephen—if only he would have asked.

⁓ℓℓ⁓

Exhausted, drained and empty, Jennifer moved to the dressing table. The maid left some time ago, so she picked up the pearl handled brush and sat on the velvet covered stool. Everything in her room was the same as when she left. Every stick of furniture, every personal item. Even her clothes looked as though they had not been touched.

Brushing her hair soothed and comforted her. She lifted one silky curl and paused as a soft knock landed on her bedchamber door. Isabella stuck her head around the edge.

"Good. You're still up." She slipped inside and quietly closed the door, scampered to the bed and flopped on her stomach upon the counterpane. "I cannot wait any longer. You must tell me about the captain."

Jen met her sister's eyes in the mirror. "The captain?"

"The man who brought you home. Who is he? Where did you meet him? He is quite large. And very handsome. He said you saved his life." She drew a quick breath. "I simply cannot wait until tomorrow for you to tell me."

Mirrors do not lie. But Jennifer was surprised to see the corner of her mouth lift in response—the first instance she'd felt her spirits rise since Stephen left. "Oh. That captain. What about him?"

Isabella rolled off the bed and landed perfectly on her feet. Treading to the vanity, she took the brush from Jennifer's fingers. "Remember when we used to brush each other's hair before we went to bed, just like this? We would talk and tell each other our secrets."

"That seems like a long time ago," Jennifer said with a sigh.

""It seems like yesterday." Isabella devotedly ran the brush through the vibrant curls twirling one around her finger.

Yes. Like yesterday.

Jennifer shoved melancholy away. Thinking to tease her sister she said, "Goodness, Isabella. I'm tired."

"No, you're not. You are still awake. I'll bet you are just as excited as I am. Gosh, Jen. I am so glad you're home." She leaned down and threw her arms around Jennifer with vigor.

"Me too." She met her sister's gaze reflecting in the mirror. "I was scared."

"Why? Was he mean to you?"

"Huh? Uh, no." Jennifer stood and strolled to the bed. She climbed upon the counterpane. "I was afraid to come home. Afraid Dad would still be mad, and maybe he would not let me in the house."

"Oh, Jen. If you could have seen him after you left. He nearly had a heart attack. He blamed himself." Isabella climbed upon the bed beside her.

Jennifer could not image her father being vulnerable.

"Johnny disappeared too, so we knew that you had run away with him. I thought it was the most romantic thing in the world." Isabella rolled her eyes in a dreamy way. "You had run off to Gretna Green."

"I did. I married Johnny."

"Then, when so much time passed without a word from you . . ." Isabella sniffed. "We hoped and prayed you were alive."

Jennifer felt like the worst kind of fool. She had brought more than embarrassment to her family. Sorrow. Heartache. Misery.

"Father said he would not accept a second son for a son-in-law. He refused Johnny. That is why we sailed to India."

"India? That seems so far away. Jen, couldn't you have sent one letter?"

One letter didn't seem like too much—now. Now that she knew her family still loved her. Now that she knew they had not forsaken her. Anguish pierced her chest. She had let them down. At the moment, this information was simply too much for her weary mind to handle. She did not deserve their love. Tears flowed heedlessly down her cheek.

"Oh, Jen. I did not mean to make you cry. I'm sorry."

"No, Isabella. You did not do anything. I disgraced Father. I am so ashamed." Jennifer hiccupped. "I made a mess of everything."

"Mother says time heals all wounds. You just wait and see." Isabella handed her a kerchief.

"I'm glad you have not changed, Isabella." She smiled hoping to relieve some tension.

"Was it so bad," Isabella asked. "Are you ready to talk about it? What happened to Johnny?"

Chapter 23

Fire had been known to hypnotize a person. Stephen watched the flames lick the burning logs. Stared, as if the intensity of the blue blaze could erase the last two years from his memory. He breathed deep. Even the comforts of home had not lessened his anguish. His uncle's favorite leather chair, the hint of tobacco permeating the room, all things familiar yet incapable of soothing his anxiety. Uncle, aunt, family. Their love consoled, but the worry in their eyes distressed him further. And Kat. The little minx.

Home, at last, only to find Kat gone. From what he gleaned from his uncle, his little sister had planned to rescue him just before she got carried off. Her and her damn hare-brained ideas. But then, that was Kat. And now she'd gone to Charity's. He still could not believe his sister's childhood friend was a Viscountess.

"Wonderful meal, Elizabeth. Roasted duckling is my favorite." Albert said as he entered the drawing room with his wife on his arm.

"Thank you, Albert. I only suggested the menu. Roasted duckling was once Stephen's favorite too. Although you didn't eat much." She directed her last comment to Stephen.

"Dinner was very good, Aunt Elizabeth. We do not get such luxuries on a ship."

"Stephen, you have lost so much weight. Are you well?" Concern filled her age-old eyes.

He tried not to wince. "I am fine. My appetite has dwindled, somewhat."

"Yes, well. I'm sure Stephen is fine, dear. We will fatten him up in no time. Katherine should be here shortly." Albert spoke to soothe his wife, and Stephen was glad for the change in topic.

"She should have been here hours ago." Lines worried Elizabeth's brow. "You sent your man to Viscount Roxborough's estate with a message yesterday."

"We are speaking of Katherine and Charity." He looked over the rim of his glass, pointedly. Obviously meaning those two were usually up to something.

"Not to mention, Charity is with child now. The Viscount will take measures to ensure her comfort."

"Charity with child?" Stephen shook his head. "I still think of her as an urchin hanging on my coattails."

"This will be her second child. She has a little boy, Zachary. He is almost two."

Reminding Stephen he'd been gone for over two years. While he'd managed to endure hell, life had gone on. Charity was a mother and Kat . . . *Damn*. Where the hell was his sister?

When he discovered his Kitten had been taken, he wanted to kill the man accountable, and everyone else in his path. She had been taken by mistake. What the hell was that supposed to mean? And the very man responsible for sending Giles to look for him—other than his uncle, of course—was the man responsible for his sister's abduction. How the hell was he to wrap his mind around that little fact?

Subconsciously, Stephen rubbed his wrists. The cuffs of his white shirt hid the marks. His aunt was worried enough, she did not need to see his scars.

"Who is this Whetherford?" Stephen crossed his arms and leaned his back against the stone.

"Morgan Langston, Lord of Whetherford Manor," Albert answered. "His brother and parents were killed in a storm when their ship sunk. Whetherford was a young man at Eton at the time. Unable to deal with the news of his family's death, he left. The manor remained empty. Whetherford only returned a short while ago."

"Just in time for Kat to get into trouble," he mumbled.

"What's that?"

"Lord Whetherford is a gentleman." His aunt boasted, clearly taken with the man. "Katherine and I visited Whetherford Manor. Lovely home. Quite large. Enormous, really. But he was a perfect gentleman, and seemed rather fond of our Katherine."

I'll bet.

Unsure of exactly how much his aunt knew, he decided not to elaborate further. Albert was a man of secrets. A man of connections. He was sure there was more to Whetherford than just Kat's relationship with the man.

And speaking of his sister, just what was their *relationship?* Katherine had better put in an appearance soon so he could see for himself that she fared well. Before he went after Whetherford and beat him to a bloody pulp.

Josiah entered and tread to his uncle. "My Lord."

"Yes, Josiah, what is it?"

"Willey has returned from Roxborough with this." He held up parchment with the Viscount's seal.

Albert quickly tore the missive open. His brows rose. "What's this? Katherine is not with Charity. The Viscount is on his way here."

Elizabeth's gasp echoed around the room.

Stephen shoved from the mantel. "Did he say where she is? Is he bringing her home?"

"Evidently not. According to his letter they will explain when they get here."

"Explain?" Stephen voice thundered off the walls. "Who is they?"

"The Viscount and his wife, Charity."

Stephen fisted his hands and marched two steps toward his uncle. "What kind of explanation can they give? Kat is up to something. And my instincts say Charity helped her." He slammed one fist into the palm of his opposite hand while turning to pace. "When I get my hands on her . . ."

"Now Stephen, we don't know . . ."

"Oh, Albert. Where is Katherine?"

"Now, Elizabeth," Albert's voice cooed. "I'm sure Katherine is fine."

"Stubborn, headstrong, tenacious little vixen," Stephen continued with a string of oaths under his breath.

"Stephen, you must calm down."

"Calm down! Katherine is missing—again." *Hell Fire.* Between Aunt Elizabeth and himself, his uncle had a devil of a time trying to appease them both. He knew he shouted. He just could not help himself.

Damn.

In order to keep his mouth shut, he turned and paced again. Only to suddenly come up short. He spun around. "Whetherford."

Albert and Elizabeth both stared—only his aunt's mouth hung open.

"Whetherford," he said again.

"What does he have to do with this?" Albert asked in a graveled tone.

"Uncle. Don't you see? He has taken her. Or the brat has gone to him."

"Stephen, please," his aunt sniffed.

"Your suspicions are not founded." Uncle gave one of his notable glares, his frown apparent displeasure.

"Based on your own words and Kat's willfulness, it is a reasonable assessment." There he was, shouting again. "Aunt, I apologize. She *is* my little sister."

"I know, son," Albert said. "She fretted over your absence, and now you worry about her. If she is with Whetherford, she will come to no harm."

No harm?

He dare not voice his thoughts aloud in the presence of his aunt. Whetherford was a man, wasn't he? The blasted earl was not above taking advantage of his sister.

Damnation.

He shoved a hand through his wild hair.

Bloody hell.

The last thing he needed was to join in fist-cuffs with the Viscount right here in his Aunt's drawing room. He had worked himself up into a fine lather pacing the floor while they waited for Charity and her husband to arrive.

Without Katherine.

Which only added to his worry. His already simmering temper shattered violently—and noisily. But Charity's husband was having none of it.

Charity placed her hand on her husband's arm. "It's alright."

Lord Roxborough lowered his head and gentled his features. "I will not have you upset."

"Stephen would not hurt me. He is distressed."

"With good reason," Stephen bellowed. At Lord Roxborough's glare, he quickly apologized. "I beg your pardon. But I know these two. She," he waved a hand toward Charity, "and my sister have schemed plenty of times in the past. Some which had us pulling our hair."

"And what a bushy lot of it you have," Charity said with a beaming smile.

How like the little imp to tease at a time like this? *Bloody hell.* Where was Kat?

"I apologize for my nephew's forgotten manners," Albert said to the viscount, "and I appreciate you coming to my home so quickly. The fact remains my niece is missing,"

Stephen grimaced from the scolding. He glanced at his aunt. Elizabeth mutilated the handkerchief she held, her eyes red from crying. Albert had stayed beside her murmuring words of reassurance since the viscount entered their door.

Where the hell had Kat gone? He had the need to pound something.

Preferably Whetherford.

He wouldn't be at all surprised—

Whetherford. Kat was with Whetherford.

"Of course." Stephen spun around and headed for the doorway.

"Stephen," Albert called. "Where are you going?"

"To Whetherford."

"Do not go charging off half-cocked, my boy."

He halted, and slowly turned. "Don't worry, Uncle. I am fully loaded and primed for bear."

"I propose to go with you." The Viscount stepped forward.

Stephen glanced at Charity's worried face, then back to her husband. "Suit yourself."

"The Earl of Whetherford," the butler announced.

Stephen's head jerked to Josiah. The butler stood there stiff as starch. No different than announcing the arrival of any normal visitor. A tall gent stood behind Josiah. Almost as tall as himself. Broad shoulders with hair as black as a raven's wing. Then Josiah's words registered. Stephen saw a haze of red. His mind reeled.

He charged.

The man's arm flew up, but not before he connected a fist to the man's jaw, knocking him to the floor.

"Stephen! Stop this at once," Albert shouted.

His hands fisted at his sides. He sucked air, wishing the bastard would get up so he could hit him again.

"Stephen, old friend."

Stephen's gaze leaped to the new voice. He had been so angered with Whetherford he'd not realized another man entered the room. Someone he had not seen in a long time.

"Well, well, well." Stephen braced his fists on his hips. "*Old friend.*"

"It has been quite a while." Wesley stepped forward, shielding the earl.

"You are with this bit of muck?" Stephen swung an arm in Whetherford's direction where he still sat on the floor. It was good to know most of his strength had returned. At least he could still throw a good punch.

"We are friends, are we not?" A full set of pearly whites flashed in the center of Wesley's face. A few years older than the last time he'd seen Wesley. Blonde hair a bit longer, not as streaked by the sun. Stephen wondered what Wesley was into these days, and how he knew Whetherford. Wesley had always been a smooth talker.

Yes, they had been friends. Close friends. Wesley had been a member of his crew at one time. The man was trustworthy, so he allowed Wesley to speak without ripping his head off.

"You helped abduct my sister?" Stephen challenged in a lethal tone.

Wesley extended his hands. "Stephen, wait! You must listen."

"Listen to who? You?" Stephen challenged.

Wesley was familiar with Stephen's temperament, yet he stood there refusing to move. Had to admire him, that.

"We did not abduct your sister. Whetherford saved the girl." Wesley spread his arms wide and resumed his melodic tone. "For old times' sake?"

"For old times' sake, you are still standing. You should know how I deal with anyone who goes against me." Hearing his aunt sniff reminded him they were not alone. He relaxed his pose—a bit.

"She was taken by mistake. Surely you will let me explain," Wesley said. After a moment's hesitation, he turned to the man on the floor, and offered his hand.

"Couldn't you have said something sooner," the earl mumbled.

Stephen took an aggressive step in the earl's direction. "Where is she?"

Whetherford's head jerked to meet Stephen's gaze. "What are you saying?"

"You are the bloke responsible. Where is she?"

"This time I'm ready for you." Whetherford braced his booted feet apart and positioned his arms for battle.

"Stop! Both of you." Albert stepped between them. "I will remind you, Stephen, you are in my home." He turned. "Lord Whetherford. Surely you understand our concern. Just tell us if Katherine is with you."

His face turned almost white. Then, his alarm turned to dread. "I came here to see her. Are you telling me you don't know where she is?"

"What blooming nonsense," Stephen thundered.

"Stephen." Albert's harsh reprimand silenced him.

Either the earl was a good performer, or he had no idea where Kat had gone.

Shouts came from the entry way. Josiah tried to restrain some man.

"What the blue blazes is going on out there?" Giving Whetherford one last glare, Stephen marched into the vestibule. "What's all the ruckus?"

The new caller side-stepped around Josiah and headed straight for Whetherford. "This came right after you left. From Juliana."

Stephen looked down his nose. "You have your doxy sending you notes here?"

Whetherford glared in response, then tore at the slip of paper. His face grew dark, his jaw tightened. He crumpled the note in his hands.

Something about his reaction grabbed Stephens' gut. Whetherford took a step forward, but Stephen blocked his path.

"Just where do you think you're going?"

"To get Kat."

Chapter 24

Stephen sat at the table staring into his mug of ale trying not to think of his little sister in the clutches of a mad woman. Whetherford's mistress, no less. To be fair, the woman had stolen Whetherford's mother's jewels. And in his search for her, he had stumbled upon Kat.

If not for Wesley, and Giles, Stephen would have killed the earl. It had taken all his will, and Wesley's levelheaded coaxing, to remind him they needed Whetherford to rescue his sister. For the woman somehow found out Whetherford cared for Kat, and she'd sent the note to him. Since she could not sell the priceless heirloom, she planned to trade Kat for money.

Giles joined them as soon as they'd left his uncle's house. His presence reminded Stephen that he should be more obliging to the man who helped arrange the search for him. After all, if not for Whetherford's affection for Kat, Stephen might still be in India, perhaps rotting in the Rajput's dungeon.

Seeing the rage on the earl's face gave him some comfort. Between the agony in Whetherford's eyes and the tension in his body, he suffered as much, if not more. It was clear Whetherford loved his sister. Guess he should take pity on the man, but Whetherford was responsible for Kat being in this mess.

Anger flared anew.

They had ridden for days. Only the need for food had them stopping at the inn. Stephen lifted the mug and took a hefty swallow, then wiped the film from his lip with the back of his hand. The bitter realization he could do nothing at the moment, did not stop him from thinking about what he would do when he caught up with the kidnappers.

Wesley slid into the chair next to him. "We're close."

"What did you find out," Whetherford spoke through gnashing teeth.

"Let the man speak," Giles said.

"With a bit of blunt in the right palms, I found out plenty."

"Spit it out."

And I thought I was livid. Whetherford behaved like a madman, ever since his fellow delivered the message from Juliana.

"A mysterious carriage showed up here about a month back. Some blokes asked questions regarding an empty dwelling a few miles east of here. Created quite a stir, because the person in this carriage refused to show her face. Kept her head covered. Although, one of the men did see her hair. Flame red, he said. Some think her a mistress of a titled gent, or a lady in hiding."

Stephen lurched from his seat. Giles grabbed his arm.

"Sit down. Do you want to alert her kidnappers? There may be someone in here loyal to Juliana. Possibly watching and waiting for us. Surprise is the only weapon we have."

"How can we be a surprise if the bloody female sent an invitation?"

"She will be expecting me to come alone," Whetherford said.

"That's right," Wesley added. "She thinks Morgan will rush to her if he is smitten with Katherine."

Morgan. If he used Whetherford's familiar name, that put him on a level of comradeship, which he did not like. *Hell.* The man said he loved Kat. His actions verified the infatuation. The man was obsessed.

And *he* called her *Kat*. That alone declared he and his sister were on familiar terms.

Guess he had to admit his little sister had grown into a woman. And if she loved the earl, damnation, he would have to leave *Morgan* in one piece.

"Are we going or not," he growled in a whisper.

"We are," Morgan answered.

Giles captured Stephen's gaze. "Slowly, without drawing any more attention."

⁓ℓℓ⁓

Hidden in the shadows, Stephen clenched his fists, then clenched them tighter. "Christ. This waiting could kill a man. I've been through hell—lived in hell. Yet the torture of waiting until I see Kat with my own eyes is worse than anything that blood thirsty bunch would have done to me." He thrust his fingers through his thick hair and pivoted on his heel. "My little sister. This standing around has my brain ready to explode."

"Waiting is always the hardest part." Morgan said in a strained voice. He had not taken his attention off the house since Giles disappeared around the back.

"That is why I am in charge of this rescue." Giles slipped in beside them. "You're too close. We both have been on too many missions to go blindly charging in without a plan."

"Well?" Morgan asked.

"Wesley, Jeremy and Piers are in position. We counted four guards in back. Two more in the house."

"What about Kat?" he ground out.

"She's there. Tied to a chair in the middle of the room. We can't get to her without being seen."

"I will kill them with my bare hands." Stephen shoved his gun in the band of his pants and charged forward.

"Wait." Giles grabbed his arm. "Juliana is unpredictable. Who knows what she might do if you go charging in there. Let's stick to the plan. Morgan, you go in the front door. Give us enough time to get in position. While you talk to Juliana, the other two guards will be distracted. Then, Stephen and I will make our move."

Morgan gave a nod in agreement.

Stephen faced Morgan. "Whetherford. Get my sister." They locked eyes in silent communication. Then the man slipped off.

With steady and silent steps, Stephen and Giles crept around to the back. Wesley and the others had already knocked out Juliana's guards. With a nod from Giles, Stephen followed him to the corner of the house, and flattened his back against the wooden planks. The moon appeared from behind a cloud lengthening shadows. What he wouldn't give for a dark sky this night.

With his head low, he and Giles scrambled to the stone steps. Looking left and right, seeing no sign of movement, he edged up each rung. Giles motioned for him to go right. Stephen inched across the porch and ducked under a window. Once he peered inside and found no one, he signaled to Giles.

Together they slithered to the door. He held his breath as Giles turned the knob. Thank God for quiet hinges. They slipped inside. Voices came from a room farther down the hall. With a jerk of his head, Giles slipped toward the flickering light. Stephen took another direction and found an entry to the room where the voices came from.

A woman's voice and . . . he recognized Morgan.

Stephen peaked around the edge of the wall. Anger sliced his gut. A red haze filled his vision when he saw Kat tied to a chair.

From what he could tell, she was unharmed. Then he nearly swallowed his tongue. For a woman stood beside his sister with long auburn hair, vastly similar to his own . . . *Damnation.* She looked like Kat.

Good God!

Giles had told him the story while they were on the ship. How the two women had the same remarkable hair. How men snatched Kat because of her resemblance to this woman. After seeing her with his own eyes, he now understood. The unbelievable story made sense.

"I'm in no mood for games."

"A man of your reputation surely has a weapon. Please remove it."

While Morgan and the redhead battled words, a form moved from the shadows.

Ahh. There is one of her henchmen. Just my size.

"You do not want my man to have his pistol go off by accident."

"Harm a hair on her head, I *will* kill you."

"There is no need to be dramatic." With a casual wave, the red-haired woman stepped closer to Kat. Then she lifted a lock of Kat's hair.

He had to keep his mind on the brute in front of him. Morgan would handle the woman.

While he searched the room, he committed every detail to memory. Then he saw Giles on the other side. Their gazes locked, and Giles gave a nod. Both men moved at once.

Stephen slapped one hand over the big brute's mouth while his other hand clasped the kidnapper's throat. At least he had regained some muscle working with the crew on the return voyage to England. Giving the right amount of pressure, the man slumped without much struggle. Stephen caught him before he hit the floor. Quiet as death, he maneuvered the body behind a curtain, and quickly took the man's place. Since they were of the same size, he hoped the woman was too busy to notice.

He glanced over to see Giles had subdued the guard on the other side of the room and was making his way to the woman. With stealth, he wormed his way to her back while Morgan and the redhead continued their heated discussion. Morgan had to see Giles, but he gave no indication. He held Juliana's attention.

"You were gone so long, we thought you dead." Juliana continued, unaware of their presence. "Of course, I gave my father the idea. Once we moved to Whetherford Manor, he became the man he used to be. Full of life. Full of power. I actually think the title meant more to him than the wealth."

"But not to you, Juliana. What happened? Did he not spoil you enough? Did he not give you your every whim? Why didn't you take the blasted jewels and keep on going," Morgan asked. "Why did you come back?"

Juliana gave a brittle laugh. "I knew you would follow me forever. You would never give up."

"You have the necklace. What do you think you will gain by taking Miss Radbourn?"

"I find it interesting *Miss Radbourn* is a replica of me."

Standing directly behind her, Giles grated close to her ear, "Pure coincidence."

Juliana's eyes flew open in shock. When she whirled, Giles grabbed her and pinned her to his chest.

"Sorry to spoil your plans, my dear." His arms tightened, imprisoning her resisting body.

Juliana screamed. "Let me go, damn you."

Stephen made a mad dash for Kat. Her eyes wide with surprise, tears trickled down her cheeks. As fast as his fingers would move, he quickly untied her bonds. Free at last, Kat hurled herself into his arms.

"Kitten," Stephen whispered and held her close.

"Stephen. Oh, Stephen. Thank God you're alive," Kat cried. She buried her face in his chest. He rested his chin on top of her head, his hands stroked her back.

"I've got you, Kitten. You're safe."

Leaning back, Kat placed a palm on his cheek. "Oh, Stephen. You're here. You are really here."

"Are you hurt? Has anyone harmed you in any way?" God, how his chest squeezed. If she had been harmed, the blasted harridan would deal with him.

"I am fine, now that you're here." She hugged him tighter. Then her cries turned into whaling sobs.

He glanced at the other woman. It appeared Giles and Morgan had her well in hand. By the look in Morgan's eye, the woman might not live long enough to regret her actions.

Stephen's concern now was his sister. She'd been through enough. Time to take her home. He tried easing Kat back, putting space between them, but she burrowed into his chest. With his arm around her, he strode to Morgan.

"I'm taking her home."

Pain filled Morgan's eyes. "Kat?"

"She has been through enough," Stephen continued.

Morgan said her name again. "Kat?"

Her fingers tightened on Stephen's coat, her lower lip trembled. "Please, Stephen. Take me home."

Stephen caught Morgan's gaze above her head. Hearing the desperation in his sister's voice, he gave a negative shake to Morgan, and mouthed the words, *not now.*

He led Kat to the hallway. Her legs wobbled. So, he bent down, placed an arm under her knees, and hefted her up into his arms. When he carried her outside, Wesley was there, waiting. Again, Stephen shook his head. Wesley gave a whistle and Jeremy pulled a landau to the steps.

"Katherine will be more comfortable in this." Wesley gave a nod toward the house. "*She* won't be needing it." The carriage must have been Juliana's. Wesley opened the carriage door and Stephen placed Kat inside.

He turned to Wesley. "You have my thanks." They gave each other a hardy shake, sending a silent message with their eyes, reminiscent of their bond as comrades from years past. Then he climbed in beside his sister.

Stephen realized how much he had missed Kat. Seeing her in his mind had kept him sane during his confinement of inhumanity. He had dreamed of his sister. Dreamed of seeing her again, holding her in his arms. He never imagined her sobs would rent his heart so.

He could only imagine the rendering of the heart of the man who held hers.

Chapter 25

The headache that threatened all night pounded in earnest. With a pensive sigh, Jennifer stared out the window of her bedchamber. A favorite spot of hers, she had spent many nights on the cushioned seat pondering her thoughts. Thoughts of marrying Johnny. A lifetime ago.

Now her contemplations dwelled on a man with a lion's mane, red as the deepest sunset blazing on the horizon of an evening sky. Green eyes that could sear the skin of her flesh, and delve into the center of her heart, demanding she give her all. And she had. Stephen may not have wanted her love, but she had given it just the same. He drained every ounce of her energy, he'd conquered her soul. She was lost without him.

How could he leave her and walk away without a care? She had not seen him in weeks. Not heard one word from him. Tossing pride to the wind, she sent him notes. Still, there was no response. Her trusted maid swore she took them to his residence. Handed them personally to another maid. Still, no answer.

Her heart ached.

A light tap and her bedchamber door opened.

"Jen. Are you awake?" Isabella slipped inside.

"Yes," she called from her alcove under the window.

"What are you doing? You did not come down to breakfast."

"I'm not hungry." She stared through the lace covering the window.

"You must eat. You will waste away to nothing. Then what will your captain think?"

A twinge plucked her chest. "He is not my captain."

"Of course, he is. I'll warrant he will not want a skinny, bony woman."

Isabella was a romantic. She would not give up on the foolish notion Stephen was her sister's happily ever after.

"I have not seen him since he brought me home."

"Well, you won't see him as long as you continue to hide in your room."

Let her think what she wants. I don't care.

"Anyway, I have something to tell you." Isabella plopped on the seat beside her. "You could at least pretend you are interested."

Jennifer looked at her sister. "Very well. What is it?"

"It's about your captain."

A spark flickered. She ignored it. "I told you, he is not—"

"You really should have come to Lady Delgrave's ball last night. It was the height of the season."

Jennifer wanted to grab her sister by the arms and shake her. Instead she pretended to be bored. "What do you have to tell me?"

Isabella frowned in irritation. "Aren't you interested? Guess who was there?"

Certainly not Stephen.

"Who?" Her voice betrayed her anxious curiosity.

"I thought that might get your attention."

"Isabella." Her sister loved to play games. "You're bursting to tell me something. Out with it."

Isabella skewed her nose in the air.

"Is-a-bell-a."

She giggled. Then she grabbed Jennifer's hands. "The talk was of your captain. His sister was kidnapped."

"What?" She ignored the *your captain* part. She had her full attention. "Are you sure?"

"Yes. The gossip of the ton is alive and running like wildfire. His sister was kidnapped by Lord Whetherford's mistress, and Stephen left to rescue her. Perhaps that is why your handsome captain has not answered your letters."

Jennifer raised her fist to her mouth and bit down on a knuckle. "Oh my. He must be beside himself." She jerked her hand down. "Stephen has a horrible temper. He is bound for trouble."

"I heard he is the man to give trouble. Not be on the receiving end of it."

Little did Isabella know. Stephen had been tortured and starved. That was a secret she would never reveal. For it was not her story to tell.

"You have a discerning look on your face." Isabella studied her. "Have you told me everything? What are you keeping from me?"

"It is incomprehensible for you to expect me to divulge years of my life in as many weeks. Tell me. What else did you hear?"

"Lord Thornton is Stephen's uncle. A very important man. Father speaks highly of him."

"If he is a man of Parliament, of course Father would know him. I never thought of that."

"Stephen's mother was Lord Thornton's sister. When their parents died, killed in a carriage accident I believe, your captain brought his sister to live with his uncle. They are here for the season, but his sister is older than me."

"Older? I thought she would be younger. Stephen speaks of her as a child."

"Well, she caught Lord Whetherford's eye. Which is another story. The on dit is he is the Dark Lord."

"What are you talking about?"

"Oh, you have been gone too long. This is like the stories we are not supposed to know about. The kind of people father protects us from. The Dark Lord is a dangerous man. Whetherford has a shady past." Isabella lowered her voice. "Whetherford is the Dark Lord." She sat back and said excitedly, "I told you the rumor mill was thriving."

"Good Lord. You learned all of this last night?"

"Yes. And if you had gone with me, you could have heard the news firsthand."

Jennifer bounded from the window seat. A million thoughts circling through her head. His sister kidnapped. He must have been in a rage to receive such news.

"Stephen is very protective of his sister. If this Lord Whetherford is a shady character, and with Stephen's temper, someone is bound to get hurt."

"My money is on your captain." Isabella's smile was more of a smirk.

Fear settled in Jennifer's gut. "He is recovering. He's not strong enough to go chasing after ruffians."

Isabella stood. "What do you mean he is recovering? Your captain looked fine to me."

Now she'd done it. *Oh, my wayward tongue.*

"Stephen was injured. I don't know if he regained all of his strength back."

"What kind of injury? What happened?" Isabella stepped closer.

"It does not matter." Jennifer waved her hand and paced the length of her bed. What was she to do? Where was Stephen? She whirled around. "Did you hear anything else?"

"That's pretty much everything. Unless you want to hear more about Lord Whetherford and his mistress."

"You know about the man's mistress? Good Lord, Isabella. What kind of company are you keeping?" She paced to her bed. "No, thank you. I only want to know about Stephen."

"Lady Marsdale is giving a ball tomorrow night. If you want to know what's happening among the ton, a ball is the place to find out."

Jennifer halted. When she turned, her sister rolled her eyes in a mocking gesture of innocence.

Isabella swiped her fingers across her chest and held up one hand. "It's the truth." Her mouth formed into a crafty smile. "You must want to go to a ball. You have been gone three years. Don't you miss it?"

Heavens no.

But then, once she had loved dressing up in fine gowns, and dancing at lively balls. For the last several years she had labored, slaved, worried for her next meal, and been scared the life she lived was her curse. Her own stupidity—she only had herself to depend on for her survival. Now, she was home. Free of her desolate life. Still young. Didn't she deserve to laugh? Didn't she deserve to be happy?

And didn't she crave news of Stephen?

"Yes. Yes, I will go."

Isabella ran to her, squealing. She threw her arms around her, bouncing up and down in delight. "Come." Isabella took her hand and rushed over to the clothes closet, throwing open the doors. She grabbed gowns by the arm full and threw them on the bed.

"Isabella, what are you doing?"

"Even if these gowns would fit you, they are out of date. We must get rid of them. Then, we will go shopping." She gave a cry of glee. "Shopping, Jen. We will find you the prettiest gowns, the latest fashion in all of England."

She ran to the door and flung it open. "Marie!"

Jennifer stared in amazement. She had forgotten how excited her sister got when they went shopping. Marie rushed through the door.

"Yes, mum."

"Marie. Take these gowns and put them in the donation box. Jennifer and I are going shopping."

~ele~

Jennifer did not have a vain bone in her body, at least not for the last few years. Before she'd left London, she had dressed in the height of fashion. Being a Marquis's daughter, it was expected. Many young swains had told her repeatedly that she was beautiful, but the only one whose words she had cared about was the man she married. What a foolish young girl.

Experience had taught her the value of life, making her realize how shallow she and her friends had behaved. She glanced at the jars of cream littering her vanity. Balm to keep her skin smooth and creamy, safe from the blistering cold English weather. She had needed them more in the harsh sun while she labored about her tiny house, to keep her sun-bronzed skin from turning to leather.

Her body may have aged only a few years, but in her mind, she'd grown much older. The little-girl-look was gone, and in its place a mature woman had developed. Standing before the mirror, she studied her reflection. A stunning creature with soulful eyes stared back at her, with full, pouting lips. Her fingers traced their outline. Memories emerged of Stephen's kisses. Soft and gentle, then eager and consuming.

Life was full of twists and turns. Luck had brought her home to her family.

She tightened her corset, achieving a fullness that came to her naturally. She had no desire to have some gentlemen ogling her breasts, dripping syrupy compliments expecting her to fall at his feet. But the modiste and Isabella argued that the latest fashion dictated a lower décolletage. Although, the only man for whom she would willingly display her wares no longer showed any interest in her.

A pair of vivid green eyes sprang to mind. Eyes that glowed with mischief, then burned with desire. Her blood heated. A fine blanket of reddish-chestnut hair sprinkled across a masculine chest. Her fingers tingled.

Closing her eyes, she rubbed her temples, driving the image away. She took deep breaths. A headache building, she needed to come to grips with the facts. Stephen left her. He would not be coming back. So, she had to go after him. Agonizing over how to manage that feat only produced another headache.

Once again, she glanced into the mirror. Her hair, done in the Grecian mode, also considered the height of fashion. She glared at the blue silk cut low in the bosom, she was about to fall out. She grabbed the top of her gown and pulled. Humph. She dug through her chest looking for a piece of linen, anything to use as a fichu. Finding a kerchief, she grabbed the thing and stuffed it under the edge of her bodice.

"What are you doing?" Isabella met her eyes in the mirror.

A flush of heat rushed to Jennifer's face.

"Turn around." Isabella rolled her eyes. "You look ridiculous."

"I know. That's why I need a fichu."

"You do not." Isabella jerked the cloth from her bosom. "That's better. You are used to ugly garb and rags for clothing."

She had not thought of her clothes as rags. "You make me sound like a beggar."

"You no longer need to live like a pauper."

Even though Isabella had not meant the offence, her slur had hurt. Supporting herself had been Jennifer's way of life. The luxurious surroundings in her parent's house seemed like a fairytale.

"You look beautiful." Isabella took her hands. "You will have your choice of gentlemen this night."

Only one would have her notice. And he would not be there.

Chapter 26

Glowing lanterns lined the street in front of Lord Marsdale's residence. A row of carriages waited, their occupants eager for their turn arriving at the bottom of the mansion steps. Guests alighted, dressed in elegant finery, sparkling jewels, capes of the finest cloth, and gowns of the grandest silk.

What the devil was he doing here?

Stephen drummed his fingers on the velvet cushion. Bad enough he showed up at all, but biding one's time while sitting in a line of courtly fobs made him seriously weigh his decision. It was not too late to back out. He could simply tell his driver not to stop. Or, one of his meaningful glares aimed at Marsdale's footman would have the man quickly closing the carriage door.

Bloody hell. He was not a coward.

By the time the presumptuous footman opened the carriage door, the man received a glare anyway. The very idea of Stephen dressing up like a dandy did not sit at all well. Thank God, his sister and aunt were too busy discussing wedding plans, they had paid no attention to his skulking about. He had no desire to explain his attire, let alone fend off their questions.

Looks like he would soon have a brother-in-law. *Whetherford.* Accepting the man as an ally was one thing, but having him for a future brother-in-law had been a resigned pill to swallow. He shook his head, still trying to digest the notion. His little sister had grown up. But married? How could he fathom that?

Strings of music flowed from the floor above. He removed his hat and handed it to the butler, then glanced up the grand staircase. Two couples ascended the steps, heading for the ballroom. To his right, three men stood in a circle outside a closed door, which probably led to the gaming room. If things took a turn for the worst, he could always try his luck at cards.

With the polish of an aristocrat, he climbed the steps, back straight, one rung then another. No need to tackle two at a time, one might think he appeared anxious. He slowed his breathing. A set of double doors, most likely twelve feet tall, stood open in welcome. Whirls of white and black swirled by the entryway. A lively tune echoed off the walls, bouncing debutantes pirouetted, while their partners—decked out in their waist coats and long tails—danced in attendance. Ladies adorned in the latest fashionable gowns in every color of the rainbow filled any obtainable space in the ballroom.

Good God, why had he come?

He had rashly ended any relationship he and Jenny might have had. Yet, here he was, attending a bloody ball. Was this any worse than when he'd attended Almacks? When he'd persuaded Frederick, an Eton chum, to hand over his voucher for attendance, the man had laughed his fool head off, damn his sorry hide. Stephen was the last person, Frederick had said, ever expected to attend a marriage mart. Convincing the fool he had no intention of marriage to a young debutante earned him another round of fits of laughter. Still, he had thrown caution to the wind, and now he was attending another foolish event which would surely open him up for more ridicule.

Leaning against the marble column, he hoped no one would find him. Since he towered above most, that was an insane wish. Still he lingered in the corner, behind the potted palm. Two dowagers seated to his right conversed on everyone in attendance. Had he been seeking gammon of any one in this crowd, he would gleam every tidbit from the pair of hens. An encyclopedia could not possibly hold more knowledge than the true background of any particular young lady coming out, how her father received his funds, or if he held a place in the upper orders. Every eligible man received the same assessment. If he were a titled lord, a nabob, a rake, a fop, or a suitable match.

No one safe from the matrons on dit. Another reason for him to stay in the shadows.

Again, he cursed himself for the fool he was. He should be in another room engaged in a game of cards. Why bother, when he could not deny his eyes even one glimpse of Jennifer. The only reason he would suffer ridicule, at attending such an event. Scowling, he searched the room. A gaggle of giggling debutantes—

He saw her.

On the other side of the ballroom, thirty feet away—Jennifer may as well have been on the other side of the moon. Knocked off his pins, he stared in fascination., not caring in the least if his mouth hung open. His eyes devoured her. A few dark curls hung down, drawing his gaze to her bare neck. His fingers tingled at the pink of her shoulders, reminding him of her soft, velvety flesh.

His brain prompted his need for air. He inhaled and nearly choked on the strong rose water of the matrons. Shaking his head, he slid around the white pillar-post. Keeping his gaze on Jennifer, he stayed close to the wall, as he inched his way closer.

Jennifer stared up at her partner. It took everything in him not to march across the floor and pound the man dancing with her. Something like dread settled in his gut. No more than a few feet away, her lilting voice trickled into his ear and down his spine. In that moment, he wanted her. Wanted to hold her, caress her, make love to her. A woman should not have such an effect on him.

He should leave. Break this hold, however captivating she may be. Disappear and never lay eyes on her beauty again. His actions did not heed his thoughts. Unable to move, he stood frozen, confined in a web of his own making.

The swain held his arm and Jennifer placed her gloved hand at his elbow. When she lifted the hem of her skirt, the bloody bore twirled her about the dance floor, holding Jennifer much too close.

"They make a handsome couple."

"The earl has been a widower for two years. He's looking for a wife."

Stephen's temples pounded. Damn gossipmongers. True or not, the earl was too handsome for his peace of mind. Then the earl's unconcealed gaze dropped to Jennifer's bosom. A red haze filled Stephen's vision. He took several breaths to calm his pulse. The blasted man would have his nose rearranged before the night ended.

Blurs of white, pink, and blue whirled into his vision. An energetic tune, the couples danced in merriment. The joy he'd felt in seeing Jennifer, now weighed like a stone in his chest. Her smiling face killed any elation he'd experienced. Obviously, she had not missed him. Every step she danced pommeled a wound into his already bruised heart. He spun around and headed for the exit.

Jennifer curved her lips and forced another smile at her partner. At least this one did not step on her toes. This evening had not gone as planned. One eligible bachelor after another—from young to old—never married to widowed with children—had asked her to dance. Smiling and laughing at their banter was expected, so she had pasted a smile on her face and half listened to their bluster.

She glanced up at her partner. Tall, inky black hair, darker than her own, and kind eyes. Quite attractive, actually.

Did she have to compare every man to Stephen?

You do when the man you see is not the one you love.

Blast Stephen and his stupidity. The very reason she came to the ball was to hear some news of him. Nothing. But then, she had not been in any group long enough for conversation before another gentleman asked her to dance. Her face grew brittle and her feet were beginning to feel like the bones had dissolved with needles taking their place. How much longer must she endure?

"Lady Gascoyne?"

Seconds ticked by before Jennifer realized the earl addressed her. The ton still considered her a Gascoyne. Didn't they realize she was a widow, and not one of the debutantes coming out into society? "Yes, my lord?"

"You drifted off somewhere. What a blow to my ego if I cannot hold a lady's attention."

"I assure you, my lord, you are most engaging. I merely gave my toes a twinkling of pity. I have not had a moment to rest since we arrived."

"Forgive me. As soon as the music stops, I will escort you to the Marchioness and then fetch you some punch. It would not do to draw attention, leaving in the middle of our dance. The gossip mill would make much of that, I'm afraid."

"Surely they will not think we quarreled. I shall keep a smile on my face."

I've been practicing all night.

"Or, they may think we have made an arrangement for a later assassination." The earl said it with a tilt of his brow. But the gleam in his eyes held the suggestion he would gladly agree to the idea.

Good Lord. How do I get out of this one?

Maybe because she was no longer a youth, or maybe because she had been married, she ascertained more open-mindedly the words and actions of men. A handsome face could hide a treacherous soul. Having a grand dream did not make one come true. Hard life had aged her beyond her years. She would not be duped again.

She ignored the comment and remained quiet through the rest of their set. Then true to his word, the earl left her with her mother and went in search of refreshment.

"He is quite handsome," Isabella said.

"Yes, strikingly dark." Jennifer watched his tall form disappear while eagerly searching for a mane of red.

"Lord Sheffield, may I introduce my daughters, Jennifer and Isabella. This is Lord Sheffield."

"It is my pleasure to make your acquaintance, ladies." Lord Sheffield held out his hand.

Jennifer placed her fingers on the edge of his index finger. He lifted her gloved hand and brushed a light kiss across her knuckles. "Lady Gascoyne." He held her gaze for long moments before he turned to Isabella and did the same. "Lady Gascoyne." Then, his attention returned to her.

"May I have this dance, my lady?"

Jennifer's toes screamed in protest. Her face must have mirrored her thoughts, for he studied her in confusion.

"If you will forgive her, Lord Sheffield, my sister has just come from dancing. She has been on her feet all night."

"I understand." He gave a half bow. "Perhaps, Lady Isabella, you would care to dance?"

"Oh . . ." She flustered with a shake of her head. "I did not mean . . ."

"Of course, you didn't. But may I have this dance anyway?" He cocked a brow in mischief and the corner of his mouth tilted in a smile.

Isabella lifted her nose in annoyance, then stood as if he'd insulted her. But she put her fingers in the crook of his elbow and glided to the center of the floor. Her intention had been to send the man on his way, yet she ended up on his arm instead. A slight chuckle escaped Jennifer's lips.

"What did you find to amuse you," her mother asked. "Lord Sheffield is a man of consequence."

"Handsome as well as rich. He should be a good match for Isabella." Her mother's gasp confirmed her suspicions that the earl had been intended for her. "Mother. Cease your match making. Have you forgotten? I am a widow."

"You are a Marquis's daughter." Keeping her voice down, Mother spoke in a reprimanding tone. "The past will not touch you here."

"You cannot sweep the last few years of my life under the carpet, Mother."

"You need not let it scar your life." Showing the onlookers all was right with the world, Mother smiled, but a warning glint in her eyes remained on Jennifer. "You are Lady Gascoyne. No more talk of nuptials."

Jennifer fumed. She would not act like her marriage never happened. Johnny deserved more than to be ignored as if he never existed. If Mother was ashamed of her . . . She glanced toward the dancers and willed her eyes not to tear. She had shamed her family. The day she ran away.

Two men headed in her direction. By their glares at each other, the dandies raced to see who would reach her side first.

"Mother, please. How much longer do we need to be here? I long to go home."

"Isabella is dancing. The night is still young."

Suddenly a tall form blocked the path of the two eager swains.

"Lady Gascoyne. Your refreshment."

Ah, the earl returned. How could she have forgotten him? But then a string of fellows, no end in sight, continued to pop before her.

"Thank you, my lord." She accepted the glass and drank half the contents before seeing the scowl on the earl's face. Oh dear. That was very unladylike to gulp like a heathen from the wild when she was supposed to be a high-born lady.

At least her mother had not noticed. A quick glance confirmed that she was in deep conversation with the matron sitting beside her.

"You *were* thirsty." The earl's voice held a ring of mirth.

"Uh, yes. I suppose I was." Embarrassment flooded her to her toes.

"I hope you have enjoyed this evening."

"Indeed, I have. With all the dancing, I believe I may have worn out my slippers."

"I would be most honored to purchase you new ones." He coughed. "I apologize Lady Gascoyne. How forward of me. I meant no disrespect."

"None taken, my lord." Jennifer gave a nod of exoneration.

"May I say how beautiful you are this evening?" Another man had approached.

"Give way, Beachcomb. Lady Gascoyne is sitting this one out."

"Who are you to speak—"

The earl grabbed the other man by the arm. "Excuse us, please." Then dragged him off. They had no sooner gone four paces before another man took the earl's place.

"Lady Gascoyne," He said as he bowed.

"Lord Hambrook," she replied.

"You remember me."

"Of course, I remember you." He was one of the few men who did not irritate her beyond measure.

"You flatter me. You have so many admirers."

She blushed. She had no idea why. He seemed harmless enough.

"May I say how lovely you look this evening. Your gown brings out the color of your beautiful eyes."

"Thank you for being so kind." Oh how tiring, the patrician chit chat expected of her.

"I am not being charitable, my lady." He cleared his throat. "I hold you in highest regard. A lady as comely as you should be told of her charming beauty and admiring character."

Oh dear. She looked to her mother, no help there.

"Lady Gascoyne, if I may be so bold." The earl hesitated, his gaze held hers.

"Yes, my lord?" Her breathing quickened in alarm.

"If you are acquiescent, I should like to call on you tomorrow."

She hesitated. How to answer? From what she remembered, he was a wealthy, highly respected earl.

Isabella had talked her into this debacle. Jennifer wished she had never come. She'd heard no word of Stephen, nor of the captain who had returned after a long absence. Did the ton know she and Stephen had returned together? Or was that a fact her family kept private? On purpose? Had Father conspired to keep the details of her sudden appearance in London a secret?

The gossip mill had no doubt been kept in full force the entire time she had been gone, so she could understand his reasoning. Still, she had a life of her own. She could make her own choices.

She searched the dancing couples for her sister. A smile plastered on Isabella's cheeky face She seemed to be enjoying herself.

Jennifer's plan backfired.

She focused on how to assimilate her answer so as not to offend the earl.

"I will, of course, ask your father's permission, if you are in agreement."

What did he think she was—a girl in her first coming out?

"Of course, you have my permission, Lord Hambrook."

Chapter 27

Jennifer propped her aching feet on the stool in front of her and leaned her head back against the soft velvet. What a night. She had danced nearly every dance, and this morning she feared her poor feet would never be the same.

A downstairs maid brought in a tea cart laden with a silver tea service. In England, tea was a daily indulgence. Often, when Jennifer was alone in her little shack, she longed for tea in the comfort of her family home. She would never take her family's time together for granted again. She tried to sit up. A little moan escaped her lips.

"Why Jennifer, darling. Are you all right," her mother asked?

"Yes, Mother."

Isabella came floating into the parlor. "Hello, Mother. Hello, Jennifer." Her sister was entirely too cheery.

"Jennifer is not feeling well," Mother said with a slight frown.

"Mother, she is fine," Isabella amended. "Exhausted maybe, after attempting to dance the night away."

Don't remind me.

"You did have a number of partners last evening." Mother's lips curved in a satisfied smile. She arched her back, a little like Jennifer's cat after lapping up all her cream. "I do believe you took Lady Marsdale's guests by storm. You had every gentleman's eye."

"And every maiden's scorn," Isabella added with a twinkle in her eye.

"Here dear. Let me do that." Mother poured tea into three cups, then added cream and sugar to each one.

Such delicacies she had lived without while in India. And the English scones. Her mouth watered. She lifted her cup hoping the tea would calm her muscles. She would never be able to walk again. Yet, her feet were not the only things making their soreness known.

"While you two were busy dancing, I received fodder from the gossip mill."

Jennifer fixated on her sister's words.

"Lord Harrywig fell from his horse at his country home on one of his hunts and broke his neck. He did not live to see his impudent daughter return."

"Did you see her gown? Indecent." Mother gave a slight shudder.

"When she attended the ball on Lord Cuthbert's arm, I thought his mother would swoon."

"The entire ton witnessed her embarrassment." Mother's back arched like any peacock ready to span his feathers. "It is rumored Cuthbert is planning to marry that harlot. He is moving his mother to the dowager house."

"Could it be true? Do you think he would ..." Isabella's eyes rounded. She bit her lip and her expression turned from curious to, almost, despair.

Her misery caused Jennifer concern. "Isabella?"

"It's just that . . . well, I rather liked Lord Cuthbert."

"I told you Isabella, not to set your sights on that scoundrel," Mother rebuked. "If he marries Lord Harrywig's daughter, his mother will be given the cut-direct. More than likely she is Lord Cuthbert's ploy in pulling one over on his mother."

Jennifer remembered Lord Cuthbert from years before. Her father had pointed him out to her as a prospect. Isabella had a fondness for him, even then. "Is he on the outs with his mother," Jennifer asked.

"Lady Cuthbert's sister, Constance, remarried last year. When her husband died shortly after, her son suggested she move in with Constance." Mother took a sip of tea and returned her cup to the gold-filigree saucer.

"I take it she was offended," Jennifer said.

"You could say that," replied Isabella.

"I think he only meant to give each woman the company of the other. However, his mother thought he wanted to be rid of her."

"She protested?" Jennifer gazed over the rim of her china cup.

Isabella added more sugar to her tea. "Revolted was more the case. She fought him at every turn."

"She tried taking over the running of the estate," Mother continued. "Rescinded his orders, issued new ones in his name. When he caught her in the act—to put it mildly—there was an uproar."

China clanked as Isabella replaced her cup into its saucer. "Mother and I were invited to their home after that. I had been excited to go. But I never wanted to go back after that day."

"Why? What happened?"

Isabella shivered. "They were cold to one another. It was uncanny. "Their home no longer maintained its warmth. The servants performed their duties in stony silence, their eyes never meeting Lady Cuthbert, or us. Then, Alicia, she had a friend on their staff at the time, mentioned her friend was looking for a new position. The girl came here in the hopes Alicia would represent her to Mother for employment. Alicia's friend spoke of the household and said, even the normal chatter among the servants had stopped. Then, she burst into tears.”

“I do not approve of gossip among the servants.” Mother scolded.

But it is alright for us to natter among ourselves.

“You did hire Alicia’s friend,” Isabella asked.

Mother gave a sniff. She stood and smoothed her skirts. “I believe I shall have a nap. It is the middle of the day. You girls may have just gotten out of bed, but I rose early this morning.”

Once mother disappeared around the door, Isabella scooted across the sofa closer to Jennifer. “I thought she would never leave.”

“You have a bee under your bonnet this morning . . . uh afternoon.” Jennifer closed her eyes and leaned back into the comfort of the high back chair. “And I am not very happy with you right now.”

“What have I done?”

“You convinced me to go to Marsdale’s ball. Instead of the news I sought, I ended up with an outing Father agreed to with Lord Hambrook. Imagine my embarrassment when the earl asked Father for his permission. I barely managed to get him to agree to tomorrow instead of today. Being a gentleman, he understood the need for *beauty rest* after dancing all night at a ball.”

“Well, this should make you feel better.”

Jennifer opened one eye. “You seem entirely too excited.”

“I have news of your captain.”

Both eyes opened as she dropped her throbbing feet to the floor. She had given up denying Stephen was her captain. “What news?”

“He’s back.”

"How did you learn that? I heard nothing. And I sacrificed my limbs."

"You were too busy fighting off droves of dandies to be privy to gossip."

"Do not remind me. I am completely done in. What did you hear?"

"Well, Lucia hid outside her father's study and listened at his door. She said Lord Thornton's nephew rescued his niece, and she was not compromised."

"Compromised? Oh, dear. I never thought of her being alone with the man. I mean, she was kidnapped. Did they think she would be . . . oh, dear."

"When did you become such a muddle head? Stop with the 'oh dears'."

"You would not want to hear some of the expletives I used in India," Jennifer said with a raised brow. "I am trying to relearn my young lady etiquette training."

"Really? What sort of expletives?"

"Never mind," Jennifer shook her head. "I forgot how easily a young girl can be ruined." She gave a slight wave with her hand.

"She is older than me," Isabella said.

"How old?"

"Three and twenty, I think."

"That's my age. You made her sound like an old woman."

"Too old for the marriage mart. She had her coming out years ago."

"Fiddle. What else did Lucia hear?"

Isabella leaned closer. "Well, Lord Thornton packed them up and moved to his country estate."

Packed them up? Stephen too?

"A place called Chelmouth."

"Where's that?"

"You are just full of questions, aren't you?" Isabella let out a deep breath.

"Oh, hush. Where?"

She waved her hands in the air. "How can I tell you if I hush?"

Jennifer glared at her sister. "Is-a-bell-a."

"How would I know?" Isabella jumped from her seat on the sofa.

Jennifer scowled, watching her sister's anxious movements. "Because you are too curious. I know you found out."

Isabella chewed on the end of her finger. "Well, Bobby said—"

"Who? Never mind." She waved her hand dismissing her question. His identity was not important.

"Bobby said it is far south. Above Brighton. That's where the captain has his ships."

"Ships?" Stephen's ship sunk. Had he mentioned more? Did he own a shipyard?

"Evidently your captain has several ships. He sailed away on *Serpents Ghost* two years ago. He returned, the ship did not."

Of course not. The Rajput prince sunk Stephen's ship.

Gossip did thrive among the ton.

Jennifer bit her knuckle. A pang of sorrow landed in the pit of her stomach, reminding her of the chief's slaughter.

"You know something, don't you?" Isabella's voice penetrated her contemplation.

Jennifer took a sip of her tea, swallowed, and set her teacup down. "Stephen sailed to India. His ship was sunk. He was . . . injured. That is how I met him."

Remembering the sight of his mutilated body caused her to stumble over the description. Her sister must have sensed her sorrow, for Isabella did not ask any more. Instead, she returned to her spot on the couch, and hugged Jennifer tight.

"I love you, Sister. Maybe in time . . ."

"Thank you." Jennifer hugged her back. Isabella seemed to understand that Jennifer did not want to reveal her secrets. Her little sister had grown up. "You have helped more than you know."

⁓ℓℓ⁓

Stephen nodded with a smirk that was becoming all too familiar to Jennifer. He leaned closer. Heart pounding, she raised her mouth for his kiss.

"Jennifer!"

The bedchamber door flew open, and her whirlwind of a mother rushed in waking her from her dream. *Arrrrrr.* Her wonderful, exciting, sensual dream. She pulled the covers over her head and wished her mother to the devil.

"You need to get out of that bed. Lord Hambrook is calling on you this afternoon."

"Go away," Jennifer mumbled.

"What's that?" She went on, not waiting for an answer. "Alicia is bringing you a tray." She marched around the room issuing more instructions, then her voice trailed off. Jennifer flung the covers down taking a huge gulp of air. Marie entered immediately upon the heels of her mother's exit. She scurried over to an open doorway and went inside to the bathing chamber. Anticipation of a hot, soothing bath had Jennifer pushing all other thoughts away. Alicia entered with a tray.

Marie stepped back into the bedchamber. "The towels are warm, my lady."

"Thank you, Marie. And please call me Jennifer. Have I been gone so long that you have forgotten me?"

Marie's eyes lifted to meet her gaze. "You . . . you married, and you are a lady."

Jennifer felt sorry for the woman, not much older than her. Once they had been friends. She never told anyone of her plans to run away. Not even Marie. Jennifer had not been in her parent's home for years, and who knew what the staff had been told.

"I am the same person." As soon as she said the words, she knew it for the lie it was. She definitely *was not* the same person.

Marie curtsied. "Yes, mum. May I help you with your bath?"

"No, thank you. I would like to bathe alone." Being on her own for so long, she had grown independent. Learned to do without. She would need to make an effort in allowing herself to be pampered.

"Can I get you anything else?"

"No thank you, Alicia." She left, closing the door behind her.

Marie spun around. "Do you have a gown in mind for today?" She moved to the large paneled doors in the wall, opening them wide." All four doors held beautiful gowns—a few remained from before, but most from her recent shopping spree with her sister. The money they spent would have fed her for years in India.

She shook off the melancholy suddenly threatening to envelope her.

"Should I lay out your under garments?"

"No. Thank you, Marie. I will be fine." She watched the maid go out the door.

She stepped into the adjoining room and sighed at the sight of the claw-footed bathing tub. Dipping her fingers, she found the water to have just the right temperature. She moaned in anticipation of emerging her body for a long, leisurely soak.

She pulled the silky material over her head, then eased her tired muscles into the welcoming warmth. She relaxed against the back of the tub, giving a sigh of pure delight. For long moments she lay there. Not thinking or caring about anything but the soothing water. She lifted the cloth drizzling oil scented water across her breasts. Ohhhh . . . that felt good. How wonderful—how different—being able to have a proper bath. The one true thing she missed during her life in India.

With her head on the rim of the tub, she allowed her mind to drift away into dangerous territory.

Stephen.

Where was he, what was he doing? Her fascination with the man had deepened in the short span of time that they were together. Blast him. He had her chasing rainbows. She had gone to a ball only on the chance of seeing his sorry hide. In hopes to gather information. Any word, any hint of his name.

As the water soothed her muscles, her thoughts grew more heated. Her bare bottom sitting on his lap, his fingers in her hair, his fingers delving lower. Her breathing quickened and she shifted causing the water to ripple. Good Lord, she needed to keep such notions from surfacing. Of course, with Stephen as the subject, carnal images were a given.

She soaped the cloth and scrubbed her arms vigorously. The quicker she got out of this tub the better.

Chapter 28

Stephen passed a group of scapegallows huddled together as he strode toward the Cock and Crown. In the deepening twilight, the dock's taverns came alive with the evenings' activities—not all entertainment. The happenings around these parts varied from drinking, rousing, whoring . . . and if a man weren't careful, he would find his throat slit for the coin he carried.

Stephen's size had always intimidated. Thieves and scallywags thought better of their actions before accosting a man of his bulk. Given time, and another ship, he'd be back to his former mammoth size.

A woman's wails echoed from a dark alley. At first, he thought a lightskirt in the throes of pleasing a randy seafarer. As he drew closer, a man shouted, then a distinct sound of a hard slap rang in his ears. He froze.

What the hell?

"No! Please!"

"I know you want it, girlie. Now stop fightin'."

"Stop! Please!" The woman's cries were panic-stricken.

Stephen rushed toward the sounds of a struggle. What he saw made his blood boil. He grabbed the assailant by the scruff of his neck and hoisted. He slammed the bloody bastard into a wall.

"Oofff."

"You're a sorry excuse for a man." Rage held him in her grasp. Fury seized his limbs. Blood thumped his temples. Lightskirt or no, beating a woman was beyond his tolerance.

"She was askin' fer it."

He hammered a punch to the cur's middle. "No woman deserves a beating," he said in a deadly tone. "I'll not stand by and allow you or anyone to pound on a helpless individual."

"She . . . she came out here with me."

"You think that gives you the right to force this woman? Any woman?"

When the man opened his mouth, Stephen tightened his hands around the miscreant's throat.

"Madam? Are you all right?"

The woman scrubbed at her cheeks and stopped her sniffling long enough to answer. "Y-yes. I think so."

"Leave us. Go on your way."

"I . . . I didn't . . ."

"I said go!"

Without a glance in her direction, Stephen heard shuffling sounds of the woman scurrying away.

"Now. You want to try your fists on me?"

The cur may have tried to shake his head no, but with the tight grip Stephen had on his person, the idiot was unable to move.

"No," the bugger croaked. His hands gripped Stephen's wrists, his legs dangled above the ground. "Please."

"Please, is it? You think I should listen to your cries for mercy? Did you take notice of the pleas from that woman you knocked to the ground?"

Good thing the idiot held his tongue. Stephen loved pounding his fist on a well-deserving bastard. To think he may have saved the poor woman from rape only incensed him further.

The woman deserved justice, and this happenstance was just the diversion he needed to release his pent-up frustration. He smashed his fist in the blackguard's jaw.

"I think I should make sure you do not get this sort of idea again. Relieve you of any physical impulse of attacking another woman." He kept a grip on the cad's throat while his other hand pulled a knife from his back. He pressed the blade against the man's lower region. A teasing glint flickered off silver steel.

The bloke's eyes nearly bulged out his head.

"You get my meanin'," Stephen growled with deadly force.

"Ye . . . yes," the sound from the rat's throat barely audible.

He dropped the vermin to the ground, the man's legs crumpled underneath him.

For a moment, Stephen considered cutting the ballocks off the gutless scum. Sheathing his knife, he stepped back, rolled his shoulders, and spat. "Get out of my sight. I better never lay eyes on you again."

Clenching his fists in disgust, he turned and strode from the alley. His hands still tense when he grabbed the handle of the tavern door. The Cock and Crown flourished with commotion. His eyes narrowed while he took in his surroundings. The man behind the bar glanced in his direction. Recognizing Stephen, Gabe gave a nod. A patch over one eye, he looked more the pirate than a barkeep. A dishonorable scoundrel had tried to take his life. Stephen interjected, saving Gabe, and luckily he only ended up losing an eye.

Sounds and accustomed smells brought back memories of another time. A better time when he'd been a willing participant of bawdy houses and drinking with his companions. Stephen scanned the smoke-filled room, and found an empty table in the far corner. Perfect. Before he reached his destination, a sailor rose, blocking his path.

"Aye, mate. You're a big un." He held up an empty mug. "Need another."

The sailor wandered off, Stephen made his way to the corner. He had survived a cruel period in his life. Damn, it felt good to stretch his limits in familiar surroundings.

Scanning the room, he studied each individual. All sorts of undesirables visited the water front. Which was precisely the reason he stopped at the Cock and Crown.

"What'll it be, luv?" A buxom blonde stood before him with a hand on her hip and a suggestive smile on her lewd lips. Once, he would have had no hesitation taking her up on her blatant charms. One thing he loved was women. All shapes and all sizes. Before he could fill his arms with her supple body, an image of ebony hair and lavender eyes filled his vision.

"A pint will be enough for now." He gave her a smile without his usual encouragement. Even if the only woman he wanted was out of reach, he had come here on business.

"Well, now. Good it is to see you've escaped the devil." Gabe gave him a hardy slap on the back.

"The devil took his due," Stephen grunted.

Gabe plopped in the chair beside him. "About your ship. Tis it true?"

"It's true." Stephen shoved down the anguish that threatened.

"Damn. What happened to ye?" Distress showed in the tightening of Gabe's body.

"I lived. Now, I'm here to gather men." Stephen made his face an unreadable mask.

"Don't know if I like the sound of that?"

Few men earned the privilege to speak freely with words challenging his actions. His jaw tightened as he lifted his gaze.

"No offense," Gabe exclaimed "The way you say it, doesn't sound like you're looking for a crew to fit a new ship like *Serpent's Ghost,* or one of your others."

The bar maid set a mug on the table. "There ya are, luv. Can I be gettin' anything else fer ya?" Stephen's gaze followed the movement of her tongue sliding evocatively across her top lip. Her intention clear.

"This will do for now." He stuck a coin in the front of her low-cut top, right between her breasts. Her eyes lit up with pleasure, then she sashayed off to the next table.

Gabe smirked. "You still have a wanton effect on women."

"I'm fitting a ship." Ignoring his friend, Stephen made his purpose clear.

"What do you need?" Gabe leaned forward, his arm resting on the table's edge.

"I need men of a certain caliber."

"A ship docked yesterday, badly damaged. Don't know the particulars. Story's a bit shady. From what I hear, her crew will be stuck here for a while." Gabe tossed his head in a direction over his shoulder. "They might be lookin' for work."

"Thanks, Gabe."

"Whatever you're up to, take care, my friend." Gabe knew better than to ask any more questions.

Stephen lifted his mug and took a hefty swallow, then swiped the foam from his lip with the back of his hand. He stretched his legs out, crossed one boot over the other and laced his fingers over his belt buckle.

Guilt assailed him. He should be with the crew of *Serpent's Ghost.* Lying in the ground beside them. He lived for the day when he would rip the guts out of the evil monster—make him suffer as he had made Stephen's crew suffer. He would afflict such pain and torment the bastard would prefer hell instead of being at his mercy.

He had other ships. Loyal men who followed his instructions. Did he want to take them to their deaths? Or should he hire a bunch of cutthroats unknown to him? Let them take their chances. Men with no families, no ties, no one to care if they never returned.

He grabbed the ale and downed every drop. With a grunt, he slammed the empty mug on the table and motioned for another.

"Word is you might be lookin' fer a crew."

Stephen raised his steely gaze to the man in front of him. Tall enough. Filled out his coat. He didn't cower. That was a good sign. The one standing next to him looked like he was made of stern stuff, too.

"I sail for rough waters. There will be a fight. The job pays well."

"What if we get killed? How are we going to collect?" The bloke standing beside him spoke up.

"If you don't want risk, don't sign up," Stephen barked. His anger stemmed from guilt.

"I am no coward."

"The notorious Captain Radbourn," a sinister voice resounded. One he recognized. A sizeable form stepped around the two men.

Clancy.

He crossed his arms over his chest, demanding attention. Never taking his glare from Stephen, he spoke to the man he had interrupted. "You best curb your tongue. This captain eats boys like you for breakfast."

Figuring this was something they ought best avoid, the two sailors stepped back, allowing plenty of room.

"Why, Captain. I barely recognize you." Clancy said with a contemptible sneer. "Heard you met with some trouble? Pirating?"

"Gossip is dangerous business," Stephen said in a deadly tone, returning Clancy's glare.

"Is it gossip that *Serpent's Ghost* has sailed to a watery grave?"

With everything he had in him, he controlled his reaction. No secret about his ship. No need to divulge other gory details. He stayed quiet.

Cold eyes stared down at Stephen "So, you're lookin' for men." Clancy drew himself up with all the righteousness of a man wronged.

"Not interested," Stephen said.

"You've got it wrong, Captain. I'm not looking for a post. Don't figure on losing my life. Nor a chance at your comeuppance."

"Didn't learn your lesson the last time you crossed me?"

"Tis true, old friend." Clancy held up a hand as he smiled through blackened teeth. "Can't blame a bloke for trying to make his fortune."

Old friend? Once a member of his crew who mutinied. Stephen made a mistake when allowing the whoreson to live.

"So, you looking for a fortune?" Stephen asked.

"It's not money I want. Have you tarred and feathered maybe. You took everything away from me. Forty lashes. It took a year to regrow enough skin to cover my back."

Clancy was an unprincipled devil. Brash and ungoverned. The man might have a reason to be bitter, but he should consider himself lucky that Stephen had not killed him. Clancy had no reasoning. The light in his eyes skirted insanity.

Every nerve in Stephen's body sharpened.

"Maybe you should know how it feels, to have the skin peeled off your back."

The bastard had no idea how close his words were to the truth.

"Some said you sailed to your death."

"Wishful thinking, Clancy? Since I am sitting before you, it should be obvious I am not in Hell's pit."

Clancy drew his pistol. "I can send you there."

Stephen's muscles tightened. "I suppose it was only a matter of time."

Fervor sharpened Clancy's features. The gleam in his eyes burned brighter. "I should have killed you then."

Stephen calculated the amount of time it would take for him to relieve Clancy of his gun before the bastard could pull the trigger. "Make sure you kill me this time. For you will never get another chance."

The distinct sound of a hammer clicked on a flintlock.

From the corner of his eye, Stephen saw a man with a pistol aimed at Clancy's head. By sheer strength of will he managed to control any sign of surprise.

"I would really hate to shoot a man I do not know," the stranger said.

"Then, I suggest you mind your own bloody business," Clancy barked back, without turning around.

"But, you see, I cannot help myself. I am a man of non-violence." The stranger spoke with a nonchalance suitable of any rouge partaking in a jest.

"Cocking a pistol is not a demonstration of non-violence." Clancy spoke with his gun still leveled on Stephen.

The man shrugged. "My father suggested I carry it. For peaceful measures, you understand."

Stephen inwardly smiled. "His finger is on the trigger, Clancy."

Clancy's sneer grew larger, but his eyes filled with uncertainty.

The stranger continued, "If you behave yourself, I will let you live."

Clancy warred with indecision. Finally, he relaxed his arm. "All right. No sudden moves. I'm putting away my gun." Clancy slowly slid his pistol into his overcoat.

Another click sounded revealing the man behind Clancy released the hammer on his own pistol. Then, he too lowered his weapon.

In a flash, Clancy bent down, grabbed a blade from his boot and whirled about, slashing out at the man. Stephen was expecting such a move. He lurched from his chair, grabbed Clancy's arm and pivoted, sending the blade into Clancy's gut.

"Damn you," Clancy cried, just before he slumped to the floor in a pool of blood.

Where only moments before the inn held deadly silence, an echo of rumbling voices suddenly boomed off the walls, and seafarers slapped the backs of their mates.

"Well now. Seems I owe you my life."

Stephen glanced to the man who had come close to meeting his maker. "Seems we're even."

The stranger held out a hand. "Jack. Jack Gordy."

"Much obliged, Jack. Stephen Radbourn." He clasped the man's hand and gave a hardy shake.

"Captain Radbourn?"

Stephen's eyes narrowed as his awareness sharpened. "That's right."

"Pleasure to make your acquaintance. Shame about your friend here."

"He was no friend of mine."

"All right. Show's over," Gabe shouted. "John. Flint. Get this scum out of here."

Several men came forward and carried Clancy's body outside. Before the tavern door closed, the room returned to the active beehive it had been upon Stephen's arrival. Sailors resumed their card games, sea dogs shouted for more ale, laughter resonated as though the incident had never happened.

Lord help him. He ignored the carnage that once had been his way of life. He longed for better.

"Blasted fool." Jack gazed down at Clancy's blood staining the floor. "Why couldn't he have swallowed his pride and lived?"

"You don't know Clancy. He would have lain in wait and killed you when you left the tavern."

Jack whistled threw his teeth. "Then I'm grateful. In my book when a man has a loaded weapon aimed at his chest, or a knife at his back, he's headed for coked up toes. Nice to be the one still breathin'."

Gabe placed two mugs of ale on the table. "Drinks on the house, you two."

Jack pulled back a chair. "Much obliged." He nodded to Gabe.

"My thanks." Stephen told Gabe, then lifted his mug toward Jack.

"A life for a life. We're even."

Stephen smiled. "Non-violence, huh?"

"A bit over the top? Can't help myself sometimes." He took a swallow of his ale. "I hear you're looking for men." He gestured across the room to a few men seated in the corner. "Others of the same ilk, same ideals. They would be willing to work for you. Sign their allegiance."

Stephen studied the man before him. Seemed a good enough sort. Just risked his neck for a man he did not know. Said a lot about the man's caliber.

Could he ask the chap to risk his life again?

Chapter 29

For three days Stephen had not slept. He'd spent every available moment getting a ship prepared with a new crew. Provisions were loaded, a crew hired, and orders given to the first mate. His mind spun with any last-minute groundwork. His aunt and uncle noted his absence. And Kat pestered him like a hound ran a fox to the ground. If he managed to avoid any more distractions, he would more than likely sail within a fortnight.

Hopefully everyone else remained in their beds. He merely needed to slip across the corridor and down the staircase.

"Stephen."

God's Truth.

He slowly turned to see his sister with her hands braced on her hips, an accusing glint in her eyes. He felt like a youth unfairly caught with his head under a girl's skirts.

His temper flared.

"Are you on another hair-brained notion rising before dawn streaks the sky?"

"And what about you," Kat accused. "What is your reason for sneaking off at this hour of the morning?"

"A man of my size does not sneak."

"ThankG od. You were a shell of your former self when you came home to us."

Ignoring her, he turned to the staircase.

"Wait. You are not running away from me. And if you take another step, I shall yell the walls down so Aunt Elizabeth and Uncle Albert will find us quarreling."

He faced her, leaning down to her height. Mere inches separated his nose from hers. "You would be in more trouble than me, Kitten."

A pout formed on her upturned lips. "Come on." She led, expecting him to follow. He loped down the stairs, through the foyer, and down the corridor to the drawing room.

He stood before her expecting . . . God knew what he expected. The top of her head barely came to his shoulder, yet her glare threatened to reduce him to half his size.

"That won't work, Kitten."

Her bravado crumpled.

"Tears neither. If you want something, just ask. I am familiar with your stratagem,and I'm sure your cunning has only sharpened while I have been gone."

"Um, that is what I want to talk to you about. You've been home for weeks and you have avoided my questions at every turn. I have missed you so. I am worried about you . . ."

"Leave it be," he said more harsh than he'd intended.

"You were gone so long." Her soulful expression mirrored in her eyes, making him feel guilty.

"I did not have much choice."

"Please. I know something happened. I am your sister. You can tell *me*."

"I think I am the best judge of that." He stepped to the windows, turning his back to her. She was too innocent to know that monsters did exist. He would not see her sad face turn to horror. He would never reveal the gruesome events he suffered.

She gave an unladylike curse. He faced her.

"Curb your tongue. Such language for a lady. Brat."

She stuck her tongue out at him.

"You are not too old for me to take you across my knee," he smirked.

"Humph. You have never done so, and you will not do so now."

"Impudent chit."

"Must I continue to worry? The sooner you tell me—"

"For the last time, I will not speak of it. Not to you. Not to anyone." He marched across the room.

"Wait! I'll—"

He spun about, glaring her into silence.

"Very well. Keep your secrets," she said in frustration.

"My first order of business is to get back to managing my ships. Then I plan to go back to sea."

"For heaven's sake. You just got home. Even if you do not tell me what occurred, you cannot leave me again."

"Did you forget you are about to be married? You will have a husband to keep you company."

"But," she lifted her chin in defiance.

"Hush, now. Trust me, minx."

She finally gave up. "All right. I will. If you will answer another question for me."

"Good God. Do you never stop?" His outburst stemmed more from mirth than irritation.

"Who is the woman?"

He raised a brow, and masked his expression. "I do not know what you mean."

"Are you going to tell me there is no woman? You have never lied to me."

"And I'll not start now. But my private life is my own." He made to turn, but Kat grabbed his arm.

"A woman disembarked from the ship with you. You escorted her home."

Jaw clenched, he glared at his sister. Where the hell did she get her information? Ignoring Kat had only wetted her appetite.

"Wherever did you find her? You simply must tell me."

He gave a brash laugh. "Must I? Imp?"

She stomped her foot.

"Why, soon-to-be Lady Whetherford. Did you just stomp your foot?"

Younger days came swiftly to mind. An image of a little girl, stomping her foot, thrusting her lower lip into a perturbed pout, demanding her due. She may have grown, but her childish temper remained.

"Your husband needs to take a strong hand with you."

"He is not my husband, yet. And do not change the subject. Did you have . . . um . . . a relationship with this woman? You were on a ship a long time."

"My God, Kitten. You cannot say things like that to a man. Especially your own brother."

"For goodness sakes, Stephen. She is a woman. You are a man. I know the desires of men."

He took a step toward her as his thoughts darkened. "How the bloody hell would you know of such things?"

"I am about to be married."

"You are not married, *yet*," he snarled, throwing her own word back at her. "Do I need to defend your honor? What has that bloody Whetherford done?"

"No. . . nothing," she stammered. "He has done nothing. We are not talking about me, anyway."

"I am not bloody well talking about a man's desire with you. You are my *little sister*, for God's sake."

She rolled her eyes. "Do we have to go through that again?"

"Well, you are." He paced back to the window, shoving his hands through his hair.

"Stephen, will you please sit down. I am getting a crimp in my neck."

"You are a spoiled brat."

"And who made me that way?" The imp stood there with a grin plastered from one ear to the other.

The corner of his mouth lifted, and he laughed out loud.

"See, you cannot stay mad at me." She plopped onto the couch and smoothed her skirts. "Come sit with me. We are both adults now. Please tell me about her. Do you care for her? What is her name?"

Unfortunately, she would not let the matter go. Had he ever been able to deny her? Truth of the matter, he could use a female's opinion. But his sister? He shoved a hand through his mop of hair and took his place beside her.

"If you restrain yourself, I suppose I could tell you her name. Jennifer. But, it is her story to tell. I will not supply fodder for the gossip mill."

"Stephen, you wound me."

"A slip of the tongue, the gossip mongers would feast on any tidbit you give them."

She lifted her fingers to her lips and twisted. "I will not tell a soul. I promise."

He studied her face for several moments.

"This whole business is new to me. I have not figured it out for myself. What I feel for her goes beyond physical . . . um . . . desire." He lunged from the sofa. "Good God, Kat. I cannot discuss my personal . . ."

"Let me see your hands."

"What?" He glanced at his hands as if he'd grown more fingers.

"Come here." She patted the upholstered sofa.

Once again, he sat beside her.

"Now. Give me your hands."

With a raised brow, he took her delicate fingers within his own. Her eyes searched, and melted his soul. A talent she had accomplished at birth.

"Stephen. I think you have feelings for this woman. Won't you tell me about her?"

He opened his mouth . . . closed it . . . and considered his words.

Kat squeezed his hands, encouraging him.

"I don't know where to begin. She is important to me. I care for her far more than I should. She is the only woman who has ever compelled me to think of marriage. I feel more for her than she could ever reciprocate."

"Maybe she cares more for you than you know. Maybe she secretly yearns for you."

What did the minx know about yearning?

A possibility he would rather not dwell on.

"Even so, a life with her is out of the question."

Kat tilted her pretty head. "How can that be?"

"She is a Marquis's daughter."

Her eyes grew wider at his statement. "Are you saying she has denied you?"

"There's nothing to deny. We have not spoken since I took her home."

"Is that your choice, or hers?"

Releasing her grip, he thrust a hand through his hair. "No matter. We are from different worlds."

"But—"

"She fled England because her father would not consider a marriage with a second son. Now that she is ensconced in the bosom of his noble household, do you think he will consider a man of lesser rank for his daughter?"

"But, if you are in love . . ."

"Love!" He leaped from the couch as if his pants were on fire. "Who said anything about love? I certainly never mentioned the word."

She jumped up right behind him. "You don't need to mention it. It is clearly written all over your face. Your eyes are filled with longing. Even your speech changes. My ruff and gruff brother turns to mush at the mention of her."

He gave her a look that had many men scurrying away in fright. But not his hot-headed sister.

"Where the devil do you get these ideas? I do not—"

"Yes, you do. You are in love."

"Will you please keep your voice down?" Imagine him, the shouter, asking her to lower her voice. "I will not have you spouting nonsense the entire household may misconstrue. Maybe a life with her crossed my mind. But, that's all. And, like I said, it is impossible."

"Nothing is impossible. I thought I would never have Morgan, and look at us." The palm of her hand heated his arm. "I love him. I would do anything for him. We had obstacles between us. But, we overcame them."

"You natter in a land of impossible things. I am not nobility."

"You are a man of considerable wealth. You are a baron in your own right, your own lands. Father saw to that. You are a man of impeccable character."

He lifted her hand from his arm and kissed her knuckles. "You give a man hope."

"Love knows no station. Your steadfastness of the ranking nobility is misplaced. It does not hurt to dream. The hard part is going after your dream."

A dream punctured by the cruel thorn of disappointment.

Could he have a life with Jennifer after all?

"And how did one so young become so wise?" he asked, his heart full of love.

"Oh, Stephen. Go to her. Talk with her."

"And what of her father?"

She gave a shameless smile. "Who could be better for her than the man who loves her? Convince him."

"Maybe I should send you in my stead. He would not be able to resist you."

"Then you will see her?"

"Enough. As I said, my business is my own."

She sneaked a peak from beneath her lashes. "You are not mad at me?"

He took a long time in answering. "I suppose there is no harm done."

She latched onto him, and his arm went around her. Kat bedeviled him, but she was right.

He could never stay mad at her.

Chapter 30

Mother could be a grouse at times. Jennifer detested all the hustle and bustle. An outing every day. A party every night. Since her return, Mother insisted she keep up appearances. The commotion this morning, landed her in bed. She had feigned illness just to spend an afternoon at home. Good Lord, she wished she were back in her quiet little shack.

Her lonely little house.

Not so lonely when Stephen filled it with his booming presence.

Stephen.

Weeks, and not one word from him. When he'd deposited her at her parents' door, the terrifying notion that she would never see him again took root. And followed her every day since. Weeks. Blast him. Her heart felt like it had been stomped by a team of horses, stabbed with a thousand knives.

Stephen had charged into her life, turning her world upside-down. How dare he make her love him and then walk away without so much as a backward glance.

What are you going to do about it?

Staring out her window held no answers. A carriage slowed, then halted in front of the house. When the footman opened the door, an elegantly dressed young lady climbed down. She shook out her skirts and patted her hair.

Jennifer caught her breath.

The same rich color of Stephen's.

His sister? She looked neither left nor right, her stride with purpose as she marched to the front door. A delightful thrill filled Jennifer's chest. It has to be her. She even walks like him.

Jennifer quickly checked her appearance in her mirror. She hurried to the bedchamber door. With a deep breath, she threw her shoulders back and stepped into the hall. She met her father's butler mid-way down the staircase. She gave a nod as he confirmed Miss Radbourn as her visitor. Then on a much slower pace, she followed him down the stairs. Only with the greatest effort, she hid her anxiety and waited to be announced.

Why is she here? What could she want? Did she have a message from Stephen?

As Jennifer entered the drawing room, she was met with a blinding smile. Green eyes, with just enough of a slant to appear exotic, beamed at her. Tropical, sea green eyes. For a moment, it was as if Stephen gazed at her.

"Miss Radbourn." The tension eased out of her body as she returned her guest's smile.

"Lady Gascoyne. I hope you don't mind my stopping by. I am Stephen's sister."

Stephen obviously had not given his sister her name. Jennifer did not bother to correct Miss Radbourn addressing her by the wrong name. She wondered how Katherine had found their home. Jennifer brushed the thoughts away, because she was too excited to care why Stephen's sister was here. "I am delighted to meet you. Won't you please sit down?"

"Thank you."

The maid had already brought in the silver tea service, polished to a glaring shine. China cups and plates adorned the center table with linen napkins. "Would you like some tea, Miss Radbourn?"

"Oh please, call me Kat. Stephen's nickname for me. And may I call you Jennifer?"

"Please do." She tired of being called Lady Gascoyne. She lifted the pot and poured steaming brew into a china cup for her guest. "Please help yourself to cream and sugar. I like to fix my own tea. One cannot judge another's sweet tooth."

"Thank you," Kat said.

Jennifer added a dab of cream and a lump of sugar to her own cup. After stirring, she heedfully placed her silver spoon on the saucer, wondering how she could ask about Stephen without blurting out her anxiousness.

Suddenly, Kat reached for Jennifer's hands. Such a forward action, she automatically conceded, somewhat surprised by the gesture.

"I have been all atwitter wanting to meet you. I practiced being demure, but let's face it. I am too impulsive."

Kat's brother had said as much. She could not help but be cheered by Kat's lively spirit. The girl blinked thick lashes over her large green eyes. "Why would you want to meet me?"

"My brother."

Jennifer mentally shook herself. But the words flew out of her mouth before she could stop them. "How is your brother?"

"Stephen is distracted. Stubborn as an old goat."

Sounded just like him. Blast the man.

"I am so glad Stephen is home. I was very worried about him for long time." Kat's voice dropped dramatically. "Please tell me you care for my brother."

Jennifer blinked. Well, that was speaking frankly. And without a blush.

"I must know what happened to him. I hope you will tell me."

"What makes you think I can tell you any more than he?" Assuming his sister had asked him. By her actions today, she had probably hounded her poor brother.

"That's just it. He won't tell me anything."

Thank God.

Surely, as a gentleman, Stephen kept their intimacy private.

"Please, Jennifer. I hope we can be friends." Kat said with fervor. Her eyes so intense, the penetrating stare reminded Jennifer of her tutor when she had been seven.

Scary woman.

"Isimply do not have the time to persuade you that I am trustworthy. You do not know me, so I understand you might question my sincerity. But I am asking you for your faith. For you to take a giant leap and confide in me."

Reeling over Kat's declaration, Jennifer roused her instincts. The girl was forthright. Downright blunt. She liked her immediately.

"You remind me of my own sister, to a certain extent." She gave Kat a smile. "What would you like to know?"

Kat's shoulders slumped with a heavy sigh. Releasing Jennifer's fingers, she plopped a lump of sugar into her tea cup.

"When I was pining away for my fiancée, I did not eat, did not sleep, I lost a lot of weight. I cried a lot. I see the same signs in Stephen." She waved a gloved hand. "Oh, he does not cry of course. He would never allow such weakness. Oh, dear. I am babbling, aren't I? Charity, my friend, she's a countess now, she is the only one who can keep up with my chatter."

"Indeed." Jennifer offered a cinnamon bread slice.

"Jennifer, I'm worried. And when I worry, I prattle. And I do impulsive things. The last time I worried so over Stephen, I was abducted by my . . . never mind."

"So, coming to see me was impulsive?" Jennifer held back a smile.

"Yes," Kat said, her eyes full of mischief. "I know this is not exactly appropriate, but I am desperate. If my brother knew of my visit . . ."

"He will not find out from me," Jennifer assured her.

"Good." She placed her cup in its saucer so forcefully, the china clanked. "I know this is um, rather personal, but I don't care. I will go mad if I sit back and do nothing. You have managed to snag my brother's attention. If you meant nothing to him, he would not be so angry."

"Kat, I do appreciate you speaking your mind, but I am afraid you are mistaken. I have not seen your brother for weeks." Jennifer hoped her pain would not reflect in her voice. "I have not heard from him. It is as though we never met."

"Balderdash." Her green eyes blazed, just like . . . Stephen's.

"That's not the only thing," she continued, her eyes pleading. "There's more he is hiding. Please tell me. He's so thin. Before Stephen left, he was a mountain of a man. I cannot bear it. I know something happened to him. He refuses to speak of it."

Jennifer smoothed her features, straightened her spine, and folded her hands in her lap. "Perhaps it is better left alone. He must deal with his own demons."

"You know. Don't you?" Kat's gaze penetrated while her soft words were spoken with trepidation.

"I will not betray a confidence. Stephen has . . . scars. You must let him deal with this in his own way." He had scars, all right. Inside and out.

"I will imagine the worst."

Jennifer seriously doubted it.

She placed her hand over Kat's. "Stephen was injured. I nursed him back to health." Her eyes stung. *Please don't let me cry.* "Listen to me. Your brother is home. He is safe. Be thankful, and respect his wishes."

The girl sprang forward and hugged her tight. "I am thankful. And I am thankful for you." She leaned back and swiped at a tear on her cheek.

Oh no.

A bead of moisture caressed her own cheek.

Kat smiled that blinding smile of hers. "We could be sisters."

"From friends to sisters all in one afternoon?" Jennifer took pride her words came out without a catch in her voice.

"Stephen cares for you, I know it. Love that is new can be exciting. Like me and my betrothed."

"Men are attracted to women for different reasons. Love does not need to be involved." Jennifer took a much-needed sip of her tea.

"I am no child. I know that men have urges."

Jennifer nearly choked on her tea.

"I told you I am impulsive, and you have seen for yourself I am outspoken. How am I to find out anything if I am not forthright? I am about to be married," she sniffed.

They were the same age, yet Jennifer felt so much older. "I have been married."

Kat's gaze turned assessing. "I was not sure. Gossip mongers said you ran off."

Suspecting gossip was one thing, having it confirmed smarted. "I married a second son. Father is a Marquis, you see. It simply is not done."

"What happened to your husband?"

"He. . . died."

"I'm so sorry." Kat chewed her lip. "Where does my brother fit in?"

Jennifer took a deep breath. "I was alone in my house when he showed up on my doorstep."

"You are no older than me," Kat burst out.

Jennifer tilted her head. She felt she had aged ten years in the last two. "I am years older and wiser in experience."

"Then you should do well for Stephen. If you love my brother, and I think you do, you must tell him."

"He does not want to see me." Drat, moisture heated her eyes.

"Nonsense. Morgan was pigheaded, too. Still is. But he is the love of my life. I made him see reason."

That got her attention. "Made him?" Jennifer asked. Feeling sorry for herself took a step to the side.

"That is a story for another day." Kat dabbed the corner of her mouth with a linen napkin. "I should go. I'm so happy we had this conversation."

Jennifer wanted to probe. Find out more about the exploit Kat had implemented. Stephen mentioned his sister was a handful. And the girl, herself, admitted to an impulsive nature.

Jennifer swallowed her unexpressed questions. "I too, am glad."

"I should go. Before I wear out my welcome." Kat rose, and linked her arm with Jennifer's, as they walked to the door. Stephen's sister was amiable. They could have been friends.

"Please come visit me again."

"I will."

The butler opened the entryway door and stood to the side. Kat turned with an emboldened smile.

"Do not give up on my brother."

As Kat hurried down the front steps, Jennifer felt lighter than she had in years.

There was still hope.

Chapter 31

By God, this time he would tell her.

If Jennifer would listen. She had been mad at him.

After Stephen's conversation with Kat, he had done a lot of thinking. So damn much his head was ready to explode. Kat assured him he was good enough for Jennifer, even if he did not have a lofty title. How had his little sister grown up so fast? And when had she become so wise? He had never wooed a woman. They came to him as naturally as breathing. But now he saw he had his work cut out for him.

With Elizabeth and Kat preparing for the wedding, and Albert in Parliament, Stephen spent most of his days alone. Giving him the time he needed to ready a ship. A few more days and he would set sail. But today he would see Jennifer. Right after . . .

"Captain. There is a young woman here to see you."

"A woman?"

"Aye, Captain."

Who knows I'm on board the Lady Mistress? Even his uncle didn't know of his preparations. He had yet to tell the family of his plans.

"Do you know who she is?"

"She said her name was Faircloth. *Mrs.* Faircloth." his chief mate said with a smirking grin.

A boulder landed in Stephen's chest.

Good God, what is she doing at the docks? What has happened?

Fearing the worst, he made short work of the steps that took him to the upper deck. His chest heaved, yet he managed to slow his breathing. If something were wrong, she would have sent a missive. Wouldn't she? He shoved his hands through his wild mane.

Like a wave breaking on a shore of rocks, Stephen slammed to a halt. His gaze landed on the beautiful woman standing smack in the middle of his ship, prim and proper as any genteel lady of the aristocracy. His eyes drank in her form. With the sun as her backdrop, she glowed in a bold crimson creation of fluff. The picturesque image took the breath from his lungs. A gentle breeze blew the few raven tendrils hanging free of her bonnet. Without touching, he knew those strands would be silky within his grasp, against his cheek. Lavender eyes glistened, shimmered with a need known only to him.

He swallowed. But the lump in his throat remained.

They were together for the first time in weeks.

Mrs. Faircloth? Lady Gascoyne? He took his cue from her. She'd given the name Faircloth.

"Mrs. Faircloth. What a pleasant surprise." He closed the distance between them.

"Captain Radbourn."

Maybe no one else would notice, but he heard the quiver in her voice. He bent and lifted her gloved hand to his lips, her fingers trembled. Another sign of her unease.

What the hell was she doing here? Why now?

A thousand questions flew through his mind. But he would not expose her vulnerability, nor air their personal business with his crew watching. She had already created quite a stir. He glanced around the deck giving each man a hostile glare. Sailors jumped to their tasks as if a squall had suddenly hit land. And one would if the blasted curs opened their mouths.

"What can I do to be of service?"

"Captain Radbourn. I wonder if I might have a moment of your time. I have an important matter to discuss."

"Of course, Mrs. Faircloth."

Saints teeth. Reputation or no. Opportunity faced him and he'd be damned if he would toss it away. He was taking her to his cabin.

Once inside, he quietly closed the door and gave a turn of the key. A magnetic field enclosed them, drew him, commanded he put one foot in front of the other, until inches separated them. The urge to touch her overwhelmed, yet he forced his hands to remain at his sides.

A whimper escaped from her luscious lips. "Stephen."

He opened his arms and she fell into them. God have mercy, how he missed her. Missed her scent. Missed holding her in his arms. Her body trembled, he realized she was crying.

"I know you are thinking of me. But . . ." she sniffed between sobs. "I cannot bear to be away from you."

"I do not want to fight my feelings any longer." He gave a growl and held her tighter.

"Oh, Stephen. Do you . . ." She lifted her tear-filled gaze. "Do you mean it? You do care?"

"Of course, I care." His gut clenched with the intensity of his declaration. "Let me show you how much."

His mouth closed over hers while his hand tightened on her hip, hauling her close. Like a man dying of thirst, he guzzled water. Like a man dying of oxygen, he seized air. He could not get enough, could not kiss her deep enough.

Her body's response was strong and swift.

Lungs near to bursting, they broke apart gasping. His chest heaved and so did hers.

"Jenny. Sweet, Jenny. God, how I've missed you. I've missed your smile. I've missed the twinkle in your eyes. I've missed your touch." He buried his face in the curve of her neck, his cheek caressing her hair. "My God, woman. What you do to me."

Suddenly he jerked back, his hands gripped her shoulders.

"Why are you here? Has something happened?"

Frightened eyes stared at him.

Bloody hell.

Was he doomed to disappointment?

"Jenny. For the love of God. Tell me."

"No. . . nothing is wrong. I . . . I wanted to see *you*."

Several moments passed before the tension left his body.

"I have been miserable. I hated this chasm between us. I needed to find out if you were just being stubborn or if you . . . if you really did . . . did not want me."

He grabbed her hand and placed her palm over the front of his breeches. "Does this feel like I don't want you?"

"At this point, I will settle for that."

Surprise had him lurch his head back. "Settle?"

"I know you want me this way." She caressed his cock. "But, I think there is more between us. I know you care for me. At least, I hope you do."

A harsh gasp sprang from his throat as he filled her hand. "Jenny, love. I want you with every fiber of my being. But, if it's pretty words you want, you have them. I care. I care more for you than I ever thought a man could care for a woman."

Her eyes misted over.

"Now don't go getting all teary eyed. Damn."

"Kiss me." She slipped a hand around his neck and pulled him down.

"Don't you want to hear more endearments? Don't you want me to declare my undying love? And what about you? Maybe a man wants to hear words from a woman about how she feels."

Until that moment, he'd had no idea how much he needed to hear the words from her. Needed to know the depth of her feelings. His chest tightened.

"Oh, you fool. You big, strong, handsome, magnificent fool." Each word was a loving caress. Her hand caressed his cheek, her gaze penetrated his soul. "I love you. I think I have loved you from the day you opened your eyes."

Could a man's chest explode from words alone?

"I love you, too, Jenny." God, it felt good to say it. "I don't know when. But it happened. I love you."

He kissed her with a fierceness born from hunger, and possession. His. Jenny was his. She loved him. He groaned deep in his throat. His hands caught her head, holding her where he wanted while he drank greedily of her sweetness.

Stephen's arms were finally around her, the most blessed sensation in the world. Passion she had been a massing these past weeks suddenly erupted. She kissed him boldly, urgently, with a determination that drew on the very life-force of her body.

His tongue stroked, coaxed, delved, aroused her further into the web he weaved around them.

I love you.

The timber of his voice when he spoke his endearment slid like warm molasses over her heated body, melting her defenses, creating a yearning beyond her imagination.

Wordlessly, he scooped her up into his arms and strode to the bed. She tightened her hold around his neck and rubbed her nose in the curve where his neck met his shoulder. With exquisite tenderness, he deposited her on the edge of the bed.

Her bonnet long gone, she pulled the pins from her hair allowing the mass to fallin long waves around her shoulders. Then she stood and spun around. Lifting her tresses, she boldly exposed the back of her gown, and peeked over her shoulder with a siren's gaze. Inviting.

Taking the hint, Stephen's fingers swiftly released the buttons. Cool air skimmed her flesh, then was quickly replaced by his heat, and open mouth kisses. Desire pierced her belly with overwhelming warmth.

Stephen. Here. With her.

Her gown fell to the floor, her chemise quickly following. When he pushed down her silk drawers, she helped him, and soon the garment landed on a pile with the rest of her clothing.

His arms came around her from behind, bringing with them the memories of the times he had done this in her tiny house, on board ship. He held her, his harsh breathing sending shivers of delight across every inch of bare skin. He palmed her breasts, weighing them in his hands while his fingers teased her nipples. She threw her head back, and moaned, lost in his caress. He kissed, nipped her neck, then traced the vein from her ear to her collarbone with his tongue. Tingles prickled everywhere he touched. She'd missed him. Missed this. She loved him. And he loved her.

He whirled her around and gave her another harsh kiss. Then hoisted her in the air and placed her in the middle of the mattress. All he had to do was look at her with those thickly-lashed, smoldering, green eyes and her insides melted. She reclined on the bed, naked and waiting. His hungry gaze swept over her with fervor.

"Your turn," she said, licking her lips. "You have way too many clothes on."

Satisfaction glinted in his eyes, and he gave a wicked smile. The devil. He reached above his shoulders and grabbed the back of his shirt, drawing it over his head. She gulped at the quiver his action produced. God, he was a magnificent creature. His scars only added to his allure.

His fingers attacked his breeches, opening his placket. Then, he stepped away, pulled out a chair, and removed his boots. Her mouth dry, she attempted to swallow. When he stood and hesitated, she raised her gaze to his. He smiled. A saucy, gloating grin.

"Well?" she asked with a hint of annoyance.

"Hmm. I was sure you had seen it all before. But, if you insist, my angel . . .although I cannot say I remember you being so eager to see me in the buff."

Arrogant poop. Just hurry.

He tugged his breeches, his manhood sprang free.

The breath caught in her throat. Tingles shot to her core. She looked her fill.

"Like what you see?"

She felt dizzy and flushed, and her body craved his touch. She held out her arms. "Take me. Make love to me."

His nostrils flared.

With slow, determined movements, he crawled onto the bed beside her. Her pulse quickened. He lifted a lock of her hair, kissed it, and tucked the curl behind her ear. Then he took her face between his hands, the pad of his thumb skimmed along her bottom lip. His gaze held hers while his fingers trailed a path along her throat, down to her collar bone.

He was a master at seduction. A skillful lover. Intoxicating to a state of euphoria. His leisurely exploration so maddening and frustrating, she yearned for more. Then he ever so slowly, brought his mouth to hers.

It was not the sort of kiss he'd bestowed on her before. His lips lingered, his tongue traced her bottom lip. Sensual, as soft as a butterfly fluttering its wings. He kissed her eyelids, her temple, as though he savored the finest wine. Who knew her rough, gruff captain could be so sensitive and sensuous?

He lay beside her, his body half covering hers. His fingers stalked a path, torching her skin from her chest to her toes. Lifting her ankle, he gave her a wicked smile. "I think you'll like this."

He held her foot and kissed each toe while his fingers massaged her skin, loosening the muscles in her limb. But, when his mouth opened and he inserted her toe, the muscles in her belly leaped to attention. His tongue curled around each toe and laved, driving her to distraction. Who knew a body could derive such wanton pleasure from a man licking her toes. Heat pooled in her belly. Each thrust of his tongue between her toes delivered a sharp stab to the pulsing between her legs.

She whimpered, her mind struggling with the maddening decision, whether to pull back or push her foot forward. After an eternity of pleasuring each foot, all ten of her digits, he worked his way up her body, massaging her calves, kissing her knees . . . behind her knees. Her belly was in so many knots, she ached for what he would do next.

With a hand on the inside of each knee, he urged her legs apart. He bit the inside of her thigh, then licked—his abrasive tongue tortured. He scooted further, bit again, and then suckled her flesh. Flaming heat licked higher, driving her desire to unknown heights.

His mouth covered her, *there*.

Her chest squeezed, she forgot to breathe.

He licked, kissed, nibbled, and sucked with greedy abandon. Demented sensations impaled her, making her want to clamp her thighs—to block out his torture—or hold him prisoner?

He made it impossible for her to choose. She could not think. Lost all reason. She could only feel.

Oh God.

She shivered, panted, arched.

Liquid fire spiraled through her loins. She jerked and cried out.

"Shhh, Angel. I've got you."

Gradually, Stephen's words drifted to her ears. When she opened her eyes, he loomed above her. He kissed her with such tenderness, she wanted to cry.

His hot palm molded her naked breast. And she knew he was not done.

"No. It's my turn." At his confused expression, she shoved him onto his back. She licked her lips, and gave him what she hoped was a siren's smile. The yearning in his face gave truth to his need. Then he grinned. He liked that she had taken the lead.

She leaned over and placed a kiss in the center of his chest. Her palms flat, she caressed and stroked his torso, moving to his collar bone, then peppering kisses from one shoulder to the other. This was exhilarating. She realized he had given her the power to do as she pleased. Her tongue fired a path down the center of his chest, and darting over to his nipple. She used the coarseness of her tongue to graze his pebble. His hand moved to the center of her back, leisurely stroking. She laved and kissed and sucked. The pressure of his hand increased with each kiss, each bite, letting her know how much she stirred him.

His arousal pressed against her, strong and vibrant. She ran her hand along the thin line of hair that traced downward over his taut belly, her intent clear. Reaching, needing to touch his passion. His sharp intake of breath emboldened her. Grasping his length, she stroked him with the palm of her hand. Thick and pulsing, her teasing strokes grew bolder. With each stroke, he swelled and expanded. Thrilled at how she could excite him with her fondling, she intensified her caress.

She swirled her tongue, and her open mouth kisses grew hotter, blazing a path to his lower region. The animal groan that came from his throat skirted close to agony.

He jerked her to him and savaged her with his mouth, lips and tongue. He cupped her mound, nestling his thumb at the apex of her nether lips.

Unbearable need for this man crashed in on her in waves, as fires began to rage again.While he plied her flesh, she grabbed his hardness, and stroked him in a frantic fashion. Hunger making her desperate.

"Enough!" He grasped her hands, rolled over, and imprisoned them above her head.

His thighs encroached between hers and he plunged into her slick body. His weight pressed her deep into the feather mattress, her breath coming in shallow snatches. Cords of steel grasped her hips. His gentle deep thrusts angled and penetrated. With each stroke, he showed her the meaning of pleasure between a man and a woman.

She wrapped her arms and legs around him. Like a man possessed, passion had him in her grip. He lost control. Together they soared, lost in one another. Shudders racked her body. She howled her release into the curve of his neck.

A second later he gave a shout. Then his steel hard body collapsed onto hers. Harsh breathing filled her ears. His heaving chest crushed her own.

Minutes passed without a sound. Only the motion of a slight sway reminded her she was aboard his ship. She sighed, her fingers dancing along his lower back.

"I am crushing you." He kissed her forehead, and rolled to her side.

"Mmm. I like having you on me."

"Good God, woman. Give me some time before you tempt me to pleasure you again."

Her fingers played with the fur covering his chest. "Let me know when you've had sufficient rest." Bringing his wrist to her mouth, she placed a lingering kiss on the angry red marks.

"Jenny. My scars are offensive."

"Not to me." She rose above him. Holding his gaze, she slid her tongue across her bottom lip. Then she traced his torn skin with the tip of her tongue, nuzzling the red welts marring his chest. When she raised her eyes to his, green fire flashed back.

"You are one of a kind. And I almost lost you."

"Never. You will not get rid of me so easily." Happiness burst within her. "You love me."

"Yes, Angel. Am I never to hear the end of my loose tongue," he said while he played with an ebony curl.

"I expect to hear you tell me every day."

"Every day!" His bellow did not alarm her. He jested.

As if to prove her point, he tossed her onto her back. "I will have you know, woman, you will not be leading me around by the crook of your finger."

Her hand slid down to caress his manhood.

"Ahh, sweet Jenny. Now that . . . is a different matter."

Then he gave her a soul searing kiss.

Jennifer suddenly remembered they were not alone. "Stephen." She tried to shove him but he did not budge. "The crew."

"They're busy."

"They will know what we are doing." She swatted him play-fully.

"Yes, my love. They do."

My love.

"Get up." She shoved again. Harder.

"What? You're not going to let something like my crew inter-rupt our interlude."

"Interlude. . ." she huffed. "Get off me."

He rolled over. "Aw, come on, Jenny. I like having you in my arms."

"Hand me my clothes."

He waved his bushy brows. "Get them yourself."

Her heart fluttered. She was lost. His naughtiness made her smile, she snuggled closer. "You are incorrigible."

"And you love me." He kissed the breath out of her.

Aftersome moments, she tried again. "Stephen. You must get up. I have to go."

He climbed from the large bunk. She ogled his backside. A pang stabbed her belly causing her to groan.

He picked up her clothes and turned. Seeing where her gaze was, he gave a near-splitting grin. "I knew you liked me in the raw."

Heat flushed her face. But she did *so* enjoy looking at him.

"Um, Jenny. There's something I've been meaning to tell you."

He stood holding her gown, and she had the insane idea he held her clothing hostage while he delivered his news.

"I think you have known all along. I have to go back."

Chapter 32

Stephen felt the sever just as sure as if an axe had been welded between them. Tension filled the space that suddenly had his life hanging on Jennifer's response.

"What . . . do you mean . . . you have to go back . . . where?"

He tossed her clothes on the bed. "India. I am going back."

Every emotion reflected on her features. Surprise—she should not be shocked. Fear—what did she have to be afraid of? He'd gotten most of his strength back. Anger—now that was one of her attributes he knew well.

"What reason do you have to go back to India? Do you still have business there?"

"If you mean, what I did not accomplish the first time, no. That business was not completed."

"Do you think it wise? Must you go back?"

He gave a heavy sigh. "Yes."

"No. You can't. You must leave it alone."

"Must I? I cannot leave it alone, Jennifer."

"But, after what happened. You cannot go back. Surely, your business is not important enough that you would endanger your life. What could possibly be so vital that you would even consider going back?" Her voice grew shrill. She swung her legs over the side of the bunk, and clutched the blanket tighter to her chest.

Grief rolled off him in waves. "Revenge." There. He said it. He would not lie to her.

Shock lit her face. "You ... you mean to face the prince?"

"My crew . . . in the midst of all that horror . . ." He closed his eyes and willed the images to go away. But he saw his men as clear as the light of day. Their blood as red as the haze of fury swarming his brain. His hands fisted in torment. "He murdered them. I cannot get that image out of my head. It stays with me all the time. I owe them."

"You owe them nothing. They are gone," she shrieked.

Indignation flared. How could she say such a thing? "I owe them a debt. I lived. They died. For me, Jenny. Because of me."

"What foolishness. You are insane. You cannot go back." She threw the blanket aside and groped for her clothes. With trembling fingers, she thrust her arms into the holes and jerked her chemise over her shoulders.

He tried to explain. "I am a man, Jenny. At least, what's left of one. That bastard nearly destroyed me. That whoreson slaughtered my crew. After he sunk my ship. The men who swam to shore were cut down by his band of cutthroats. The ones they did not kill right away, he butchered right in front of me." His voice grew with each vile deed he listed.

The shock registering on her face made him realize not only was he shouting, but his harsh words—the deeds of a madman—were not meant for her ears.

She recovered quickly, but her voice quavered. "And he can do so again."

"Have you so little faith in me?"

"I have all the faith in the world in you. If not, I would not have given myself to you." Tears pooled in her eyes. But, the woman had backbone, and the strength of a termagant storm.

"I do not want to argue with you. This is not for discussion."

"What?" She jerked to a halt. Her eyes flashed fire. "Is that why you told me you loved me? To smooth the way for your revelation?"

He fisted his hands. "What the bleedin' hell are you spouting, woman?" His anger rose to fury. He allowed her to see a side of him that he had shown no other. He had allowed her into his heart, and now she lanced it with her scathing temper.

She picked up one of her stockings and aimed it at him like a weapon. "You think I am so flustered in my desire for you, you think I would kiss you, and then send you merrily on your way?"

"Now you're just spouting nonsense."

"Nonsense?" She braced both hands on her hips. He recognized the stance as his, the way he stood when every nerve in his body cautioned him of imminent battle.

His own temper surfaced. But, she was just too damn fetching. She shoved her glorious hair out of her face and thrust her dainty chin into the air.

"Do you remember the shape you were in when you were brought to my doorstep?" She struggled with the back of her gown. "But then, how could you? You were barely alive."

"I will be in your debt, Jenny, till my dying day, but I am going back."

"You will thank me by letting him hack away at you again," she screeched. "You have lost all sense. There is no reasoning with you. I saved your life."

"And I thank you. I am stronger than you think. My revenge is what kept me breathing."

"Oh, you mulish, poop."

He chuckled. When he saw her reaction, he realized he should not have done so.

"I hate you."

"You just said you loved me."

"How dare you make light of this situation. If you go back and find him, he will kill you."

"Turn around." She did. He made short work with the buttons on her gown. "I have already proven that I am hard to kill."

"Your arrogance will get you killed."

He pulled her around and into his arms. "Jenny. It is not arrogance."

All her steam seemed to sizzle away. She snuggled, just the way he liked her. "You suffered more than I realized. Please, put it behind you."

"I made a vow for my crew. I will avenge their deaths. The man was brutal. To the point, no sane man can comprehend."

She jerked her head from his chest to meet his gaze. "That's just it. The prince is insane. Please, Stephen. Do not go. I'm afraid."

"There is no need."

"There is every need."

"I will be careful. I will plan and take precautions."

"No. Promise me you will not go."

He glared down at her. "I will have my revenge."

She chewed on her lower lip. Something stirred in her mind. "Then you cannot have me."

He stilled. His arms became steel bands, as an alarm went off in his head. "What?" When she pulled away, he released her.

"You heard me. You cannot have both."

"Because I care for you I allow you more liberties than most. But do not make the mistake of thinking I will permit you to lead me around like a bloody dog."

She whirled. "I do not want to tame you, or lead you. But I will not sit here and wait, wondering if you are alive or dead. I will not dither for months, pulling my hair out, not eating, chewing my fingernails, pacing the floor—

"I get the picture." He came close, his hands stroked up and down her arms. "Jenny. I'll be fine. I will come back. I promise."

She shoved away. "Hear me well, Stephen. If you seek your revenge, do not expect me to remain in a state of repose."

Several moments passed before he could grasp what she meant. Cold dread seeped into his bones.

"Explain yourself."

"I will not wait for you. If you leave . . . we . . . we are through."

Every word struck him a telling blow. Emotion he'd denied—had not wanted to deal with—reared up and threatened to take him down. She had given her uncompromising demand as though she had not pummeled a hole in his gut—right beside the open wound from the Rajput prince.

"You issue an ultimatum?" His palms shook with righteous indignation.

"What choice do I have when faced with a fool?"

"I am a man of my word. I vowed revenge for my crew."

"They are dead."

"No less, a vow spoken is not broken. Not by me!"

"Did you hear me?" Now she was screaming. "You do not love me. If you choose revenge instead of me, that will prove you do not love me."

Despite everything that had passed, this was the deciding moment. Fury crawled into his blood and pounded through his veins. Still he controlled his rage.

"You want me to choose?" His cold voice sounded lethal to his own ears. No man had ever dared to challenge him in such a manner. "You dare to give me an ultimatum," he thundered. "Who the bloody hell do you think you are?"

When she spoke, her words were soft. "Evidently someone of no importance."

"Hear my words, woman. No one threatens me. No one orders me about. I have received one blow too many."

"Stay with me now . . . or leave, and never see me again." Her chin thrust into the air. Her chin wobbled, but in his blinding rage, he ignored it.

"That is your only choice?" he asked in a deadly calm.

"It is the only one I will accept."

Blood pounded his temples. Pain squeezed his chest. The leash on his temper threatened destruction.

"Done!"

He turned on his heel and stomped to the cabin door. With the tempest of a storm, he jerked the door from its hinges. He glared over his shoulder.

"Take your decision to bed with you tonight."

⸙

The raging wind outside matched the bluster whirling around inside of his brain. Stephen pounded a fist into the palm of his opposite hand while he glared through the window of his uncle's study. This business with Jennifer had him frustrated beyond his imagining. He'd given her what she wanted. Then she took his words of love and defiled them. Mocked him.

How do you get over someone who has left a hole in your soul?

"Your ship sets sail with the morning tide." Wesley dropped into a chair. "You haven't been on your feet long enough to get your land legs back."

Stephen glanced at the blond man sprawled in the chair on the other side of his uncle's mahogany desk. His posing presence was one of debonair, even suave—a gentleman of the finest order. Stephen knew Wesley before he became a refined gentleman. Wesley was good with his fists, and sharper with his wits—as he'd proven many times while serving under Stephen's command.

He turned at the sound of thunder crashing outside to see rain slashing against the windowpane.

"Seems to me you lost your edge," Wesley continued. "Surely you are not going to let your lady love keep you from revenge?"

Stephen gave him a glare. "Would you like to keep your tongue in your mouth?"

"I will admit I have gotten a tad used to having it there. I thought your temper had cooled."

He turned back to the window. "The blasted woman gave me an ultimatum."

Wesley whistled through his teeth. "Cannot imagine why you would ever listen to a mere female."

"Be careful, Wesley, or I'll wipe that smug assurance off your pretty face."

"Can't stand it, can you old man?"

Stephen scowled at Wesley seriously considering the idea of removing his tongue.

Wesley pulled the top from a decanter and poured a generous amount of brandy into a glass. "You allowed her to get firmly under your skin."

Yes. Firmly entrenched.

Stephen gave a sigh. "To think I was actually contemplating marrying her."

"At the time you had this foolish notion, were you vertical or horizontal?"

He smiled at the memory of Jennifer lying in his bed, purring like a kitten. Then shoved the image aside. "You would be surprised to know I did most of my *foolish* thinking on ship, on the way home from India."

"Usually the sea air clears one's addled brain." Wesley's blue gaze never wavered as he held a glass toward Stephen. "Come now. Tell me about this ultimatum."

"You seem mighty interested in what *a mere female* had to say," Stephen said accepting the drink.

Wesley ambled back to his seat. "Ultimatum or no, evidently she did not change your mind."

Stephen regarded the figure lounging in the chair before him. He appreciated Wesley's worth. His friend had proven his allegiance many times when their lives had depended on each other. But with his smart mouth, the chap pushed his boundaries.

"Nothing, and no one will change my mind," Stephen said.

"Not all is lost. You are returning to India. For Revenge."

The tone in which Wesley spoke did not match his words. "You do agree with me."

"Are you asking me?"

"Well?"

Wesley frowned. "I am going with you aren't I?"

Raising a brow, he ignored Wesley's cocky attitude. "With your eyes open. There will be trouble. This time I'll be prepared. The *Lady Mistress* is equipped with man-o-war cannons. Nothing will stop me from taking my due vengeance."

Wesley was smart enough to remain quiet. Although Stephen expected Wesley to ask how he had managed to get cannons from a man-of-war ship.

Stephen stepped in front of his uncle's desk and gave Wesley a sly grin. Leaning back on the wooden surface, he placed his arms over his ribs and crossed one booted foot over the other. "All is ready."

"You've picked a tough crew. Jack is an unusual sort. Appears trustworthy."

"He saved my hide." Stephen grated the words through his teeth. Thinking another man had just been added to the list of saving his arse.

All humor faded from Wesley's expression. "He may need to do so again." He took a gulp of his brandy. "I know you think this voyage is necessary, my friend. I, for one, will be glad to get this over with."

Stephen hoped against hope his new crew would not meet the same fate as his last.

Chapter 33

North Sea, 1826

His features a mask of intent concentration, Stephen rocked to the motion of the *Lady Mistress*. A gentle wind stirred his rust colored hair about his face and shoulders. His firm resolve made a startling contrast to the calm summer sea.

Finally, he would have his revenge. Killing was too good for the Rajput prince. The whoreson deserved to be chained, tortured, have the flesh stripped from his bones.

Agony resurfaced at the senseless killing of good men, who'd never stood a fighting chance. Who were never given the opportunity to defend themselves. A stinging image pierced his mind and chafed his chest at the same time. His jaw ached from gritting his teeth, reminding him of broken bones.

Bones healed. Scars remained.

"Good night for sailing."

Lost in dark thoughts, Stephen had not heard Wesley approach. "Hmm," he grunted in response.

"Two days and I've not seen you move from this spot. You still set on this course of action?" Wesley asked.

"You expected me to change my mind?" His brows rose in disbelief.

"I know how you are once you have made up your mind."

He studied Wesley closely. "Why did you come with me?"

Wesley gave a nonchalant shrug. "If for no other reason than to keep the same outcome from happening again."

"What makes you think you could make things any different? I am the only member left of my entire crew. The only man left alive." He turned into the wind. "There were days I wished for death."

"That does not sound like the captain I know."

"I am the same man," Stephen grumbled.

"No. You're not."

He whirled with an angry scowl, his voice bitter. "Wesley, you are my friend. But if you spout nonsense to me, you will soon join the list of adversaries." Men normally cowered when Stephen's temper flared. Wesley seemed undisturbed in the least.

"I know little. I suspect a great deal. It is because I am your friend I must ask."

"Ask what you already know? I want to kill every mother's son of the bastards who tortured me and killed my men. I owe it to them." Stephen breathed deep, fighting the battle raging within his soul.

"You owed them your leadership. You gave them that."

"I led them to their deaths." Pain engulfed anew, the way it did every time he thought about the senseless slaying.

"Every man under your command would have given his life willingly."

"Bah. You know not of what you speak."

"I know because I served under you. I know what kind of man you are. There is none better." Wesley stared into the distance.

"You are a man of smooth words. What do you think flattery will get you? If you know me, you know nothing short of my desire will satisfy me."

"Seems a fool's errand. Yet, no one knows better than I once you've set your mind on a course, there is no changing it."

Stephen grunted in acquiescence.

"You know what I say is true. You had the loyalty of your men. No captain cared for his crew more. None more fair."

"Some would not agree with you."

"Who?" Wesley turned to face him. "Knaves like Clancy? He had not an upright bone in his disreputable body. He tried turning the crew against you in mutiny. He deserved what he got. Another captain might have taken his life instead of flaying him."

"I did kill him."

Wesley glanced over. "When?"

"Before we sailed. At the Cock and Crown."

"I'm surprised he didn't come to his end sooner."

"There was a pistol aimed at his head. The fool lowered his guard, and Clancy struck. I brought him down."

"The night you signed on a new crew?"

"Yes. T'was Jack." Another crew. He prayed this bunch would not see the same fate.

"Let the guilt go," Wesley said.

"Let go?" Stephen roared. "Are you out of your bloody mind?" He shoved his hands through his hair. "I cannot *let it go*." The same thing Jenny had asked. "How can you ask that of me?"

"Because I was once a member of your crew." Wesley's gaze impaled his.

"Can you say you would have accepted death, and been in favor of life for me? I told you. Stop spouting nonsense."

"Is friendship drivel? Is a man's loyalty rubbish?" Wesley shouted back. "Do not belittle the admiration your crew gave you. Do not permit their deaths to be pointless."

"But they were pointless! Senseless. The damned Prince . . ." His anger was so great he trembled from the force of it.

"Hear me, Stephen. You are my friend. I am speaking to you as my brother. Your men valued your judgment. They would not have followed your orders without question if they felt disdain. They may have been rude, or audacious at times. But, the crew respected their captain. And they would have killed anyone who said otherwise."

"Good God, Wesley. Enough!" Stephen stomped across the deck and back. Too many arguments filled his head. He could not think straight.

How much more was he expected to take? He rubbed his temples, his brain ready to explode.

Must he endure ridicule from everyone? He could still see tears in Jennifer's eyes. She refused to let them fall as she pleaded with him not to go. He had forced her to issue her ultimatum. Then he cut out her heart when he chose revenge, making her believe his thirst for vengeance more important than her love.

Bloody hell.

What an ass?

What a bloody fool?

A sailor's life was uncertain, the past year had proven that. Until he walked away from Jenny, leaving her in her father's house, he had never been lonely. But he missed her. Missed her smile. Missed running his fingers through her ebony strands. Missed her warmth, her kisses. The woman knew how to send his body up in flames.

Nothing had charged his adrenaline like *Serpent's Ghost* swashbuckling on the high seas. Being on the *Lady Mistress* did not hold the all-consuming appeal sailing once did. Because he embarked on a mission for vengeance? Or because a pair of lavender eyes haunted his soul?

Jennifer enticed him beyond all imagining. She didn't give a whit for his lack of title. Even entrenched with her family, she had stayed true to him. She'd gone against her father once, he did not presume she would do so again. Yet, their sweet joining only a short time ago more than implied her choice. Had he not sailed out of the harbor, he might even be with her this moment.

Her father's approval or no.

But then, perhaps her father might accept him on the consequence that Stephen had returned his daughter to him.

Jennifer—a dream come true. She could become a reality. Once he'd tasted her, a sweet fire burned within. Having known such fire with his angel, he was willing to burn in her fire for the rest of his life. He could not allow her to slip away.

Would she accept him? Would she forgive him?

A life with Jennifer. The idea was ludicrous, building castles in the clouds for sure.

But, what if . . .?

Jennifer meant more to him than anything else in the world. More than vengeance. More than any glad tidings he may gleam from taking the worthless life of the monster who'd caged him.

Revenge would not bring back his crew. Retaliation would not heal the grief within his heart. No matter how much he tried to convince himself he did this for the men who sailed with him, the concept of triumph left a sour taste in his mouth. Victory? Success? What exactly would he accomplish? And horror of all horrors, what if he were captured again? What then?

He refused to even consider that ghastly thought. For if the Rajput prince did not kill him, Jennifer would.

A corner of his lip lifted in a smile.

Jennifer.

A small glimmer formed in the shadow of his black heart. Trust and caring were fragile between the two of them. Where his sweet Jenny was concerned, he had ignored all logic, all reason, all sense. He cursed himself for the insensitive fool he was.

Her tactic had been ineffective. His stubborn pride would not accept her demand. She'd cut him to the quick. His temper had flared. What else was he supposed to do?

A curse escaped him.

Why couldn't she leave well enough alone? Why couldn't she let a man make his own decisions? A man had his pride. He could not give her what she wanted.

Then.

Mayhap he would have given in had she used other methods of persuasion.

When hell froze over.

An ultimatum issued was a challenge accepted.

At what cost? The restlessness inside him fed his cold heart. He'd risked everything. He couldn't think straight for wanting her. Her hair loose about her shoulders, wearing nothing but the blanket she clutched to her naked breasts. His scars did not offend her. Closing his eyes, he groaned at the vision of her tongue tracing the marred flesh. That image shattered by the hurt in her eyes, the despair he had put there . . . He slammed his fist against the ship's rail.

He had exposed his heart to her. Bared his soul, spoke the words she wanted to hear. Yet she had flayed him. Ripped his guts out with her *ultimatum.*

His thoughts battered his brain. This teeter-totter motion of a pendulum twisted him into knots.

Revenge had brought him to this? Did he dare risk the same thing happening again? Jeopardize the lives of these men? Was he taking them to their death?

Had he not done this very thing, not so long ago? Stood, just like this, contemplating his fate? Swearing he would never take his freedom for granted again? What the hell was wrong with him? Surely, he had lost his mind. A loving woman of his dreams—his for the taking—and he'd chosen revenge.

He ached for her. He ached for what might have been. Could he make such an enormous change for her?

Hope warred with wariness.

He'd inherited an estate from his father. He had lands. True, Chelmouth was a far cry from English society, but she had run off with a second son, had she not? If he explained his wealth, if he did this for her, then maybe . . . just maybe . . . Was it too late?

What if she wanted nothing to do with him? If he gave up this counterblow, he might have some chance of winning her. If he continued on his current path, he would have no chance at all. He could prove his love by returning to England without retribution. And if she accepted him, he would savor her love for the rest of his days.

Giving up his revenge did not concern him nearly as much as his worry whether Jennifer would forgive him. Blasted woman.

Yet . . .

Even when she settled back into the bosom of her family, she had stayed true to him. Genuine, authentic, firm in her allegiance. Unwavering in her love for him. She'd stood by him, taken care of him, loved him even when he least deserved her affection. Sincere in her dedication. Steadfast in her support of him.

She'd been a constant in his mind, in his heart. She did not give a whit for his lack of title. During his pain and grief, she was the one true thing that remained in his heart.

"Silas!" He charged up to the quarterdeck.

"Come around. Hard starboard," he bellowed.

More shouts directed the crew. Men scurried about, hauling ropes, tautening whipping sails against the masts to change direction.

The *Lady Mistress* lurched at the sudden turn of the wheel. Her side dipped low into the rampant water as she circled around, heading back to England.

Chapter 34

On unsteady legs, Jennifer stepped away from the dressing table. Her body went through the motions—get up, sit down, dress, undress. Sleep? She had not slept a wink since she had carelessly thrown down that gauntlet. How had she expected Stephen to react? He was a man, after all. And men never used the head on their shoulders to think.

Her behavior had been appalling. But he'd given her no choice. She had panicked. Loneliness pressed down on her. Not like the isolation she felt when Johnny died, and she'd been left alone. During that time, she had grieved more for home than her husband. This was despair—ripping her heart out like nothing she had ever known, or could ever survive.

He never even knew she stood on a hill watching his ship until the vessel was only a small dot in the distance. Without looking back, he'd sailed across the water and out of her life. If not for Kat's arms around her, she would have crumpled, her harsh words, the last words she spoke to Stephen, echoing through her mind. Had she allowed Stephen to go to his death thinking she did not love him? Knowing he quite possibly sailed to his death sucked the life right out of her.

Self-pity reared its ugly head. Would she ever see him again? If he did accomplish his vendetta, if he did survive, and if he sailed back to England, would he come back to her?

She yearned for his laughter. Yearned to see the corner of his mouth lift in that oh so endearing way. She yearned for his touch. Craved his body next to hers. Her last impression of her love had been his sneering tone. Not an image she wanted imprinted on her memory.

There were no tears left. Her body had racked with sobs for hours. Even embarrassment had not kept her from curling into a ball upon the floor, and having Marie find her. The gentle woman scooped her up, tucked her in her bed, and sat with her through the night. A duty beyond a maid's obligation.

Jennifer tied the bed hanging back to the heavy post. A light rap drew her attention to the door. Marie entered carrying a tray of tea. The woman had been with Jennifer's family as long as she could remember. The sadness in the maid's eyes matched her troubled movements.

"Yer mum said you'd be wanting tea."

"Thank you," Jennifer said in a low hoarse voice.

Marie twisted her fingers in her apron. "Can I get you anything else, Miss Jennifer?"

"No."

"Tis good to have you home."

"I am glad to be home." Where else did she have to go? She was miserable without Stephen.

"You're mum and your family missed you something fierce. We all missed you." She lifted the corner of her apron to dab at her eyes.

Wallowing in her own self-pity, Marie's distress had escaped her notice.

"Marie, what is it?"

"I know I shouldna say anything. I cannot help it. I cannot stand the black circles under your eyes. Forgive me, but I heard you and your sister talking about the captain. Your heart's breakin', ain't it?"

Jennifer put her arms around the tearful woman. "Marie. There is no need for you to worry. I will get over it."

"Do you forget I found you on the floor?"

"And you comforted me. I am better now."

Marie sniffed. "At least, you're home. Safe and sound as a bug in June. We all love you."

Jennifer's heart swelled. "I know you do. And I love you too."

"Your mum . . . didna send the tea." Marie took a deep breath. "I brought it to you."

"Just like when I was young." Jennifer smiled in remembrance.

"You shouldn't stay cooped up in your room, like this. Why don't I get your riding-habit, and you go for a nice ride?"

She seemed so enthusiastic for the idea, Jennifer hated to disappoint her. She wanted to ease Marie's mind. Jennifer had been cooped up within these four walls. She needed to clear her own head, as well.

"Very well. Pick one for me."

Marie's smiled with relief. She scurried over to the wardrobe.

Jennifer led her mare from the stall and the groom helped her to mount. No side saddle for her. Determined to have a vigorous ride, she had specified her preference, and the stable boy eagerly granted her request. Hopefully the pounding of the horse's hooves would pound the misery out of her soul.

Fanny was her favorite. The spirited mare took off at a furious gallop. She raced across the open field and headed to the line of trees. Wind pulled at the pins in Jennifer's riding hat and she gloried in the frantic pace. A delightful thrill spurred her on. Freedom. Excitement. Long denied pleasures began to surface. The faster Fanny flew the more Jennifer's spirits lifted. Carefree and stimulating. Oh, the thrill of feeling alive. She had repressed living for so long. The glorious sun brightened and cheered her.

Time zoomed by as she soared over the ground without thought of consequence. She slowed Fanny to a walk before the mare ran out of steam. They ambled to a clearing with a stream close by. She dismounted, loosened the reins, and led Fanny to the stream for a drink.

Tinkling sounds of water trickled as the translucent liquid rushed over the rocks. Spring buds sprouting on tree limbs had burst open forming blooms. A plump robin sat on a limb, his chirping tweet a song. The cloudless blue sky encouraged a brand-new day of life. Buoyancy took over her limbs, like the weight of the world had been lifted off her shoulders. A sense of elation filled her. She silently thanked Marie.

Getting out of the bedchamber had been the best thing for her. Moping around did a body no good. She should take a lesson from Kat. Pursue her wants. And she wanted Stephen. She had to make a plan. God willing, he would survive his foolish vendetta. And when he came back to England, she would seek him out. Demand he listen to her.

Well, her last demand had not worked out so well.

She chewed on the end of her finger and stared across the trickling stream. Entice. Yes, that's it. Use her womanly wiles. Whatever it took . . ."

"Jenny?"

She whirled around with her hand on her throat. Her heart stopped.

Stephen.

When he opened his arms, her feet took wings. She hit him with a thud.

Stephen laughed, his arms squeezing the breath from her.

Tears ran down her cheeks in rivulets. He was here. This was real. Her hands roamed over his frame for assurance.

"Jenny, my love."

She lifted tear filled eyes and tried to focus. "You're real. It is really you."

"Yes. I am real." He gave her a bone melting kiss to prove his words.

When he finally allowed her to breathe again, she wobbled on shaky legs.

Then she hauled off and slugged him.

"You beast. You left me."

If she weren't so mad, the shocked expression on his face could have been amusing. His mouth hung open. Then his eyes blazed, his jaw tightened, and she knew his quick temper had surfaced. Well, she would not stand for it.

"How dare you! Do you think you can waltz back into my life as though you never tossed me aside?"

"Jenny, I . . ."

"And don't Jenny me. You left me. For your blasted vengeance."

"You threw an ultimatum at me."

Blood heated her face. Her cheeks puffed out with indignation "And you chose vengeance!"

"I chose you, my angel."

"You said you loved me. You filled my heart near to bursting. And then you ripped—"

"Jenny." He grabbed her shoulders. "Did you hear me? I chose you."

Now it was her turn for her mouth to hang open. "What?"

"You are more important." His eyes claimed her soul. "You, Jenny, are more vital than life itself. My blasted temper would not allow me to back down. I realized before I reached Indian waters . . . we were still in the North Sea when my temper cooled enough for me to think rationally. For me to realize that you were more crucial than any misplaced vengeance."

"Then . . . you chose me?"

"I chose you."

Her knees wobbled and she grabbed at his open neck shirt.

He lifted her as though she weighed nothing and strode to a tree. She refused to relinquish her hold around his neck. He sat on the grass and settled her on his lap. Then, smoothed her wild hair from her face.

"I was afraid you would not forgive me." He searched her eyes. "You do forgive me, don't you?"

"I was afraid I would never see you again," she hiccupped on a sob. Her palm caressed his bewhiskered cheek. "You chose me."

He clasped her palm, turning it to his lips for an open mouth kiss. A thrill raced up her arm and straight to her belly.

"Let me enjoy the feel of you in my arms." He buried his nose in her hair and kissed the skin just below her ear. "I never thought about love and the desperate emotions caused by love. Until, you. You have been steady in your allegiance. True to your heart. And you forced me to accept what is in mine. I love you."

"And I love you, you stubborn . . . adoring man." She cuddled in his embrace. He was alive and he was here. Holding her. Caressing her. He loved her.

"You are my life, Angel. You're in my bones, my blood. You never gave up on me."

"You were worth the wait."

"Sweet Jenney. You stayed true to me. I promise, I will always be true to you."

A tear slipped from her eye as he sealed his vow with a passionate kiss.

Epilogue

London, 1826

The church erupted with cheers startling Jedediah from his sedate surroundings. Most weddings were a quiet affair with decorum followed to the letter. In London, he found propriety must be above reproach. The ton demanded good behavior, and respectability. Any taint upon one's name resulted in the cut' direct. The English upper class lived by a certain code. One did not dare cross that line. Scandals were simply not forgotten—or forgiven.

Although he'd heard stories of a noble Lord, or two, who had dared to flaunt propriety. And one of those just happened to be the captain's brother-in-law, Lord Whetherford. Evidently, he had kidnapped his lovely wife, then had to rescue her from his ex-mistress. But that was neither here nor there.

This happy occasion clearly overlooked bad manners. For the noise within sounded more like a rowdy celebration resembling one of the pubs he had visited while looking for Captain Radbourn. Several men from the back row, directly across from Jedediah, yelled, whistled, and threw their hats into the air. At least the bunch had removed the coverings from their heads upon entering a house of worship.

Jedediah stared as the captain grabbed his bride and took a long time in letting her go. He smiled. Ah, to be young and in love. Jedediah recalled the image of when the captain had returned to England. If not for the flowing red mane, he may not have recognized the man it took months to find. With food, and the love of a good woman, Captain Radbourn would regain his size. A man with his strength and determination was to be admired. He wished the couple a long happy life together.

Jedediah slipped out of the church without being seen. With the commotion going on inside, no one would notice a stranger that had not been invited in the first place. He had the information he needed. Once he reported that Captain Radbourn had indeed recovered, and in good spirits, Jedediah could embark on the next step in his employer's plan.

Overcome with guilt, his employer blamed himself for Captain Radbourn's capture. His reasoning—he had contracted *Serpent's Ghost,* its captain and crew, and sent them to Indian waters. His intention—information.

Nonetheless, Jedediah would begin a new quest. Find another captain. And hope the next voyage would not turn out like the last.

He may well have the next candidate in mind. *Jack Gordy.* Lord Wesley Hatheridge was not only a friend of the captain, but a comrade to his brother-in-law, Whetherford—also with a somewhat shady background. Astounding what one could learn when one dug deep enough. The Duke of Nethersall would require more looking into.

For now, he must return to the country, and report to his employer.

My Prince.

THE END

Thank You

Thank you for reading my story. I hope you enjoyed reading it as much as I loved writing it.
And, if you did, would you consider leaving a review online? It really would mean the world to me.

Thank you!
Samanthya

longing for the woman who branded his very soul, he returns to claim the love he'd carelessly thrown away.

A girl's determination triggers a woman's desire

From the first moment Alexandria saw him she decided he would be hers. A feisty girl seduces the lord with a woman's passion determined to get the man she wants.

Turn the page for a SNEAK PEEK of *The Only One My Love.*

The Only One My Love

New Orleans, 1825

I t was a day to try a man's soul.

Giles Heathcliff Montague Litscomb, Duke of Nethersall, wondered for the hundredth time why he'd volunteered for this venture. He had visited the Americas before, so he'd been accepting of the unexpected trip, if not excited. Perhaps boredom prodded the root of his disquiet.

His life had grown considerably dull since his spying days; years of dangerous assignments, which brought him more than satisfaction. Hell, he had lived for the thrill and risk without a care for his own safety. He'd learned a set of critical skills, managing to deliver his comrades through hell and come out alive.

Although, days of adventure were not necessarily in his past. Remembering his latest endeavor brought a smile to tug at the corner of his mouth. The familiar leap of exhilaration pumped through his veins from the mere thought of a precarious situation. The mission involved danger and mystery in the rescue of his best friend's bride.

Giles' brow furrowed in thought. His friend had a spitfire on his hands, but the two were well suited. The couple deserved an extended bride month—which led to his agreement in taking care of the groom's business in New Orleans. The first part of business had been simple enough to handle, and took less time than he expected. There was only so much a man could do in a foreign land with an abundance of time on his hands.

Thus, the boredom he now felt creeping in.

Only by chance had he found out about Hudson's auction. The young clerk from the shipping office informed him of an event where owners came from all over, displaying horseflesh. He also hinted there would be a certain gentleman in attendance with an animal of special interest. His hope lifted with the prospect of something to look forward to. Morgan would be pleased if he brought back some thoroughbreds.

Giles found himself amazed at the number of patrons attending the auction. By the size of the crowd, either a great number of horses were to be sold, or this event marked the highlight of the New Orleans Season. With a large quantity of steeds, perhaps the day would turn out not to be a waste, after all.

The shipping clerk, Joe, had suggested they ride horseback, and now Giles understood why. Carriages filled the meadow. Men waited in line for stable hands to help with their mounts. Numerous horses had been tethered helter-skelter to trees scattered over the field. Giles waited while Joe took care of their steeds.

"Told ya."

Giles turned to Joe, coming up behind him. "Yes, I see what you mean. Quite a crowd."

"Anybody who is anybody, and then some."

A mass of men, seemingly from all cultures, attended the auction. Some were dressed in proper suits. Some of the dandy peacocks Joe had mentioned strutted about. Even some of the lesser class who looked as if they could not afford their next meal, let alone a mare or stallion.

"You mentioned some of the best horseflesh. After seeing this crowd, I hope you were not exaggerating."

"Naw. You won't be disappointed. Come on." Joe led him around a building and over to a fenced-in meadow. Several hastily made structures—a stables of sorts—sheltered stock.

A stallion captured his gaze. His coat shiny, like black silk. He swished a fine tail, that when it was still, it nearly touched the ground.

Now there was a handsome creature.

A lad stood beside the beast, his hand brushing the horse's mane. Farther down, two more steeds caught Giles' notice. A big grey and an Arabian. He needed a closer look.

"This way," Joe said.

Giles jotted a mental note of the horses' location, then followed Joe in the opposite direction.

With only a few clouds in the sky, the sun blazed hot, making him glad he wore a wide brimmed hat. A slight breeze helped keep the day pleasant, even with the smell of horse and dung swimming in the air.

"Who is that gentleman?" Giles gestured to a large man in the center of a group. Important gent, if the others vying for his attention was anything to go by.

"That's Mr. Carmichael. Owns a spread two days' ride from here. Over a thousand acres just for his horses. Some say his plantation covers ten times that. Plenty of money. Has a family. Wife, three sons, and a daughter who's a hoyden."

"A thousand acres just for his horses? Does he have a breeding farm?"

"Has a sugarcane plantation, and breeding besides. He employs some of the best trainers, too. One imperative fella has his own way of training. Some new-fangled idea he conjured up himself."

Giles gave a low whistle through his teeth.

Wonder if the chap would want to share his ideas. Or better yet, if he would be interested in a job—on the other side of the ocean.

"Is he someone I should meet?"

"Yes, sir. The very one. You might be especially interested in his private stock."

"Private stock?"

"One in particular, if you like the white Mr. Morgan got."

It would appear many knew the story of how his friend gained a magnificent white stallion while on one of his business ventures to the colonies. Seeing an owner beating his horse, Morgan had trounced the man, then gallantly relieved the cur of his animal, paying him good money, of course.

Giles' jaw tightened. "Don't tell me he is the previous owner of Pegasus."

"Nope. Morgan scared that man out of the county. Mr. Carmichael would have loved to get his hands on Pegasus. Come on, I'll introduce ya."

Filing the information away to mull over later, Giles followed Joe over to the crowd of impressively dressed men. Giles towered most men, but the largest man in the group was just about his height and broader in width.

Joe called to him. "Are you buying or selling this day?"

The large man turned around. Bushy dark brows shot with a hint of silver, kind brown eyes. When his gaze landed on Joe, he gave a blinding smile.

"Joseph, you old son-of-a-gun. How are you?"

"Just fine, Mr. Carmichael." Joe shook the man's hand. "Just fine. And I hope your family is well."

One brow rose in reproach. "There's no 'mister.' My name is James as you well know it."

"Yes, sir." Joe flashed a set of white, even teeth.

"My family is fine as well. Around here somewhere." James glanced over the crowd, searching, then gave a slight wave of his hand.

"James, I'd like you to meet Giles Litscomb, the Duke of Nethersall."

Bloody hell. He had hoped to keep his title quiet.

"Mr. Carmichael, I'd rather no one knew of my title." Giles frowned briefly at Joe as a gentle reminder. "Which, by the by, means little in this land."

"I'm James." He thrust out his hand. "What shall I call you? Nethersall? Litscomb?"

"Giles will do," he said as he grasped James' hand.

"So familiar? An aristocrat of noble birth?" James shrugged. "So, you prefer an image of mundane circumstance. But, one of wealth?"

"Enough to buy some blue-blood." Giles offered a crooked smile, all the while assessing the man.

"Very well." James slapped him on the back. "Welcome to Hudson's horse auction. The best of the best. You'll find your blue-bloods here."

"I am looking forward to it."

"Giles, here, is a friend of Morgan." Joe spoke as though the information were important. Giles supposed James must have met Morgan.

"So, you're a friend of the man who owns Pegasus."

Another person obviously impressed with the story. "You know Morgan Langston?"

"Everyone has heard the tale concerning the man who saved the white stallion. Called him the *Dark Devil*. But a man who does not allow another to mistreat a horse is more than all right in my book."

"Glad to hear it." Giles wondered how Carmichael had heard of the Dark Devil. That bit of news should have stayed in England.

"Well now, Giles. Since this is your first visit, allow me to be your guide. I even brought a few of my mares for the auction."

First impressions usually rang true, and Giles prided himself as a good judge of character. There were times when his life had depended on sizing up his opponent rather quickly. His assessment of Carmichael described him profitable, educated, with a fondness for horses, a cared-for family, and by his group of associates, he possessed moral fiber.

He followed the man with an air of indifference, a single question burning uppermost in his mind—why Joe seemed to think he would be interested in *one in particular* of James Carmichael's private stock.

Alexandria brushed her hand over the horse's mane. He was a beauty. Nothing caught an admirer's eye quicker than a shiny black coat of silk. She glanced down. *And white stockings*. Her lips turned up in a smile. Only a year old, and the most stunning horse she'd ever seen.

She didn't like his name. *Blackie*. How unoriginal. And with four white feet? The owner could not have appreciated this fine animal, saddling him with such a name. She would change that at once. The black tossed his head as if he agreed. She stroked her fingers down his nose, determined he would be hers. Now she just needed to find her father.

Alex hurried around the building, searching the crowd. With so many heads towering above her, she darted this way and that, seeking a broad back larger than most.

Her father, tall with wide shoulders, had dressed in dark blue today. As she scoured the lot looking for a blue coat, she encountered her father's good friend.

"Mr. Barnum."

"Why hello, Alex. Fancy seeing you here today." His smile was warm with affection, and his lip quirked up in a hint of teasing.

"You know me. I couldn't stay away."

"Never seen a girl love horses as much as you. Has something caught your fancy?" His eyes twinkled.

"Sure has." She couldn't hide her excitement. She wanted that black. "I'm looking for my father. Have you seen him?"

Mr. Barnum gave a nod over his shoulder. "Last I saw, he was over by the presenter stage. No doubt getting a look at the first lot."

"Thanks." She turned to go.

"Alex?"

She pivoted on her boot and gazed up at him.

"Be sure and ride over next week to show me your new mount."

"Yes, sir." Anticipation bubbled in her chest. Her father was here to buy horses, wasn't he? She'd just add Blackie to his list. She cringed at the thought of naming such a glorious mount anything that boring. Instantly she pondered a list of new names. Midnight, Night Fire, Black Velvet, Night Dancer—of course she would need to see him run first. If he ran as fast as she hoped, maybe Lightning.

With names for the black occupying her thoughts, she nearly slammed into the back of a rather large body. She quickly side-stepped and jerked her head up. A man scowled, then suddenly his eyes widened. The apology died on her lips. Obviously, he had mistakenly thought her a boy, then suddenly realized the blundering muttonhead who bumped into him was a girl. Her lips tightened and her face flamed.

Probably never seen a girl in trousers before. With a toss of her braid, she stepped around him.

Eagerness overcame her embarrassment when she remembered her mission. Then she glimpsed her father just ahead. A tall man stood beside him. Black hair, the same shiny hue as the horse she wanted to buy. He turned just a bit . . .

Alex stared in shock as the breath left her lungs. She stood immobile, her feet frozen to the ground.

The sun silhouetted him in profile.

The duke.

He was back.

Order your copy of *The Only One My Love*,
Scan the QR code below!

About the Author

S amanthya Wyatt writes sizzling hot romance with suspense. Intensely emotional characters with a deep passionate love for friends, family, and most importantly—between the hero and heroine. Although her first love is historical romance, this award-winning author also writes contemporary romance under the pen name S. R. Wyatt. Additionally, she has written a book of one family's struggle based on true life events.

Samanthya left her accounting career and married a military man traveling and making her home in the United States and abroad. She now lives in the Shenandoah Valley. On a sunny day, you can find her and her husband driving on the Blue Ridge Parkway or going to car shows in their 1969 Mustang convertible. She loves long walks, and a book to read on a sandy beach. Starbucks is her favorite drink and she likes hearing from her fans.

She invites you to lay the worries of the world off your shoulders and get lost in the pages of a romance, where you embark on a journey with the hero and heroine, become involved in a dream, plunge into a world of fantasy, and live an adventure your heart can share.

To find out more about Samanthya Wyatt and her books, please visit her website: https://samanthyawyattauthor.com/

www.ingramcontent.com/pod-product-compliance
Lightning Source LLC
Chambersburg PA
CBHW022011310726
48972CB00006B/1603